BLOOD PROPHECY

One: Queen's Destiny

BARB JONES

WCP

World Castle Publishing, LLC
Pensacola, Florida

Copyright © Barb Jones 2013
Print ISBN: 9781629891521
eBook ISBN:9781629891538
Second Edition World Castle Publishing, LLC, October 1, 2014
http://www.worldcastlepublishing.com

Licensing Notes

Editor: Maxine Bringenberg
Cover: Kip Ayers

PROLOGUE: THE PROPHECY

Sidon, Phoenicia, 1129 B.C.

Eshmun'azar leaned back in his chair and studied the grey outlines where masonry had covered the open windows of his study. He watched the candlelight cast shadows on the rock and reached for his little brazier. The sun hadn't shone through those windows in eighty-three years. He lit his incense with one of the candles and sighed. The child would be there soon, smuggled into port in one of the many ships the small community within these walls controlled through various daylight entities. Abibaal had been insistent— *Eshmun, the child is most certainly the one the stars foretold.* He recalled the look on Abi's face...excitement.

It was, on reflection, an interesting and rare occurrence. Prior to that conversation seventeen days ago, he hadn't seen him excited in more than a century. In fact, not since Abi's early days when he was coming into his power had Eshmun seen more than calculation and sober contemplation in his son's features. It was a welcome change. He cupped his hand and drew smoke to his face, inhaling. The incense, herbs caked in ghee, had come from Crete on one of the boats. The shipping enterprise had been remarkably successful, not only allowing for discreet movement of goods and persons that suited the community's particular needs, but also from a monetary standpoint. Merchants had followed suit, and Sidon was rapidly becoming the most important port in the world. That was fine with Eshmun'azar. More shipments made none worthy of special attention.

A knock came at the chamber door. It was a servant offering refreshment. He waved him away. "No child, I'll eat later." As the servant turned to leave he added, "But bring a pot of wine and cups. Abibaal will arrive soon with a guest. See that he knows where I am." The young man bowed and mumbled his understanding, and Eshmum was again left alone. He thought of the girl. Could it truly be her? Nearly seven years they had sought for her, this child who would bring a message of great significance. *Great import.* That was the way the astrologer had explained it, *import*. He had opened the charts and explained the positions of the stars — a child would bring a message of great import not just for their community, but also for the scores like it that existed throughout the world.

He heard the gates open below and knew that his son had arrived. It would take a moment to open the carriage, which had been locked securely against the sun. The servant appeared a moment later with the wine and reported that Abibaal had arrived safely with his guest and would be up presently. Eshmun took the pot, dipped a cup, and sipped the wine. His mind was racing and he checked once more that his parchment and quill were ready and the inkpot full. He drained his cup, wishing not for the first time that wine still affected him and his kind. Finally, he dipped the cup again and sat in his chair. It would do no good to let his son see him nervous.

A few moments later, the servant was back. He announced Abi and opened the door to allow him to enter.

Abi carried the girl in his arms. She was wrapped in light linen secured by a clasp at her shoulder and a rope at her waist.

"She was in Athens, then?"

"Yes, Father."

"Has she spoken?"

"I have heard her myself, Father. I believe she spoke in the old tongue." Abi's eyes were wide and he couldn't suppress a smile. He placed the girl on cushions at the side of the study and stepped back, gesturing for his father to examine her.

Eshmun studied the girl. She looked about seventeen or eighteen, hair black and curled in the Grecian style. She was slender, almost waifish. Her wrap—he was pretty sure the Greeks called it a *stola*, or perhaps a *palla*—had bunched at her waist, revealing her legs from ankle to the middle of her thigh. Her legs were shapely, rising smoothly from ankle to knee to thigh. He sighed. The ghosts of memories of the life he had left centuries before haunted him more frequently lately. He looked at her face, the high cheekbones giving way to a smooth jaw line right above…. He stopped, noticing her throat, long and extended as her head reclined over the cushions. He could hear the blood coursing through the vessels in her neck.

"How much did you drain her?"

"Only enough to ensure she would cause no difficulty in the journey, Father."

"What else did you learn of her? What is her name?" Eshmun brushed a stray hair from her brow as he spoke.

"She was abandoned as a child. Evidently, the Greeks do that. The women at the temple call her Diana. She's a mute, except for those times when she speaks the old tongue. The temple women assumed she was some kind of oracle, but none have been able to divine the language." Abi stepped to the wine pot and dipped a cup.

Eshmun considered the girl again. "When do the trances occur? Will we have to wait long?"

"I don't think so, Father. She has yet to be in my presence without going into the trance. "

"Well, then...let us wake her." Eshmun walked back to his desk and lifted his quill.

Abi smiled and walked to the girl. "It's time to wake up, Diana," he said, and turned her head so she faced the ceiling. He brought his hand to his face and bit deeply into his wrist. Holding her head steady, he positioned his wrist over her mouth and watched as blood dripped over it. The Greek's lips parted almost immediately, and her tongue flicked out. Abi smiled at his father and put his wrist to her lips. The girl sucked eagerly and moments later, her eyes opened.

Abi withdrew his wrist and looked at her. The girl sat up on the cushions, frightened. Her eyes grew wide and she looked around the room nervously. Then, her eyes rolled backwards into her head until only the whites showed, and she began to speak. It was a harsh, guttural language, more animalistic than human, and Eshmun scribbled furiously on the parchment. She spoke for nearly thirty minutes before he put down his quill.

"Silence her, Abi."

Abi bent down and grasped her head. He brought his mouth to her throat and held her tightly as his father watched him feed. Finally, when her heart had stopped, he stood and wiped his mouth. Eshmun had finished writing and was reading the words on the scroll.

"Was it the old tongue, Father?"

"It was. It must be her, son. The human tongue should not be able to form some of the words she said." Abi scanned the document. "She said the message twice. You stopped her as she started a third repetition."

"Was it as the stargazers said?"

"Oh yes," Eshmum said. "Of great import." He handed the scroll to his son. Abi took it. Strange symbols he'd only seen in his father's old books were written, but at the bottom, Eshmum had translated into Phoenician. He began to read.

In the hour of the wolf will come the Queen of reconciliation? In the birth of her death the joining will commence and great will be the hatred of her words....

He looked up. "Father, what does this mean?"

Eshmun'azar dipped his cup and took a long swallow. "Keep reading, my son."

CHAPTER ONE

Approaching

Amber, New York, Present Day

Amber started to pull her ponytail out of the hair band but stopped herself, sighed, and stepped away from the mirror. It was her last chance to run in New York, and she was not going on a run with her hair down. She sat on the edge of her bed and pulled on her running shoes, lacing them carefully and tightly. One more run and tomorrow she would be in Seattle. She stood up and began stretching, reached down to her ankles, gripped them tightly, and felt her calves and thighs gradually loosen. She straightened her body and caught a glance of her desk. It was strange to see it bare, although she used it more as an end table than a desk. The movers would arrive in a few hours to load up all of the possessions she'd accumulated in college and get them started west.

It was strange to think that school was over. She'd entered college at sixteen, and Amber had completed a bachelor's degree in archeology and a master's degree in cultural anthropology in just over four years. Her pacing kept her removed from most of the other students, and she'd opted out of consideration as valedictorian, though she would have won. She picked up her master's diploma at the dean's office, shook his hand, and called home.

Her parents—well, her adopted parents; they'd taken her from the orphanage when she was nine—were proud and insisted she drive the three and a half hours north to their farm to celebrate. There, she suffered through their embraces and the nine-day flow of neighbors with casseroles and cakes, all coming to see the Stones' girl genius. They bought a cap and gown and snapped pictures one after another. No fewer than thirteen boys were introduced or reintroduced, and she politely smiled and laughed on cue. Twenty-seven meals, and not even one had her family alone at the table. The Smiths for lunch, the Frosts for supper, the Antons for breakfast—a steady stream of family friends and acquaintances come to gawk and to plan her future.

She didn't mind too much. Honestly, for the four years she was gone, she'd only visited a few times. If her mother hadn't called every Sunday morning, Amber believed they might have talked only once or twice the entire time. She loved her family—who wouldn't love a couple who had adopted a nine-year old girl? Kids at the orphanage called the fourth birthday the "deathday," because the chances of adoption past that age disappeared. Not the Stones—they had seen Amber helping with the toddlers and insisted on her. They were good, honest people. Still, after twelve years and countless evidences of their love and affection, she still felt out of place, like a guest at the house rather than a daughter.

She'd returned home to find mail waiting for her. Six schools had already commenced recruitment campaigns to get her into PhD programs, and fourteen unsolicited job offers had come within two weeks. Headhunters called almost hourly until she finally let all of her calls go to voicemail. In a day, the voicemail was full and she still hadn't cleared it.

The Seattle Museum of Science and History approached her a little differently. An overnight package about the size of a television set had arrived just four days ago. Within, she found a human skull, six crude flint knives, a bag full of pottery shards, and eight clay masks. An attached letter indicated that the museum had acquired a collection of nearly eighteen thousand pieces from six digs originating in ancient Macedonia. If she found the task of organizing, cataloging, and analyzing the collection of any interest, a curator position was available to her. In addition, the museum would pay for her tuition, field research requirements, and even her dissertation printing for the PhD program in socio-cultural anthropology at the University of Washington, which was prepared to incorporate the curator position into her course of study. A loft apartment, a museum car, and a staff of five interns rounded out the package. Inside was a one way plane ticket for a flight out of Kennedy and a $5000 check for moving expenses.

She hadn't wrestled over the decision. Grasping the skull and studying the pre-mortem fractures on the anterior half, she had dialed the museum and accepted, but not before negotiating a seven percent higher starting salary, just on principle. The flight was tonight, at eleven forty-five. After a quick change in Denver, she'd be in Seattle in time for breakfast.

One more run, then, she thought, and opened the door. The air was cool against her neck, and she imagined the wind targeting her birthmark. She started a slow jog, and then quickly ramped up to a fast run.

Chloe, Yakima, 1993

Chloe held tightly to her mother's hand and they walked

through the pines. She stepped around the occasional drifts of snow that stubbornly refused to melt even now at the end of March. Six others walked with them, heading deeper into the woods. Chloe looked at their feet, trying to match the sound of the needles and brush crackling under their boots to each particular step. She concentrated on the sounds. When she was satisfied she could identify each of the walkers by the noise of their footsteps, she turned her attention to their breathing. Her mother was easy, and she recognized the pattern without having to think much about it.

The others took a little work. The man ahead and to the right breathed shallowly and regularly, while the one behind them wheezed a little. The woman next to her mother breathed purposefully, as though every exhalation resulted from conscious intention. The others —

"Mommy, stop." Her mother looked down at her and Chloe began to tug at her arm, pulling her south. "Come on." Her mother looked at the wheezing man and he nodded, so she allowed Chloe to guide her and the others followed. In a few minutes, the bubbling of the Yakima River reached Chloe's ears. In four or five more, the others heard it as well. She pulled her mother through a last copse of trees and stood at the bank, staring at the water.

"What is it, honey?" Chloe's mother knelt beside her and studied her face.

"The whitefish is about to die." Chloe pointed at the water.

"What whitefish, sweetie?"

"The one right there." She was still pointing at the water. Her mother followed her finger to the water and squinted, but couldn't make out anything below the ripples of the river.

"How is the whitefish going to die, Chloe?" It was the wheezer. He'd walked up to where the girl and her mother stood on the bank. He pointed at the water. "Will another fish come and get it?"

Chloe reached out and took the man's hand, still pointing, and lifted it up, pushing it as far as her reach allowed. "The sky will kill it."

The man looked up and studied the sky for a while, then turned his attention on Chloe's mother. "Marlene, I'm just not sure. She feels intently, I know that. Still, it's not just…what? What is it?"

Marlene's eyes had grown wide and she stared at the sky. "Look, Tom."

He looked up. It was an eagle, and it circled above the river. Suddenly, it dove, and Tom gasped at the speed of the thing. In only a second or so, it was flying back upward, a whitefish in its talons.

He looked at Chloe. "You were right, she has the Sight."

Michael, Brussels, Present Day

Michael rested his head against the velvet of the coffin and sighed as it was closed. The flight from Brussels would arrive in London in just over three hours, and from there he would travel to New York. His agents in America had already completed construction of suitable dwellings in Hartford, New Orleans, Las Vegas, and Seattle, and it was time for him to leave Europe. Not forever—no, nothing could keep him from Bruges, though the city was little more than an amusement park now. Still, he knew the quest was reaching its fruition, and he knew that he would find the queen on the other side of the Atlantic.

It had been good to see Kabos again, despite the old one's constant retelling of stories heard thousands of times and his insistence on reciting all of the joys that modern day Bruges had replaced with ills. "The finest restaurants serve tripe for the tourists now. There has been no good food in Flanders for four hundred years."

"Do you still eat then, Kabos?" Michael had asked the question with a sly smirk, but Kabos missed the sarcasm and continued.

"I tell you, Machiel, there is not a chef left in Flanders! Bruges is dead. Did I tell you I saw a child ask her mother if *Gruuthuse* was where Belle and the Beast lived?" He had. He'd told that story to Michael when he'd visited nearly a decade earlier. "There is nothing left in this place for you. Go ahead to America. Find your queen. Soon, I think I shall climb to —"

"Shall climb to the top of the *Halletoren* and greet the sunrise." Michael had chuckled. "Don't you think that's too Flemish? I mean, even for you?"

"Machiel, sometimes you try —"

"What was it Longfellow wrote? *In the market-place of Bruges stands the belfry old and brown; Thrice consumed and thrice rebuilded, still it watches o'er the town.* There must be a better place to die."

"Why must youth constantly mock age?" Kabos had shook his head, and then brightened. "Do you know, I was there when he saw the bell tower? Longfellow, I mean. He was still mourning the death of his wife, a lovely girl. She died in childbirth, I think. I actually considered feeding on him, so sad was he. But as I came behind him, I heard him forming those words. Machiel, I think there may be nothing so profound as the sound of a poet forming verse."

"Perhaps, Kabos. Why do you call me young? I think next month I shall be three centuries old. We are both relics now."

"Bah! I was fifty-two when I left my life for this, and that was three hundred years before you, a whelp, were born. You have never lost that youth. I think should you live a thousand more years you will still be young."

The two men had sat in Kabos's parlor, a soft room, lushly decorated with ornate furniture he'd acquired over the years. A soft knock and a shy servant reminded Michael of his flight, and Kabos had hugged him warmly before he stepped into the car. Michael was leaving Bruges, again.

In a half hour, the plane would lift off, and in two hours the sun would rise. Michael closed his eyes and thought about New York. He'd been there once with Kabos, at the turn of the century, but that was it. Outside of that and an unconscious trip to Panama in the midst of the Napoleonic wars, he'd not crossed into what he still considered the New World. He sighed.

Machiel. Francis will ensure your transfer in London, and Marcus has already made arrangements for New York. Kabos's voice sounded softly in Michael's head. *Has your plane left?*

Not yet, but I hear the engines have started, and – Michael stopped mid-thought. *Kabos, will I hear you in America? Can we speak... well, this...so far from each other?*

Oh, I have communicated with many in America, my child. Still, you and I will not speak. I do go to Halletoren this morning, Machiel, and I will greet the sun. Michael was silent. *Six hundred and seventy years, Machiel. It is too long for a man, and no matter what I have become, I was born a man. I will greet the sun and die in Flanders.*

Father, please! Even in thought, Michael's voice was plaintive. *There is too much I must learn from you, too much I must know.*

There is nothing left to teach you. Sleep now, and remember. You must be strong for your journey. Michael felt his eyelids grow heavy. Kabos had done this before, when Michael was new – when he still called himself Machiel and still thought of himself as Flemish. Michael felt calmness replace anxiety as he fell into slumber. Then, as promised, the remembrance came and Michael's grief left him and let the images wash over him.

CHAPTER TWO

Beginnings

Amber, New York, Present Day

As she had on nearly every morning for three years, Amber ran the six blocks that made up the college neighborhood, streets lined with brownstones like the one she rented. *Used to rent,* she thought as she reached the corner of the development and crossed the street to the campus proper. From there, she ran through the faculty parking lot and into the hills the university had owned for nearly a century but had left undeveloped. The strong smell of the leaves and the brush filled her head with memories of her mornings in New York.

She wondered briefly why she wasn't feeling nostalgic for New York. In fact, she couldn't remember feeling nostalgic for anything or anywhere, unless ancient civilizations counted. Those she longed for, for times so distant that extant texts describing them were rare and day to day life had to be gleaned from shards and tools and sites buried beneath centuries of soil.

She was running faster than normal, and perspiration had soaked her white t-shirt, making her dark sports bra stand out lewdly. She pulled the shirt off as she ran and tossed it in a trashcan. Somehow, she felt less exposed in the sports attire alone.

She regretted her haste a few hundred yards later as she felt her crystal—no longer contained by the shirt—bouncing on its chain against her chest. *Damn.* The shard of rose quartz had come from her parents, her real parents, and she had worn it as long as she could remember. The nuns at the orphanage said it had been around her neck when she arrived. It wasn't very beautiful, just a semi-opaque cylinder of pink stone, even with the ornate gold setting and chain she'd added a few years ago. Still, she felt incomplete without it, disconnected. She even found herself out of sorts in the shower when it lay on the sink next to her toiletries, waiting for her to dry herself and wear it again. Now, the damn thing was bouncing on her chest like a finger poking her repeatedly against her sternum.

She heard steps approaching her and saw another runner, a man...a massive man. Amber had to turn around in mid-step to get a closer look, but she didn't want to be obvious, so, she stopped abruptly and bent down to tie her shoe. He passed her, but not before she got a good look at him. *Christ, the guy's a poster child for Charles Atlas!* He wore blue jogging pants, expensive New Balance shoes, and a tight sleeveless shirt that seemed barely able to contain his chest and arms. He was attractive enough, in his way, but Amber had always gone more for the intellectual types than for muscle. *Still, muscle has its uses.* She chuckled and shook her head as she started to run again, and the man smiled at her. His face was startling, really, with thick sideburns that reminded her of something—yes, that comic book hero with the metal claws. She smiled, nodded, and kept running, but the man raced ahead and disappeared around a bend in the trail.

Amber ran on and briefly considered trying to tuck the

crystal under her sports bra, but decided against stopping to fiddle with it. She felt good, actually…really good. The dirt trail crunched nicely beneath her feet and the wind felt good enough that the tapping of the stone on her chest was bearable, even helpful as it measured her pace. She breathed deeply, felt her body reacting to the air and the exertion, and wondered, as she did almost every day, at how running relaxed her rather than exhausting her.

As she crossed the bend she heard voices, and in a moment saw four men in hooded sweatshirts standing along the trail. As she approached them, they began their catcalls, whistling and hooting at her. She looked at the dirt and gravel and the trail and kept running, but one of the men, a rat-faced man with acne scars covering his face, ran backwards in front of her, forcing her to slow down and finally stop.

"A pretty girl like you shouldn't be running alone out here. Who knows what could happen?" The voice was full of false concern, but his eyes scanned Amber's body. He drew in his lips and even licked them lasciviously.

Amber began a retort but realized the man's three companions had drawn near. They surrounded her now. Her heart began to beat at an impossible pace, adrenaline coursing through her. "Let me go," she said, trying to appear unafraid. "Get the fuck out of my way!"

Rat Face laughed at her. "Look at the dirty mouth on this one, guys." He turned his attention back to Amber. "Didn't your mother teach you any manners?"

Noise suddenly filled the air. A deep, guttural growling reached Amber's ears, and she found herself strangely comforted by the sound. The four assaulters looked around, and Rat Face's eyes grew wide as a large dog bounded from the brush and leapt at him. Amber stood wide-eyed, watching as the animal knocked her tormentor to the ground and the other three scattered. The dog was large and looked almost like a German shepherd, but was at least twice as big as any she'd seen, with dark brown fur — so dark it was almost black.

It seemed to lash out at the man's throat, but at the last minute bit his shoulder instead, drawing a scream of pain from Rat Face. Amber leapt over his legs and ran hard, figuring that if she could get the next half mile behind her, she'd reach McGuffin Street and people everywhere. She ran, felt the wind whipping her hair behind her, and felt the crystal tapping between her breasts.

Michael, Bruges, 1712

You must remember your early days, Machiel. If you are to make the queen, you must remember what my negligence cost. Kabos's voice washed over Michael like a dream, and he remembered.

***

Machiel awoke with a start. The girl lay next to him, her left breast partially exposed, an arm over her eyes. He didn't remember having her last night, but he'd had her before. He'd had her and the three other girls who lived on his father's estate. He'd also had the four servant girls he found desirable, and one that he hadn't particularly liked but who had done his laundry with skill and care. The old cook had avoided his attention, and he'd not taken any of the married servant's wives, but this one and the others were ready options when his luck at the taverns or the marketplace failed him. Still, had he been so drunk that he'd taken her without knowing it? He'd been drunk before, completely drunk. The beer flavored with fruit that was the staple of Bruges had on more than one occasion left him sleeping on the streets. He'd even fallen in a canal once and woke soaked and shivering, scrambling for the cobblestones.

He couldn't imagine being so drunk that he would lose memory, but not so drunk that he could not perform his duty to the girl. She breathed shallowly, and he pulled the blankets down slightly to completely reveal her breast. She moaned and mumbled softly at his touch. His head ached from the beer, but he moved his mouth to her nipple and playfully kissed and nibbled at it. He felt her hand stroking his hair. "More?" she asked, "After last night, I would have thought you'd had your fill of me for months."

"Oh? Was I vigorous, my dear?" Machiel mumbled the words, feeling her harden against his lips. She tasted strange this morning, alive and fresh…wonderful. He nibbled at her nipple and pulled the blankets down to her thighs, moving his body to rest one leg over her.

"Vigorous? Sir, vigor does not describe you yesterday. You approached the enterprise with a vehemence that a soldier might have in a campaign, a—oh…." Her words trailed off as his attentions became more focused and less playful. "You were a conqueror, and I was your conquered and your prize." Machiel realized he was ravenous, and he sucked hungrily at her.

"As you are now, sir…you—" Her sharp cry interrupted her thoughts. "Wait! Ouch. Ah—wait."

Machiel felt his teeth ripping into her nipple, felt her blood, hot and thick, coating his tongue. It was salty and rich and he sucked hungrily at it. He was vaguely aware of the girl beating at his shoulders with her hands and screaming, but the blood called him and her cries were soft compared to the roaring in his head. His headache had vanished. He felt strength and joy unlike any he had felt before. She was crying, but why would she be crying? How could she not feel what was happening?

He moved his hand to her waist, then to her thighs, pushing them apart. He felt attached to her breast, and a great river of joy flowed from it. She writhed beneath him, and his fingers found their goal. She didn't stop screaming or crying, but she was softer now, the sound growing weaker. He felt a surge of energy and moved his hand faster. Ah, she was his! She was hi—

A sudden impact on his temple lifted him from the bed and onto the floor. He lay there for a moment, and the roaring in his head gradually subsided until he heard the girl, still weeping. Other voices were there as well. He stood up, disoriented, his vision clouded by a red tinge that made the room a hellish vision of crimson haze. He staggered, caught the back of a chair for balance, and shook himself, blinking hard.

The haze parted, and he saw the girl sitting on the bed. One of the servants had wrapped her in the blankets, and a wet red stain seeped from within them. His father stood at the foot of the bed, a lead candlestick in his right hand. The girl continued to weep.

"I said get her out of here." His father never looked away from Machiel as he spoke. The servant helped the weeping girl to her feet and took her from the room, and the door closed behind them. A streak of red painted the floor where they had walked. The older man turned to his son. He was strong, even at fifty, and he eyed Machiel with narrow eyes. "Are you back with us, then?"

The younger man collapsed on the chair that had kept him standing. "What happened?"

"I yelled at you for four or five minutes, Mach, four or five minutes and you never heard me. That girl screamed and beat at you, and it was as though you felt nothing. God! What if Bauwens hears of this? Can you remember nothing of what happened?"

"Father, I...I remember the tavern last night. I remember fighting with a braggart; I remember stepping out with a beer in hand while his friends dragged him away. Then nothing. I woke up, and Pauweline was in the bed. I didn't intend to hurt her. I—"

"You must avoid beer again until after the wedding. I have worked too hard to arrange this, and the wedding price—for all that Bauwens needs it, the rich prick—is already paid and not refundable. Stay away from the taverns." His eyes softened. "Son, I understand youth." He put the candlestick on the bed and sat down beside it. "Before your mother, I had servant girls. I had houseguests. Well, not with as much success and frequency as you." He laughed. "I don't suppose too many will be eager to share your bed after this."

"What of Pauweline?" Machiel wiped his mouth with the back of his wrist. It came down covered in blood.

"Oh, I suppose she'll enjoy a rather large endowment now, won't she? You need to get cleaned up and dressed. If the story has yet to spread, I'll see if I can convince anyone to bring you a washbasin." The old man chuckled. "I haven't felt my heart beat like that in ten years, Machiel. I suppose I should thank you." He stood and walked to the door, but he stopped before he opened it and looked back. "I know you don't want to marry Lysbette, son. I didn't want to marry your mother. In time we grew to love each other, and the wisdom of your grandparents proved itself. Please—"

"Mother wasn't fat, Father, and Mother was the daughter of a fruit dryer, not a banker."

"All right, all right: Lysbette is no prize, son. Still, take a mistress if you must and be discrete. But do not despair of your life for a marriage. Whatever the bishops might say, it's a business arrangement. For God's sake, try to stay sober." With that he left, and Machiel sat in the chair waiting for the servant with the washbasin.

In an hour, Machiel left his room and walked into the library. Since his teens, he had taken breakfast there, gradually wresting control of the books away from his father, who rarely took time to read anymore. A kettle of tea was already resting on the short, ornately carved table next to his chair. He remembered when his father had the table made. They had journeyed to the east to Halle to see the bluebells carpet the forest, and his father took rooms in an inn and sent for carpenters. When they arrived he took them to the Hallerbos, the forest, and told them he wanted a table for the library, carved with bluebells and made from the forest's birch trees.

Machiel chuckled to himself, and ran his fingers over the bluebells carved along the legs. The carpenters had recommended oak, but his father would hear nothing of it. The table had been commissioned and delivered and placed in the library, utterly out of place with the other pieces. For the next three years, his father had decorated the library in blue. Machiel looked at the far wall, where rich, blue tapestries hung. Christ and his disciples, dragons, birds, even an Arabian marketplace…the subject didn't matter: Blue. That was all. Even blue pillows had been commissioned to adorn the high backed oak bench that stood on the far wall of the library, their flowers a laughable contrast to the menacing knights carved into the back in iconic squares.

He sat and poured himself a cup, but let it sit to cool. The cup seemed strange. It was blue, of course, sparrows surrounding blue flowers and a blue sun, with very little white between the shapes: delftware from Antwerp. The blue seemed richer than he recalled from yesterday, as though it lived on clay, a pulsing and growing being rather than the tin glaze the Dutch potters had fired to imitate porcelain from the east. He studied it; it didn't move, but it seemed to have movement. He touched it, and it was unusually warm to the touch. It was warm, there was something—he stopped himself. The tea was making it warm. Machiel blinked his eyes and shook his head, smiling at himself. The *kriek* he drank the night before had been good, sour with Brussels cherries, and dry as hell, but he guessed he'd not drink another beer for a while.

He sipped the tea and frowned. The servants had brewed it poorly. It was nearly as tasteless as hot water. He set the cup down and stretched his arms. He found he was still aroused after the interrupted episode with Pauweline that morning. Well, he wouldn't be revisiting her for a while, if ever. What had come over him? The memory wasn't clear.

A servant stepped in...Rosalia, the French girl who'd been brought to Bruges by a scoundrel promising marriage and family, but abandoned. Machiel had prevailed upon his father to let the girl work in the kitchen, and he'd had many opportunities over the two years since to receive her gratitude. She carried a covered tray and set it on the table for him. She turned to the window, and as she did, Machiel swatted her bottom playfully, and she squealed and scowled at him. He smiled at her and she smiled back, blushing.

"Perhaps, after you've finished in the kitchen, you might like to help me in my chambers?"

"Sir! You are to be married!" She was mocking him, and she walked to the window, sweeping open the heavy drapes and hooking them over the iron catches at the sides. Early morning sunlight swept into the room, illuminating Machiel's father's blues in fine contrast to the dark stained woods and leather bindings. "But perhaps you need instruction for your

wedding night. If you promise to be an attentive pupil with —
Mon Dieu! What is wrong? *Mon trésor*, speak to me."

Machiel writhed on the chair, arms covering his face.
"The light...please...too bright." He felt his eyes burning as
though they had been filled with smoke. The brightness was
overwhelming. Pain lanced through his forehead. "P—
please." He croaked out the word and continued to squirm on
the chair. Pressure was mounting at his temples, like a great
vise had been placed on his head and a carpenter turned the
lever, screwing the vise tighter and tighter. The lever turned,
the screws moved. Surely his head would explode like a
melon. He opened his mouth to plead with Rosalia again, but
as quickly as his mouth opened, the pain was gone. It didn't
fade, it didn't dissipate, it was just gone.

Rosalia stood at the window. The drapes hung again, and
the chamber was again illuminated only by the oil lamps and
the fireplace coals. She rushed back to him and cradled his
head in her arms. "Are you okay now, my light?" She cooed
softly, stroking his hair, and felt the bump his father's
candlestick had left on the side of his head. "Machiel, you are
hurt!"

"I'm fine now, my dear. I'm fine." The candlestick must
have done something to his eyes. He looked up at the girl and
smiled. "You called me your treasure." She stared down at
him, confused. "*Mon trésor*, you said, *my treasure*. Am I your
treasure, then?"

Rosalia kissed his forehead softly. He heard a soft rushing
sound at her throat, almost saw the blood coursing through
her neck. He had a terrifying and dark impulse to lash out, to
grab her and tear at her throat, but it passed when she stood.
"No Machiel, you are not my treasure. You are to be
Lysbette's treasure."

She lifted the copper dome covering his breakfast, and

Michael saw the rich *boudin noir*, the rich pork blood sausage he loved. It sat on the plate (delft, of course, with blue girls dancing along the rim) next to his favorite *stoemp*, potatoes mashed with leeks and sprouts. "Not my treasure," she was speaking softly, sadly, but she brightened a bit and added, "But perhaps when I have attended to my duties we can pretend for a while that you are." She lifted a blue cloth napkin to reveal a plate of breads, waffles dusted with sugar, and berry pastries. He smiled at her and watched her leave, focusing on the sway of her hips and feeling again the arousal he'd not consummated earlier.

His meal passed strangely. The bread and pastries that Machiel loved held no appeal for him at all. He stared at them, then took a small slice of the dark brown bread and brought it to his mouth. It took a great deal of effort just to take a bite, and it was nearly tasteless. He tried a piece of waffle, and he may as well have chewed on parchment...the *stoemp*, soft clay. Only the *boudin* held any flavor, and even then, he thought it was quite overdone.

He left his tray on the table and stood. The tapestries called to him. Like the blue on the cup, the embroidered birds seemed alive. He envisioned a breeze rustling through woven trees, and the image was so strong he could almost see the leaves moving. Dragons seemed to fly, knights galloped over threads, and he could almost hear Peter and John murmuring prayers at the feet of the Christ.

I'm still drunk, Machiel thought, and he walked out of the library. Back in his room, he splashed water from the washbasin over his face and lay down on his bed. A servant had already changed the bedclothes, and Pauweline's blood was gone, a memory. Machiel inhaled deeply and believed he could still smell it, the coppery, rich, and thick aroma that had so flooded his nose even as her blood flooded his mouth. *My*

God! What the hell was I doing?

He drifted off, and when he woke Rosalia was in the chamber. She had pushed out the shutters, and moonlight streamed in. She was in the middle of stepping from her dress when he opened his eyes and saw her. She truly was beautiful, the soft light and shadows giving alternately clear glimpses of her gentle curves and obscuring them in a way that made his desire for her almost maddening. He felt the bed shake a little as she got in, moving the blankets out of the way and climbing on top him. He reached for her, stroking her back, her hips, her shoulders. She opened his shirt and kissed his neck and his chest. "You slept all day, *amour*. I would not wake you earlier, but I must have you before that *vache grosse* has you."

He smiled as she moved lower. She was removing his trousers, and he felt himself responding to her touch. "Lysbette is a fat cow, isn't she?" He reached down and lifted Rosalia's head, gently cupping her chin. "I have no choice in this, love. My father arranged it, and I must be a son to him. Tell me, though, will you come with me to the house my father in law has built for us? Will you run the kitchen and be my treasure there?"

Rosalia smiled at him, kissed his hand, and moved it to his side. "I will," she said, and she began to kiss him, to tease him with her mouth as she had that first time a few years prior. Machiel felt the urgency within him growing, and she grew more pointed in her ministrations, her mouth no longer teasing, but working diligently, pointedly. When he cried out, she stayed there, her hands gripping his legs, her mouth still moving as he finished. She kissed him a final time and looked up at him. "I will."

Machiel's breath came heavy, and his eyes were glazed for a moment. It had never had that kind of power before, not with her or any of the other girls. He looked at Rosalia. She was kissing her way up his abdomen to his chest. He felt himself growing again, and he gripped her hips, lifting her up and onto him. Machiel could tell she was surprised by his vigor, and she cried out before kissing his neck and moving on top of him. She was flushed, her pale skin a soft pink. Machiel could feel the heat of the blood bringing color to her cheeks. He heard it as it coursed through her, quickened by her exertion.

She gripped his shoulders and cried out, and Machiel felt her body, hot with blood at the surface, just beneath her skin. He held her tight, moving his arms to her back, pulling her forward. There. There on her neck, the blood was powerful, strong. He smelled it. He felt it. He lifted his mouth to her neck and bit into her throat. Blood rushed into his mouth, even as her cry was strangled by the blood flooding her windpipe. She shook briefly, still gripping his shoulders, and Machiel drank deeply. It was, in just a moment, all of the substance and flavor that had been robbed of the food he'd tasted earlier. It was rich. It was strong. It was Rosalia...he was drinking her, and she was good.

Finally, the last of it flowed out, and Machiel realized he was still inside of her, in fact had culminated his passion a second time while he drank. He gently pushed her to the side. He felt full, glowing, burning with power as one of his lamps might burn with oil. Ah! Rosalia, her —

Rosalia! He looked at her. Her throat was torn as Machiel had seen sheep torn by wolves. What had he done? He looked at himself; blood covered his chest, his arms. He backed away from the bed, recoiling from the girl's body, and tripped on his chair, falling on the floor but still crawling backwards, away from the body.

"You'll want an explanation now, I imagine." A tall man

about his father's age stood on the windowsill. "Come with me." Machiel, panicking, reached for a weapon, any weapon, and came up only with a small clay vase, but he reared back to throw it. "No. Come with me." A sudden calmness swept over him and he found himself compelled to obey. The man handed him his clothes and he put them on. Together, they stepped through the window.

CHAPTER THREE

Inklings

Chloe, Seattle, Present Day

Chloe studied the fetish doll. Dark wood carved with a bulbous abdomen led to a thin torso and an oversized head. There were no arms carved or attached, but the body of the doll was adorned with strung beads, small bits of metal, and a few tiny pieces of glass. In 1964, a worker, probably a volunteer, had incorrectly categorized it as Zulu and dated it in the late 1700s. Chloe gingerly lifted it from the table and brought it to a shoebox sized plastic container lined with soft cotton. She carefully placed it in the box and reached across the table for a label.

Fertility Fetish, Dinka Tribe, Sudan, c. 1890. She smiled at the label. She could have written August 23, 1887. She could have added that the fetish was carved by a man named Achak and decorated by his seventeen year-old wife. She could have written that couple gave the fetish to a Christian missionary in exchange for a large kettle. She could have listed the eleven owners who'd had the doll. She could have written about the Dutch businessman who bought it at a curio shop in 1927 and brought it home to his sick daughter to offer her comfort in her last weeks of life. The image of the little girl lying weakly on her bed, pillow damp with sweat, hands so weak that her father had to place them on the doll for her to hold it, brought tears to her eyes and she reached for a tissue.

Not all projects carried with them clear visions as this one had...most of the time, the Sight came to her in vague impressions and cryptic thoughts. Chloe wasn't sure why a tricycle or even a cigar might give her a slight feeling of foreboding, but a brass door knocker or this fetish would offer clarity so intense that in the five minutes or so she'd handled the thing it felt to her that she'd lived every life that touched it. Years of learning, exploring, and training at the coven had done nothing to illuminate the erratic nature of the Sight.

She stood, picked up the box, and walked to the shelf. She had already categorized about twenty items today, and she needed to slow down. Three days' worth of work in a single day brought questions, and she wasn't ready to tell curious museum officials why she identified the artifacts with such ease. She chuckled to herself, thinking about the conversation.

"You see, sir, I'm really a witch and I've been gifted with the Sight, and our coven leader believes it only comes along every sixth generation. Evidently, I'm a child of prophecy. By the way, the prostitute you see every Thursday — you know, the one who gave you that tie — she told seven other men last week that they were her favorite customer."

She sighed. The new girl-genius curator from New York was arriving tomorrow and Chloe was assigned to pick her up and show her around. She hoped they got along. There weren't any women her age on the museum staff, and she could use some youth among the agelessness of the place. She glanced at her watch. Time for lunch.

Amber, New York, Present Day

Amber stood naked on the hill, her hair darker than normal, almost crimson and flowing with the breeze so she felt it brushing against her breasts, her shoulders, and her back, soft bristles of sensation that clung to her for moments at a time, as though her skin refused to release the touch in time with the wind. The wind was brisk in fact, and she wondered why she wasn't cold...freezing actually. She could feel it blowing against her thighs, her waist, between her legs, and over her face, but the trail of touch it left was almost devoid of temperature. She lifted her hands to touch her face and noticed that her nails seemed long, manicured to a sloping point about three-quarters of an inch past the cuticle, and colored with the same dark red of her hair. She stared at them. It wasn't right. *I don't wear my nails like this.*

She looked down at herself. She wasn't naked after all but wore a single item...a gauzy strip of red silk so insubstantial that she felt it now only when looking at it wrapped around her waist, secured by her family's crystal. It only hung down about seven or eight inches, and the wind caught the edge of the silk and blew it open and closed, alternately exposing her completely and then almost but not quite obscuring her with the transparent cloth. Vaguely, she realized she should feel uncomfortable or at least a little self-conscious, but she found herself completely at ease. In fact, she felt a bit empowered; her body had never looked this good before, and she imagined the college boys eating out of the palm of her hand. The thought brought a tinge of desire to her, and she felt the breeze at her breasts create a slight tingling.

A growling sound floated through the air to her, and she looked up to see the man from the park. He stood in a field blanketed with snow, bare to his waist. His hair also moved with the wind, the sideburns a little more pronounced than they had seemed in the park. His chest, the giant barrel of a chest, moved with his breath, and she followed it to his neck and then his face. He stared at her impassively...no, not impassively. *Just not lustfully.* She felt a little foolish but wished his face, just staring softly at her, would transform itself into a leer.

Snow! How could there be snow on the ground? She looked down. Yes, she stood on snow. Still, she was not cold. She reached her hand to her right breast and touched her nipple. It was soft. Neither the cold nor the vague stirrings she felt for the comic man had — wait. The man was gone. The field was empty now. Snow still covered the ground, but he was gone.

A line of trees lay about forty yards in front of her and curved around to the left side of the field — was it a meadow? She could hear birds chirping softly. A movement caught her eye. Two deer stepped out of the trees, a buck and a doe, and walked slowly into the snow until they paused at a small patch of green, lowering their heads to graze. She smelled blood, imagined she could hear it coursing from their hearts through their necks.

The breeze died, and Amber felt her hair settle over her shoulders. Something was different about the sky. Clouds had simply appeared, and they were changing from white to red, casting a strange pinkish glow over the snow. She heard growling and noted that the deer had stopped, ears pricked up. Eleven black shapes burst from the trees almost as one, and she watched the buck jump forward as the doe jumped backward. The shapes, giant black dogs — no, not dogs, wolves — split, seven chasing the buck and four cutting off the doe's retreat. She saw the doe try to leap over and away, back into the woods, but a wolf leapt at the same time, and she heard the bones in the doe's neck crumble as the wolf's jaws clamped down. The others gnashed at the body, one pulling a foreleg clean off and the others tearing huge pieces of flesh and gore from the back and rear. The killing wolf had nearly pulled the deer's head from its body.

For a moment, Amber thought the buck would escape, but as it neared the trees, a new wolf appeared and leapt at it, its mouth opening impossibly wide and coming down right at the shoulder. Amber licked her lips at the sight of blood pouring through the wound, and the remaining wolves clamped down on its neck, fur, sides, and back. The new wolf, the large one, released his bite and lifted his head. Amber looked at it, its eyes deep yellow even in the strange tint of the clouds. Blood dripped from its jaws and its muzzle was encrusted with gore. It stared at her for a moment and then lifted its head and howled a violent, jarring, and impossibly loud mourning that strangely thrilled her. The other wolves stopped their feast and lifted their heads, joining the howl until an eerie and melancholy chord filled the field.

Amber felt movement beside her but didn't turn. Eleven or twelve men and women were walking past her and down the knoll into the field. The wolves started to growl and to circle them, and the newcomers' eyes seemed to glow red. One opened his mouth and hissed, and Amber saw fangs instead of teeth.

A hand touched the small of her back, and she turned to see a man dressed in black. His face wasn't distinct, but somehow obscured through the red haze. He pulled her toward him, and she felt his lips on hers, felt his tongue pushing into her mouth. She could hear the wolves fighting with the newcomers, yelps mixing with screams and growls and roars. The man's hand moved lower, cupping her and pulling her even closer to him. She could feel his hardness through his black slacks and she kissed him hungrily. His hands were travelling now. He placed one over her breast, and she felt him reaching lower with his other hand. He pushed her away for a moment, and she heard him say, "Because the traffic downtown won't wait for anyone!"

She looked at his face, still incomplete, amorphous. "What?"

"And now, it's another block of ten uninterrupted songs."

The radio blared and Amber sat upright on the bed and clicked it off. The wolves were tearing at the throats of the people in black, and the people pushed their long nails into the wolves' coats, tearing red strips of flesh...no. It was her room. She rubbed her eyes and saw the man disrobing and walking up to her. She blinked. She was on her bed, alone. The clock read 4:30. It took a moment for the dream to fade and for her to recognize her room confidently. Her bags sat next to the door where she'd put them just a few hours before. She had to get moving. She called for a cab and stepped into the shower.

Michael, Over the Atlantic, Present Day

The scraping of the wood of the lid woke Michael, and without conscious thought, he extended his nails and his fangs. With a slight push, the lid flew off and he sprang from the coffin, landing lightly on the metal of the cargo bay landing. A girl in a stewardess uniform stood behind the coffin, her eyes wide, and he stared at her, her thick brown hair pulled up severely in a bun, exposing her neck. She looked terrified, and he could hear the sound of her blood rushing through her. His hunger was becoming too real.

He licked his lips and approached her.

"Wait!" The word sputtered out of her, half a choke and half a sob. "Marcus sent me. Marcus sent me."

Michael forced himself to calm down, burying the hunger

deep within. "Didn't he tell you what happens when girls play with coffins?"

She was weeping completely now. "He...he said...to wake...wake you...you up...when it was safe...for you." She looked down at the metal tiles. Through her sobs he heard her say, "I'm sorry."

"Marcus should have told you that we are hungriest when we rise, and we're not accustomed to waking at the whim of another." The poor girl was shaking. Michael reached out to her and pulled her into an embrace, stroking her hair. "There, there. No harm done."

She looked up at him, her eyes red and her mascara running a bit on her cheeks. "He told me you'd be hungry," she said softly and extended her wrist, bending her hand back and placing it in front of his mouth. Michael could smell her blood, and he flicked his tongue out at the vein and then bit softly into her. He was still holding her and he felt her sharp inhalation as his teeth pierced her skin. He sent soft images of calm to her and felt her relax.

Her blood was fresh, rich, and tender. She was a drinker—he could taste the alcohol in her blood, and he enjoyed it. The blood flowed softly into him and he felt his strength growing. Finally, he removed his lips, released her, and kissed her wounds. She stood back a moment and gingerly pulled the sleeve of her uniform over her wrist.

"I'm sorry I startled you," she said softly.

"Let us speak no more of it." Michael considered what else she might offer, or give whether or not she offered. She was still shaking a bit as she reached down to the floor, recovered her handbag, and pulled out a ticket.

"You're in first class. We'll be landing in about five hours, but Marcus thought you'd like to be upstairs since the sun won't shine again on this trip." She handed him a few folded papers, and he placed them in his jacket pocket.

She was attractive, her waist curving to her hips, her legs long. He looked at her, and she saw his intentions. She blushed and said quietly, "We don't have to go upstairs right away."

Chapter Four

Journeys

Chloe, Mount St. Helens, 1998

Chloe stood in the center of the valley, the wind causing her long black hair to flow behind her in a surreal way. Tom stood in front of her. "Focus now, Chloe. Only notice what the stone tells you."

Chloe stared at the rock in her hand and tried to concentrate. "There's too much to see! It's like every pebble and tree and even the water is yelling at me. I can't see what the rock says. I can't!" She stamped her foot and stared belligerently at him. "I just can't do it, Wheeze—uh, Tom." She threw the rock down at the ground and folded her arms at her chest.

Tom sighed, walked to where the rock lay, and picked it up. He looked at it for a moment and brought it back to the girl. Gently, he unfolded her arms, opened her hand, put the rock back in place, and closed Chloe's little fingers over it. He closed his hand over hers and whispered softly to her. "Chloe, do you know what it's like when the television is on really loud and when music is on in another room and when people are having conversations and then someone talks to you?" Chloe nodded. "When that happens, sweetheart, do you turn the TV off and tell everyone to shut up?" She shook her head. "That's right, Chloe. Instead, you concentrate on what the person is saying and your mind makes everything else quieter. That's what you need to do now. See, this place is filled with stones and trees and everything else yelling and shouting because of what happened here. You need to try to make all of that noise get quieter."

"Like when someone talks to me at a party?" Tom nodded.

Chloe pulled her hand from his and sat cross-legged on the ground. She closed her eyes and concentrated on the rock, squeezing it in her hand until it began to hurt her palm. A tree a few yards away was burning, but she knew that had happened in the past, not now, and she tried to make the image get quieter as Tom told her. It was hard, but she pushed it to the background. She felt the ground underneath her. It rumbled, shook, and grew warm. She closed her eyes tighter and made the ground quiet as well. She began to get a picture from the stone in her hand and focused on it, willing the images around her to fade.

The stone grew louder and Chloe began to speak. "The stone is silent until it was mixed with sand and glue and became part of a house where people walked on it almost every day, and every day a little girl walked on it and played with Barbie dolls and a bear named Buttons. She had tea parties on this stone, but there wasn't really tea in any of the cups. A day came when all of the people went away and nobody walked on the stone. A little later, the whole house blew apart and the sand and glue melted away until the stone was all by itself again. It was covered up with ashes until rains came and washed them away. Sarah, that's the little girl's name, is all grown up now and studying vetera…vetra…she's studying to help sick animals in a school for big people somewhere far away. Her daddy died, but her mommy misses her a lot and cries at night because she misses her." Chloe looked up at Tom, tears welling up in her dark brown eyes, eyes that seemed deep-set and distant as though she were ninety years old instead of nine. "It's so sad, Wheezer. It's so sad!" The girl burst into tears and threw her arms around her teacher. He held her, stroking her hair and softly humming to her.

"That was very good, Chloe. Don't you worry about Sarah and her mommy. Children grow up and move away. That's what happens, and mommies everywhere are sad. But those same mommies grow proud of how their little girls grow up and do wonderful and important things."

"Like helping sick animals?" Chloe asked, wiping a tear from her cheeks. "Like Sarah is gonna do?"

"Yes, honey, like helping sick animals."

"Will I do wonderful and important things?"

"Oh, yes, sweetheart. You will do very wonderful and very important things. You are a child of prophecy, and you have the Sight! You will do things that will be important to many people." Tom found a handkerchief in his pocket and handed it to Chloe. "Now, blow your nose and let's go get some ice cream."

Amber, New York City, Present Day

The airport was awash in chaotic activity. Amber stood in line to check her bags, looking around her at the mass of people milling about. A middle-aged woman stood as though paralyzed, looking around her, then at the ticket in her hand, and then around her again. Skycaps moved in and out of the crowd with flat hand trucks loaded with luggage. People of every color, shape, and size moved as though purposeless, and Amber couldn't help but think of them as ants or bees swarming—no, that was not right. Ants and bees had purpose in all of their movements, and nobody here seemed to have any idea where to go or what to do.

The airline employee finished with a customer, and the line moved forward a bit. Amber pulled her suitcases forward and stood again. She hated waiting. She always had. Her mind raced to a thousand things she could do, even with nothing in particular necessary. She wasn't going to miss her flight; there was plenty of time left before it would board. Still, to her, productivity was almost a necessary aspect of every second of her life. She shook her head and chuckled at herself. Even relaxation became a means to increase her personal productivity.

As she stood, she recalled the first time she'd recognized that fact. It was late in her first year in college. She was still five months from her eighteenth birthday, and boy after boy had tried to be the one who first took the little girl genius. While completing a term paper on the influence of third-party observation on a cultural construct, she realized that a lack of recreation affected her ability to write concisely on the subject. With no particular desire for companionship or even for a break from her studies, she nonetheless selected one of the boys at random and called him over. The two watched a laughable horror film and ate pizza at her apartment. As the evening drew toward a close, she'd let the boy lead her to the bedroom and clumsily work his way through sex with her. She'd enjoyed the night, and she liked the sex. Nonetheless, she was unable to approach the whole experience without a clinical detachment. The movie, the pizza, and even the student moving on top of her were all designed to make her work more effective and effortless.

I haven't ever had fun without a purpose. Amber wondered if she should feel strange about that, but the ticket agent was calling her name and she returned to the present as she lugged her bags up to the counter. In a few minutes, her bags were checked, her ticket accepted, and a boarding pass issued. She thanked the woman who had handled the process, and instead of receiving a pleasantry in return, the woman gave her a cold look as she walked away and searched for an escalator. It took her a while to find the gate, but she still had nearly forty-five minutes before her flight would board, so she strolled to the newsstand to find something to read on the flight.

Michael, New York City, Present Day

Marcus stood at the gate as Michael stepped out. He had one of his agents with him, a tall man with dark eyes, dressed in a suit that looked absurdly small for his build. When Marcus saw Michael, he stepped forward and embraced him. "Ah, I'm glad to see that Hanna woke you, Machiel."

"Call me 'Michael' here, Marcus. I am not in Flanders, and only Jacob...." Michael stopped and drew a breath. Kabos was gone now. "Only Kabos called me by that name."

"He finally climbed the tower? I can only imagine how you feel, Michael."

"I'm pretty certain," the dryness of his tone wasn't lost on Marcus, "that you'll not feel the same the day I leave this world."

"Please, Father, don't be cruel. I do share your pain, and as hard as it is sometimes for me to recognize the purpose in your actions, I do not wish you harm. No—it's good to see you after a decade of separation. Did Hanna see to it that you fed?"

"You should have warned that poor girl about waking me, Marcus. I almost killed her." The alarm in Marcus's eyes softened Michael's tone. "She saw to it that my every need was met, Marcus. Thank you for arranging it."

"You'll be happy to see how things have been arranged in the States for you as well. Tonight we will stay at your estate in Manhattan. As we research where your queen will turn up, we'll determine which of your other estates will become our base of operations." Marcus gestured to the man beside him. "Wilhelm came over with me from Germany. He's been with me for nearly twenty years. Wilhelm, take Michael's baggage ticket, please."

Michael handed over the claim ticket and studied Marcus. He hadn't changed. Of course he hadn't changed. None of them ever changed. "Let's get some wine while your man gets my bags."

The two walked out of the international terminal and found a terminal sports bar. Michael sat as Marcus left. This was the New World. The mass of humanity was overpowering. If he hadn't fed from Hanna's wrist, he might have had difficulty containing himself. As it was, it felt as though he were surrounded by a great sea of blood. He decided to hunt later tonight, to feed from live prey and to feel the life leave its host and fill him instead.

Marcus returned with two glasses of red wine. He set one in front of Michael and raised the other to his lips as he sat. Michael reached out and took the glass. Wine was the only mortal food that still held appeal for him…for any of his kind, really. Something about the fermentation allowed pleasure to taste buds altered by…by whatever it was that made them. *Jesus, how did we start?* It was such a cliché and unanswerable question that Michael shrugged it away as he always did. He turned his attention back to the wine and took a sip.

It had been nearly three hundred years since Michael had tasted red wine with a mortal tongue. He was fairly sure it tasted the same, perhaps a little sweeter than when he was alive. Kabos said — *used to say* — that something about fermenting fruit sugars agreed with the new body. Still, even the sour limbic beers of his youth, beers flavored with fermenting fruit, tasted like stale water now. Only red wine held any appeal, and even then, the wine did nothing to the body. As far as he knew, only blood could bring drunkenness. That drunkenness was fleeting though, lasting only a moment after feeding and so filled with energy that —

"The bags are in the car, sir." Wilhelm was back. The man stood impassively as they drank.

"Thank you, Wilhelm. You may wait at the c —"

"Marcus!" Michael was on his feet too quickly, and Marcus looked around to make sure nobody had seen the movement. Michael ran to the door, and Marcus struggled to keep up.

"Michael, you're moving too fast! Someone will see." Michael stopped and turned around. His eyes were blazing, nearly shining with excitement.

"It's her, Marcus. It's her!"

"What? Where?"

Michael turned and pointed, and Marcus saw a young woman stepping through an entry gate.

"The redhead?"

"Yes. We must get on that plane!" Michael was moving quickly again, and Marcus grabbed his arm.

"We can't, Michael. We haven't prepared. Look at the sign." He pointed to the board above the gate, which indicated Destination Denver. "It will be dawn before the flight arrives. Without a coffin in place, you'll join Kabos."

Michael whirled on Marcus, curling his fingers in his jacket and lifting him from the ground.

"Marcus, it is her. *Her!*"

Marcus looked down at Michael and sighed. He placed

his hands over Michael's and said, "We will send Wilhelm to follow her to Denver. He will keep an eye on her until we can travel there tomorrow." Michael still stared. "Be reasonable, Father. The time may come when you will die for your queen, but that time is not tonight."

Michael slowly lowered Marcus to the ground. "Send him."

Marcus walked away and Michael watched him conferring with his charge. Wilhelm nodded and made his way to the gate. It was not until long after Wilhelm crossed the threshold that Michael stopped staring. He stood wordlessly until the doors closed and Destination Denver was replaced with another indicating Chicago O'Hare.

"I cannot lose her, Marcus. It is my destiny."

CHAPTER FIVE

Layovers

Amber, Denver, Present Day

Flames surrounded her. Amber floated among them, naked again. She could smell the sweet and nauseating odor of burning flesh, but it was not her flesh. She looked at herself, saw the flames surrounding her body, and still felt inexplicably cool. Flames caressed her legs, licked at her back, and mingled with her hair, but she remained undamaged. From beneath her she heard screams, loud and torturous, rising to a feverish pitch and then ending in gagging coughs. As soon as one faded others began, and Amber tried but failed to look through the fire to see the people consumed by the flames.

From above, Amber heard more cries of pain, but these were different. Howls and whines replaced human voices, reminding her of dogs squealing in pain. A new odor assaulted her, the deep smell of burning hair. Finally, the yells, howls, and squeals came at once, a cacophony that grew in intensity and power until she shut her eyes, pulled her hands to her ears, and screamed herself.

The noise of Amber's scream was unearthly; even as she opened her mouth it seemed to her that the voice came from elsewhere. She opened her eyes and put her hands down, but found her lips still parted and the hollow, overpowering eruption from within didn't stop. It grew in volume until she could no longer hear the cries of those dying in the flames. She felt her throat growing strained from the effort and wondered why she hadn't stopped screaming. Finally, she placed one hand on her chin and one on the top of her head and pushed her mouth shut.

Silence — it fell like a blanket over Amber, smothering the flames beneath it. She was still floating, but below her was an ocean of bodies. Men, women, children, dogs — all charred beyond recognition. *Not dogs, wolves.* Some were still locked in battle. She saw a wolf, body still smoking from the flames, with its mouth still locked on the throat of a man burned so completely that his arm was only an ash covered skeleton. There were at least a hundred dead people and twice that number of wolves. The stench was overpowering, choking her, and tears flowed down her cheeks as she tried to breathe.

Suddenly the ground was clear and she sat on a bench watching small children playing on a jungle gym. A little girl in a bright orange shirt and white Capri pants skipped along singing, "The hour, the hour, the hour, born without knowledge of power." She watched a toddler at the top of the jungle gym climbing unsteadily. *He's going to fall!* Amber tried to stand and found she could not. She watched in horror as the little boy fell. It was about a nine-foot drop, but the boy fell slowly, his overalls rippling with the wind, his dark brown hair flying up over his face.

Suddenly a wolf was there, and it caught the boy in its mouth. Amber braced herself for the sound of teeth tearing into bone and flesh, but they were gone. The jungle gym was gone. The singing girl was gone, and Amber sat on the bench surrounded by a misty red fog.

"You're the child of prophecy." Amber stared. The man from the park, the one with the sideburns, sat on the bench beside her and held out the little boy. No, not a boy — it was a doll with a ceramic head.

"What did you say?" Amber looked earnestly at the man.

"I said it's time to land, dear." The stewardess smiled at Amber. "Please put your tray table up, and make sure your seat belt is securely fastened."

Amber rubbed her eyes. *Why the hell don't I dream about Gerard Butler like a normal girl?* She lifted the cup of water that still sat on the tray table and drained it before pushing the tray table shut. She put the cup in the pocket of the seat and made sure of her belt. The mists were finally fading, but she rubbed her eyes again and the cabin came into focus. Around her, passengers packed away their laptops and papers and sat a little straighter. A tired young mother was trying to get her daughter to sit still long enough for the seatbelt to be buckled. A young man was staring at the stewardess' rear end as she walked, and....

The man! The man from the park sat three rows ahead in a window seat. He sat straight, occasionally glancing out of the window, but it was him. She recognized his sideburns, his build, and his profile. He was dressed in a charcoal suit, remarkably well-tailored for a man of his size, and she noticed an expensive watch on his wrist. Why was he following her? *My God, get a hold of yourself. It's a coincidence, Ms. Genius.*

It was the damned dreams. They'd been with her for at least as long as her adoption, maybe longer. There were always wolves fighting strange people, and she was usually naked or changed. Hell, there was always something weird about her in the dreams. Her nails, her teeth, flying, handstands...God, she was sick of it.

She closed her eyes as the plane landed and she tried to push the last vestiges of the dream from her mind. She glanced at her watch…ninety minutes before her connecting flight. She lifted her window shade and noticed that dawn had just begun to creep over the Colorado Mountains.

Michael, Italian Alps, 1772

Michael rode slowly on top of the chestnut mare. She was skittish, and he had to reach out constantly with his thoughts to calm her. Jacob (Kabos insisted on that name now) told him animals were far easier to influence than humans were, but the effects were much more fleeting. "A charmed man is loyal to death, but calm a horse and it will need calming again in just a few minutes." Up ahead, the old man rode a smaller black horse, his stooped figure atop the saddle belying a speed and power Michael had witnessed time and time again.

"Where are we going, Kabos?" He'd asked the question several times to no avail, but it was late into the night and he was bored and frustrated.

"Jacob."

"Of course. Where are we going, Jacob?"

"It is only a mile or two down the road now. Be patient."

The mare whinnied and started to rear. Michael reached out with his mind, sending thoughts of calm and peace.

"It's not you Michael," Kabos stopped his horse. "We appear to have company." He looked to the trees beside the road and called out loudly, "Well, get on with it, if you can."

From the shadows stepped two men. One, a hulking brute, towered over the other, a rat-faced man holding a dagger. Both were dressed in dull grey cloaks, and the brute held a large wooden branch fashioned into a club of sorts. "Step down from your horses and stand back." It was Rat Face who spoke. "Do as you're told and Victor won't need to use his little stick on you."

Michael sighed. "Jesus, Kab...Jacob, we don't have time for this."

Rat Face took a step forward. "If you don't dismount, you'll find yourself without time for anything."

Michael glanced at the robber and then back at Kabos, but the old man was gone. A gurgling sound came from the brute, from Victor, and Michael saw him flailing wildly and beating at Kabos's back. He was a good two feet in the air, and the old man's mouth was locked on his throat. Michael looked back at Rat Face, who stood staring at them.

"Shall I dismount as well?" he asked dryly.

The small man turned to Michael, his eyes wide with fright. He lifted his dagger, but shook so heavily that it fell to the ground. Desperately he turned and ran toward the trees, but only made three steps before Michael was on his back, his teeth tearing through the wool hood and finding the flesh of the small man's neck. Michael's eyes opened wide at the first rush of blood. He was hungry, and the blood was warm and thick. He drank deeply and stood.

Kabos was just finishing with the big one. In a moment, he pulled his mouth away and casually tossed the body into the trees. "Get rid of it," he gestured toward the smaller robber, and Michael threw the other body after the first. "Well, Michael, we've saved a bit of time then, haven't we? No need to hunt later."

The two found their mounts, but Michael had to exert a deal of effort to get the damned mare to forget about the smell of blood. Finally, the horse relented and Michael climbed up and took his place behind Kabos once more. The two travelled silently until the lights of a camp came into view ahead. Michael heard voices and singing.

"What is this, Kabos? You told me to avoid the gypsies."

"Jacob."

"Damn it! Does everything have to be cryptic with you? Why are we here?"

"This group has come from Flanders, Michael. My agents there have paid them to deliver to me a message."

"God, Kab…Jacob, was that so hard?"

Kabos waved him to silence. Two men were already walking up to the horses, long torches in their hands. Kabos raised an arm in greeting, but one of the men was already speaking with a thick Eastern accent. "If you'd like to rest your horses or have a meal, we can help. If you want to sleep, you'll have to camp elsewhere."

"I am Kabos van Gruuthuse. Besnik has something that belongs to me and I am come to fetch it."

The man lifted his torch so that light fell across Kabos's face, and looked intently at him for a while. While his companion had a long scar over one eye and down his cheek, this one was young with fair and unblemished skin. "Why do the blood drinkers come to our camp? I warn you, we are not the helpless prey you usually hunt. There are—"

"Tell Besnik I have arrived. We're not here to hunt, and he's expecting us." Kabos turned his horse toward Michael and said over his shoulder to the men, "We'll wait here." Michael sighed, but Kabos winked at him. The men returned to the camp.

"We have a long history with the Romani, Michael. They may be the only people in this world who know of us. Of course, they distrust us, but they have their uses. Take care not to overreact to their behavior."

"When have you ever known me to overreact?" The old man chuckled and turned his horse around again. The men were already returning.

"Besnik would like to invite you to his wagon." The other

man spoke this time, the scarred man. "Please allow my son to take your horses for you." He stepped forward and Michael readied a protest, but Kabos wordlessly dismounted and handed the man his reins. Michael did the same, a little warily, but Kabos was moving quickly so he turned and followed.

The camp was loud, and it occurred to Michael that the people within seemed to pay no notice to the visitors. As if sensing his thoughts, Kabos said, "Make no mistake about it, Michael. Every eye is on us."

"Not mine," the scarred man said. "My eyes are on Besnik's wagon. It stands at the end of the camp past the cooking fire." The man pointed and Michael followed the direction to an ornately decorated wagon with bright silk sides. He and Kabos walked forward and Michael noticed an impossibly old woman struggling to lift an iron pot onto a ring above the fire. He stepped forward, then paused, glancing at Kabos.

"Go ahead Michael. We bite; gypsies don't." Kabos continued to the wagon while Michael walked up to the crone, reached forward with one hand, and easily lifted the pot into place. The pot was filled with water.

"Usually, a woman would lift an empty pot and fill it afterward." Michael smiled at himself and turned to walk away.

"Usually, a night creature would walk past without helping." The woman's voice was guttural and thick. Michael turned and saw her pouring herbs of one kind or another into the pot. "Why did you lift that pot?"

"I...." Michael thought for a moment. "I'm not sure. I just saw that you needed help and I helped."

"You are not ancient yet, then. Come with me, I will read you." The woman turned and hobbled toward a wagon a few yards away. Michael glanced at Besnik's and then followed the woman, who climbed inside with a dexterity that seemed impossible for her age.

The wagon was bare inside except for a few cloth bags, two stools, and a small table. The wooden planks of the wagon looked newer than its contents. The woman walked to a stool and seemed to take hours to sit down. Finally, she gestured to the other and Michael sat as well. "What is your name?"

"Michael."

"You are not like your kind. You are chosen. You will find a girl, an important girl." The woman sighed a long exhalation and closed her eyes before continuing. "Not in this lifetime. A hundred years, two hundred years, more even will pass, but you will forsake all other women in search of her. You will be alone, but not the solitude of your kind. You will find many women, but this one child, this girl is special. She is chosen as well."

The woman licked her lips and opened her eyes. She stared at Michael. "Give me your hand." Michael extended it and she took it in both of hers. Her skin was rough and dry and Michael was amazed to find he could not hear her blood as it ran through her wrists.

"Listen to me, Michael, she is young and old. Her life is the soul of an old life. Her hair is the color of the blood you steal, and her eyes are the forests of your youth. This girl is your soulmate, your imprint. You must find her and make her one of you. You must give her your power."

"How will I find her?" Michael didn't think before he blurted the question out, but the hag smiled up at him. He imagined were he still alive the blood would be rising on his cheeks.

"She is your destiny. You will find her. She is marked

with the tongue of ancients on her neck, but you will know her before you see that mark. Find her. Her history is long and old. If you find her, and if you give her your power, your love will be eternal. You must—"

Michael shuddered. "But what if I don't?"

"Oh, you will find her. You are young, but you are strong, very strong for your kind. Perhaps in a century or two there will be none among the blood drinkers stronger. If you fail to turn her, fail to give her your power, your love will end, and perhaps all of the night dwellers will suffer. Perhaps love for all of you will end." She sighed and released Michael's hands. He sat silently for a moment and then stood, but before he could speak, the old woman looked up at him again.

"Wait. There is more. There are wolves here as well. She is a child of prophecy, and the wolves and your kind are all...if you fail, you fail all of them. I cannot see more. The power is beyond me. Seek out the prophecy, Michael. There is a prophecy. I see it. It is written. There is more."

Michael stared at the strange old gypsy as she closed her eyes and seemed to fall asleep on the stool. A knock at the wagon was followed by the face of the scarred man. "Your friend is finished, and my son is fetching your horses." Michael nodded and stood, but before he stepped from the wagon, the old woman wheezed and spoke again.

"Machiel of Bruges. Do not fail the child of prophecy. Do not fail yourself."

CHAPTER SIX

Connections

Amber and Chloe, Seattle, Present Day

The black wolf was friendly. Amber knew that right away. She knelt next to a large evergreen, feeling the pine needles crinkling beneath her bare knees. *Bare?* She looked down at herself. *Naked in the forest like some kind of nymph.* The wolf was approaching, whining softly. Amber noticed a luster to her skin. *At least I'm a hot nymph.* The wolf was nearly to her now, whining and looking up at her with...well, with puppy eyes. "Are you hungry, boy?" As soon as she said the words, she felt stupid. She was naked in the forest. Where the hell was she going to get food? *My God, I am the food.*

The wolf reached her and began nuzzling her extended hand, still whining. "Oh, you are hungry, boy." The wolf pushed Amber's hand to the left. Inexplicably, a joint of beef, still glistening with blood, lay by Amber's leg. She lifted it up and handed it to the wolf, which took it between its jaws and began to eat. She started to stroke the thick, dark fur on the back of his neck, which brought grateful half growls as it ate, more and more intent on the meat in front of it.

Amber watched as the powerful jaws closed around the joint, and she heard as the force of the bite set it to straining, almost creaking, until finally the bone gave with a sickening crunch. The wolf turned to look at her with an almost satisfied look on its face. *If you could smile, you would, wouldn't you, boy?* The wolf whined again and turned its attention back to its meal, and Amber glanced toward the meat and screamed.

Where seconds ago had been a joint of beef laid the body of a small child, neck crushed and face unrecognizable beneath the torn skin and flayed muscle.

The plane landed and Amber awoke with a start. *What the hell is happening to me?* The dreams were changing, images growing more profound and disturbing. *Disturbing? They're fucking scary!* As the plane taxied to a stop, she went over images of pictures from an archeological dig of an Andes village conducted in 1911 and cataloged by a Lima museum in 1973. She'd included a number of cultural conclusions based on that dig in her master's thesis, and the pictures of pots, baskets, and flint tools gradually drove the bloody child's face from her mind.

As she stepped out of the arrival gate, she looked around, expecting someone to be there to meet her. Sure enough, a sign with her name on it got her attention, and she made her way to the attractive young woman holding it.

***

Chloe saw her as she stepped out of the arrival gate. *Oh great. Twenty-one years old, two degrees, and she looks like a supermodel. Yeah, that's fair.* She stood waiting, holding the sign from the museum until Amber read her name and walked up. At this distance, Chloe realized the flight hadn't been kind to the new girl. *Amazon Princess has red puffy eyes. At least she's not perfect.*

"Hi, Ms. Stone?"

"Hi, call me Amber." Amber extended her free hand and

Chloe shook it warmly. She didn't get any visions, which was weird.

"Okay, Amber, welcome to Seattle." Chloe dropped the poster board sign in a wastebasket and began to walk. She glanced back at Amber. "The baggage claim is this way, and I paid a skycap to let me keep the car in the loading zone. Was your flight okay?"

"Well, I slept a little, but I didn't get any rest."

***

Amber followed Chloe and studied her. Straight black hair reached down just past her waist, half-obscuring her rear, but the long gray dress the woman wore clung so tightly to her that nothing could obscure her body completely. *I think I'd kill to look that good*, Amber thought. Chloe led them to an escalator and down until they stood by the benches surrounding the baggage carousels.

"Are you a cab driver?" Chloe wasn't dressed like a cab driver.

"Oh no, I work at the museum. I'm the designated female employee young enough to share common interests with the new girl genius superstar assigned to make you feel welcome."

Amber stared at her for a moment, her cheeks reddening. Suddenly, simultaneously, the two burst into laughter. The laughter turned to giggling, and Amber dropped her carryon and collapsed onto the bench, lost in the laughs until tears formed in her eyes. "Well," she said as her breath returned haltingly. "At least I know Seattle cab drivers don't walk around dressed like actresses on Oscar Night."

"Oscar Night? I bet you didn't even do anything to make yourself look like Ms. All Men Must Have Her Even After A Transcontinental Flight." This set off another round of laughter that didn't end until a carousel a few down started up and the two got their bearings up enough to walk over. Amber watched for her bags and felt Chloe staring at her with amazement.

"Okay, I guess this means we're going to be friends, but even if I like you I'm going to ask for a bonus for genius management."

Amber smiled. "Is that what you do at the museum, genius management?"

"Indigenous artifacts and tribal art. I'm the curator."

"We might do some work together on the digs I'll be cataloging. How big is your collection?" Amber reached down and grabbed her suitcase. "One more bag to go."

"The museum buys collections three or four times a decade, but they stopped cataloging them back in the sixties. This rich family endowed the museum just to buy the stuff, and in the fifties they hired one of the family's kids to catalogue it. The kid worked on it until his dad died, and left to go be a multi-gazillionaire. The museum has to spend the endowment interest every couple of years, but it was just last year they decided to do something with the pieces they'd collected. That's where I come in. I'm a couple of weeks from finishing with reclassifying all the stuff the kid screwed up, and then I'll start on fifty years of other purchases."

***

Chloe saw another bag on the carousel. Images flashed through her mind. The little duffel bag held the skull from the Macedonian collection. *Wonder how that got through security*? She reached down and picked it up. "Okay, let's get out of here, I'm starving."

"How did you know that was mine?" Amber was staring at her, and Chloe scrambled for something to say.

"It matches the suitcase, doesn't it?" Amber looked down, and nodded in agreement. "You should see me at a mall."

"I've never been to a mall."

"What?"

"Grew up on a farm and lived in a college town. This is only the third place I've ever been." Amber smiled shyly.

"Oh great. Smart, redhead, hell of a body, *and* innocent. It's like you were designed just to suck away all of the attention I usually get. You know, I bet there are museums hiring in New York." Another laughing fit overtook the two as they made their way to the car. The skycap was standing by the trunk, and Chloe slipped him another bill and popped it open. They stowed the bags and Chloe noticed the man hadn't left but leered at Amber. "Hey, pervert! Keep staring and I'll charge you that sawbuck I just gave you."

More giggling, and the two finally took their seats. "You know," Amber said, "I think he was staring at you, not me."

"Yeah right. Look Amber, when you bend over all men become blind to everything else." Chloe started the car and pulled away from the curb. "Seriously, though, what's your secret? Did you sell your soul or did you make a deal with a dark magician?"

"Says the girl who looks like a mad scientist combined Crystal Gayle, Megan Fox, and Jessica Alba and then dressed her like Audrey Hepburn." Amber looked at the cloudy sky, which foretold the frequent Seattle rain.

"Oh, I don't always dress this way. I get pretty outrageous sometimes, actually. The other day I had this bright yellow tube top over—"

"Tube top?"

"Yeah, yeah, tube top over a striped t-shirt, and—"

"The tube top was over the t-shirt?"

Chloe smiled. "Stop interrupting. The point is, today is Meet the Genius Day, and so I'm dressed nicely. Most of the time I'm just crazy...either some Goth punk princess, or a

Barbie doll whose owner mixed up all the outfits." A left turn brought them onto the freeway. "I'll tell you, Amber, if I couldn't tell the difference between a 17th century slave carving from Barbados and a Haitian fertility fetish, there's no way the museum would keep me around."

Amber sighed. Chloe thought she looked tired from the flight. "Where are we headed?"

"The museum is checking you into a hotel tonight and tomorrow, and your stuff will get here on Tuesday, right?"

"Yeah. The movers wanted an extra $800 to get it here today, but I didn't want to sleep a whole week in an empty apartment back home...I mean, back in New York."

"Okay, I'll drop you at the hotel and get you settled in. You get some rest and tonight I'll show you the town."

Michael, New York City, Present Day

"He lost her? What the hell is wrong with your agent, Marcus?" Michael flung the glass of wine from his hand and it crashed against the wall. A young woman, on whose wrist Marcus had placed his lips, sucking hungrily and deeply, fell back against the couch in fear. Marcus looked at her gently and gestured to the door. She gratefully bolted through it and Marcus calmly reached for a cocktail napkin, dabbed blood from his lips, and turned his attention on Michael.

"Well, Michael, right now what's wrong with Wilhelm is that his throat has been torn from his body. He was found by my agents in Denver lying in a toilet stall. It took a great deal of effort to dispose of the body without any involvement from the authorities."

"Jesus! I saw her. I was so close!" Michael looked at Marcus. "What now?"

"She's not in Denver. My agents would have seen her leave the airport. She must have caught a connecting flight. I have some inquiries working now."

Michael sighed. "Marcus, I can feel her still. This is maddening. Two hundred years I've searched for her. Two hundred years!"

Marcus walked over and put a hand on his shoulder. "And I have searched with you for nearly all of that time, Father. We will find her."

"Where the hell is she?"

Amber and Chloe, Seattle, Present Day

As the fire streamed from her fingers, Amber spoke in a low voice. "You will do as I say and will fight no more." She was naked again, and her whole body seemed to glow with fire. She moved her arm in a wide arc and the flames found wolves, people, plants, and—

The phone rang. It was four o'clock. The formal and polite voice on the line informed Amber that this was the requested wake-up call and asked if she would like to have anything sent up. Amber mumbled a no and sat up on the bed. The museum hadn't skimped on the hotel. *Who ever heard of wake-up calls that aren't recordings?*

She stood and walked to the mini bar, pulled out a single-serving bottle of cabernet, and unscrewed the cap. The dreams were changing, and so strange now. She drained the wine in a single drink, shuddered, and walked to the bathroom.

By the time Chloe knocked on her door an hour later, Amber felt like herself again. Her hair had reclaimed its tight wavy curls, and the bags beneath her eyes had been replaced by the pale freckle-less skin that belonged on her face. Chloe looked at her. Amber was dressed casually in a cream-colored blouse and jeans. "Well, Ms. Genius, are you ready for a little fun and relaxation?"

"Sure. What's on the agenda?"

"Happy hour."

As she said it, Amber turned around and reached for her purse. As Amber picked up her purse, she could feel something from Chloe but wasn't sure what it was. She'd had this feeling many times in the past, but she had only been a child. She shrugged the feeling off, but then it hit her like a bolt of lightning. She could feel Chloe's thoughts. Her new friend was feeling like the *ugly friend*.

***

Something fell out of Amber's shirt...a crystal on a small chain. Images flooded over Chloe in a wave, and she stood transfixed for a moment. None of them made sense. None of them were distinct. It was like a slide show flashing thousands, millions of photos one after the other, twenty-five per second. Amber absently tucked it back into her shirt and the images ended.

"Where?" Amber was looking at her.

"What? Where what?"

"Happy hour. Where are we going?"

"Oh, God, Genius Girl, does it matter?" Chloe smiled as Amber shook her head and followed her to her car.

CHAPTER SEVEN

Dreams

Michael, Rome, 1773

Michael sat on the hard bed and looked at Kabos. The package from the gypsies had been wrapped in cloth and bound with string.

"What is it, Kab...Jacob?"

Kabos looked at Michael; his eyes seemed sad and heavy. "Did I tell you of my maker, Michael?"

"You said he was a merchant, or something like that."

"Well, that's true, in a sense. You have seen me speak to my human agents, yes?"

"Of course."

"My family controlled the market for dried fruit in Bruges. Not a beer was made that didn't have something from our warehouses. Usually, such a market would be cultivated by our kind with agents, our daylight agents. The success of *Gruuthuse* was such that the Avalani wanted an heir."

"The Avalani?"

"Oh, you'll know them soon enough, within a century or so."

"Who are they?"

Kabos smiled at Michael. They had left Bruges so quickly and kept moving for so long that he hadn't taught him anything of the old ways. "The Avalani rule us. In any case, they rule us as much as our kind will let itself be ruled. They were formed thousands of years ago by a group of prophets, but nobody cares much about their origins anymore." Kabos paused and shook his head. "Pour me some wine, Michael."

Michael reached over to the jug on the little wooden table that came with the room and poured a cup. He handed the cup to Kabos and poured one for himself. The old man took a long drink and smiled sadly.

"Thank you, Michael. The group formed to guard a prophecy and to see it come to pass, but when their leader died a half century ago, the group changed. Now, they're just a group of politicians enacting rules for the sake of rules."

"What was the prophecy, Kabos?"

"Call me Jacob." Kabos took another drink. "The prophecy told of a queen who would come. A few hundred years back, we thought she had come, but she fought with the king and he killed her. The Avalani were devastated, and the queen's husband, her human husband, killed the leader. After a few decades, the original purpose just faded away."

"What of the king?"

"Oh, the king is alive and well—or I should say 'dead' and well—and he still reports to the Avalani, which still rule us, though their purpose has become one of separation and…what do they call it? Oh yes, purity. Separation and purity. No mingling of our kind with any other. They even report to the Covenant."

"The Covenant?"

"A council of creatures such as we are. They formed to protect—oh, to hell with them. They're politicians like the Avalani." Kabos drained his cup. He pointed at the clothbound bundle on the bed. "That is for the Avalani and for the Covenant. It's a last accounting of the glorious house of Gruuten." He almost spat the last word. "All of these silly laws, Michael. Only kill if we must. Don't mix our blood with other races. Don't reveal ourselves to men. They are not enforced except for political gain. The Avalani are powerful, but they're just a lie now."

"Tell me about the queen, Kabos."

"The king loved her, and she loved him. But this girl, her powers were strong. She was stronger than the king, and she didn't wait for permission from anyone. She consorted with wolves, Michael, and the king loved the war between the wolves and our kind. He actually kept a number of them chained in his palace as pets. The queen opposed that. One day she freed them all. The Avalani leader supported her, while the rest opposed her. In the end, the leader was killed, anyway. A few years later, the king did some kind of dark sorcery, and the queen was consumed by fire."

"So the prophecy is still unfulfilled?"

"It appears so, Michael. Come with me. Let us hunt."

Amber and Chloe, Seattle, Present Day

In the dim light of the bar, Chloe looked even more mysterious and alluring. "You know, you're like something out of an old black and white movie." Amber smiled at her.

"So what's wrong, Amber? Are you nervous about the new job? Are you tired from your flight? Is it just a whole hell of a lot of work to be so damned perfect?"

"No, I—" On the patio, Amber saw a man lighting a cigarette. The flame from the lighter seemed to grow larger and larger. Her dream returned to her and she shuddered. "I just…. I…. What were you asking?"

"What's wrong, Amber?" Chloe stared intently at her.

"I've just had a hard time sleeping lately. Well, always, actually."

"Tell me all about it." Amber sighed as Chloe signaled to the waitress and gestured for another round. She drained the beer from the glass on the table and set it aside. "You'd be surprised at what I can help with."

"God, it's stupid." Amber took a sip of her beer and shook her head.

"Come on, Genius Girl. Help some of the rest of us feel useful once in a while."

"All right, listen, but no laughing. Ever since I can remember, I've had the same dream over and over again. It's the same damn dream every time. There's this man and he keeps saying something about fulfilling a prophecy. It's irritating as hell, but I could live with it. Now, though, the dreams have been changing. Now, it's driving me nuts."

***

Chloe listened and reached her hand out. "Go on, tell me. You've already made it clear that you're crazy, so what could it hurt?" Amber looked at Chloe, but the waitress appeared with fresh beers. After she left, Chloe said, "Look, I'm serious. I think I can help. Keep going."

"Well, it's the same dream, kind of. There are these dogs, but they're really wolves, I think. Then it always changes, and people appear. They're not quite people, though, and there's a man that keeps showing up. Like I said before, he just talks about some prophecy. It's like a horror movie, some weird surrealistic horror movie. I don't get it. Then, the man changes. Sometimes I change. I never really see his face, but I can sometimes see his eyes, and it's like they're in a trance. Then, he gets claws and fangs and — "

"Fangs? You mean like a vampire?"

Amber looked like she was going to cry. Chloe breathed a

deep breath.

"I guess so. Sometimes I have the claws and fangs. I guess I sound pretty crazy."

"Not as crazy as you might think." Chloe drained her beer. "Look, bottoms up. I have something I'm going to tell you, but not here in the bar. Tonight's on me, tomorrow's on you." She opened her purse, pulled out a twenty, and tossed it on the table. "C'mon, I'm right up the street."

Chloe led a drunk Amber to the car and seemed to notice the dazed look in her eyes. She didn't speak at all as she drove but whistled Sonny and Cher softly as Amber kept staring out the window.

In a few minutes Chloe had parked the car and the two climbed the stairs to a small apartment. Once there, Chloe opened a bottle of red wine and Amber sipped from her cup. Chloe's dark hair swayed against her back as she began to light the candles and incense. She eventually stepped into another room and left Amber to herself for a brief moment. When she returned, Chloe had changed into a black dress and was more ethereal than earlier that night. She was in full power and hoped that wouldn't alarm her new friend.

Amber sat on the sofa and sipped her wine. When Chloe was finished preparing her place, it looked like something out of a movie, with the candlelight throwing shadows against the walls and the smell of sage and jasmine and who knows what other hippie crap coursing through the air.

"Okay, let's get started." Amber looked up and had a strange look on her face.

***

"Relax, Amber. I'm going to tell you a secret. I'm not just a brilliant curator. I'm also a witch."

"A what?"

"I practice witchcraft. It's not all the crazy junk you think

71

it is, and I think I can help you to understand your dreams."

"Oh, Jesus." Amber stood and started for the door. "Are you drunk? This is too insane for me."

Chloe put a hand on her shoulder. "Sit down, Amber. I can help. There are things that people think are imaginary, but I assure you, they are real. Please let me help you. Please."

"Chloe, what are you saying?" Amber sat, but in the process she spilled her wine and started to cry. She tried to hold back, but her lips began to quiver and she ended up giving in to the sobs. All at once, she realized how badly she wanted the stress and the lack of sleep and the fear to go away.

"Amber, there are things in this world that are beyond what we think is normal. There might very well be vampires like the man in your dream. My mother was a witch. Her mother was a witch. Her mother was a witch. We go back for hundreds of years. I can help."

"How can you help me?" Amber looked at Chloe, whose eyes were wide. Was she crazy? Chloe gestured and the candles in the room seemed to flare before burning more steadily than before. Amber noticed an old clock sitting on a shelf with two candles on either side. It was 8:45. *I haven't even been in Seattle for twelve hours.*

Chloe gestured again, muttering something under her breath. A warm breeze blew through the apartment and seemed to settle on Amber. She felt her hair blow across her cheeks, and her body began to shiver. Chloe approached Amber and took her hands.

"Close your eyes and breathe in deeply. Listen to my voice and only my voice. Breathe, okay Amber. That's it. Relax and listen to my voice. Let me take you back to your dreams. Amber, you are dreaming, okay? You are dreaming again. But you're awake in my apartment, and you're safe. Tell me what you dream."

Amber stood in the woods. She was naked, again, and she felt the hot breath of dogs — no, wolves — blowing against her thighs, her ankles, and her hands. She looked down at the wolves, hundreds of them, covered in red fur, brown fur, grey fur. They snarled at her, some coming close and bearing their teeth, growling menacingly. A large wolf, enormously large with black fur and deep yellow eyes, stepped from among the pack to stand in front of her. "He's giant, Chloe." She saw its body moving as it breathed, and felt its breath against her breasts. It stared at her for a moment and then dropped its forelegs as though bowing.

"Wait, now a man is stepping out of the trees. The wolves are going crazy." Amber shook on the sofa. "They're stepping between me and the man. He's laughing and pointing at me."

The man waved his fingers at Amber and smiled. She saw sharp teeth, and the man licked his lips and blew her a kiss. His face was still obscured, unknown, unreal.

"Amber, calm down. Are you still there?" Chloe's voice seemed distant. "Nothing is going to hurt you, Amber, you're still dreaming. Take me back to the woods, Amber."

"The man is very close now, and the wolves are gone. He's touching me and kissing me. He tells me he's been waiting, and I am his. He's calling me 'Queen.'" Amber shook on the sofa. "I can smell his blood, Chloe. God, all I can smell is blood."

Amber sobbed and mumbled incoherent words as Chloe held her on the sofa.

CHAPTER EIGHT

Resistance

Michael, New York, Present Day

Marcus tossed the paper on the table. "Your girl's name is Amber Stone."

Michael picked up the paper, a color printout from a computer. Her picture was there, long red hair flowing along her face. She had perfect features, full lips, and high cheekbones. Her eyes, deep green, seemed alive even in the grainy inkjet print. Below the picture was the name and an address in New York. "She lives here?"

Marcus sighed. "Not anymore. She left that apartment yesterday. My agents have tracked her ticket. She was headed to Seattle. I've already alerted the estate there, and we'll be heading that way tomorrow. We can pick up the search from there."

Michael studied the picture. "Nearly three-hundred years, Marcus. I'm almost worried about finding her. What will be left for me once my journey has ended?" A girl walked into the room, slender and waifish. Michael looked at her short brown hair, her boyish features. She set a tray with wine and glasses down on an end table and started to walk away, but Michael gestured to her and she came to him.

"I think you'll find a new journey will begin when you find her, Father."

Michael sighed. "Perhaps." He reached forward and trailed his fingers across the girl's cheek. He reached lower and unbuttoned one, and then two of the buttons on her blouse, and she shivered. Michael smiled at her and continued with the buttons until her shirt was open. He slid it over her shoulders and she stood, shaking slightly as her small, delicate breasts were exposed. He stroked her neck, let his hand trail down to one of her breasts until he found her nipple, and pinched it. She winced, and color flooded her neck and her cheeks.

He pulled her to him and bit into her left breast, feeling the flow of her blood into his mouth. It was young and fresh, and he felt her unease. *What has Marcus told all of these girls that they fear me so?* Her blood was rich and strong, and he drank deeply.

"When we arrive in Seattle, we'll be able to track her down fairly quickly, Michael."

Michael murmured against the girl's breast. He could hear her heart, strong and beating faster now. She was trembling, and he put the palm of his left hand against her back and pulled her tightly to him. With his right hand, he rolled the nipple of her other breast between his thumb and forefinger and felt it harden. She was shaking badly now, and he glanced up to see her eyes widen. *She's terrified.* Michael sucked harder at her wound. *Poor girl.*

"If you're going to finish her, Father, I'll need to make arrangements for the body." Marcus said it drily, and Michael considered drinking until the girl was dead. It had been a while since he'd taken a victim completely. He saw tears welling in the girls eyes and took his mouth away.

"No, Marcus. I could not kill a flower as pretty as this."

He leaned forward and kissed the girl, who recoiled a bit from the taste of her own blood on his lips, but he held the back of her head and pushed his tongue into her mouth for a few seconds before releasing her. "Perhaps she could join me tonight for a little entertainment before we leave New York."

The girl reached to the floor and took her blouse from where it lay. She held it against her body, covering her nakedness. Michael smiled at her embarrassment. "How old are you, child?"

She looked on the verge of tears, but she managed to whisper, "Nineteen."

"Well, what do you say? Will you help me say goodbye to New York tonight?"

The girl turned red, looked toward the floor, and whispered, "As you wish, sir," before turning and running from the room.

"Was that necessary, Michael?"

Michael looked at Marcus, who had that irritating long-suffering look that had irked him on more occasions than he could remember.

"The cruelty."

"She's food, Marcus. Food and other sustenance. You're the one who talked about killing her." Michael walked to the wine, poured a glass, and took a long drink.

Amber, Seattle, Present Day

A mild shock made Amber stir from her sleep. She pushed off the blankets, but it took a moment for the disorientation to fade. Slowly, the evening came back to her and she recognized her surroundings. *The tribal art girl's apartment. Why am I on her couch?* Her arms and her legs were still asleep. Tingling sensations moved up and down, and she shook herself to end them. Finally, Amber rose from the couch and walked to the kitchen, where the welcome smell of coffee hit her full force and cleared what sleep was left.

Chloe sat at the kitchen table with a mug in her hand. "Help yourself. Cream and sugar are on the counter."

Amber found another mug and took the pot. The coffee was thick and black and steam rose from her cup. *God, that smells good.* She took a sip. It was far stronger than she was used to, but it warmed her and tasted great. She looked around and was amazed at how different the apartment looked in the daylight. Chloe was some kind of Martha Stewart homemaking artist. Her kitchen, though small, was a lovely shade of yellow and lime green. A number of expensive cooking appliances lined the counters. *She must be one hell of a cook.* She added cream and sugar to her cup, had another sip, carried the mug to the table, and sat down. She took another sip, savored it for a moment, and began to feel human again.

"Chloe, I don't understand. What am I doing here?"

"At the bar, you talked about your dreams and we came over here to help you out."

Amber studied Chloe. This was the girl who had wandered around the apartment last night like some kind of matinee horror pin up girl. She didn't seem crazy, but who the hell dressed up for Halloween in June? Still, it was probably the first night in ten years…. "I actually slept well. Last night was the first night I can remember not dreaming. It feels good to be awake."

Chloe listened, pulled a stray strand of her hair from her face, and tucked it behind her ear. "You did dream, Amber." Amber paused mid-sip and stared at her. "But I got some guidance for you, and you told me about your dreams. I think there's more going on than what I heard, but we got a big chunk of it."

"What the hell does that mean, you 'got me guidance'?"

"I'm a witch, Amber. I come from a long line of witches — all the way back to the witch trials at Salem. I — "

"The kids in Salem were victims of ergot poisoning. They weren't practicing witchcraft."

Chloe smiled and shook her head. "I thought you were supposed to be some kind of a girl genius, Amber. If the ruckus in Salem came from tainted rye, why didn't everyone in a family get the symptoms? Why was it that only the symptoms that could explain witchcraft were manifested? Not a lot of diarrhea in the history books. Not a lot of vomiting. Did the ergot decide only to affect the girls in ways that would make them seem like witches? Hell, why wasn't the whole damn town in a trance? Why didn't the — ?"

"Come on, now. You can't possibly believe that — "

"Why didn't the symptoms appear gradually? Biological symptoms don't show up on cue, Amber. The testimony says the convulsions and trances did."

"This is crazy." Amber shook her head, rolled her eyes, and took another sip.

"Look, Girl Genius, you need help and I can help you. Amber, I want to be your friend. The man in your dreams could be a — "

"I can't deal with this, Chloe. It's not real." She drained the last sip from her coffee and put the cup down.

"Look, Amber, give it a chance. I know — "

"Leave me alone!" Amber rose from the table, knocking the chair over, and ran to the bathroom. She locked the door behind her, sat on the floor, and felt the tears begin to flow. *This is too intense.* She was a university student and a museum curator. Jesus, she studied cultures that believed this crap. *This is too much.* The first friend, real friend, she thought she had made believed she was a witch. *What's next, fairies and elves?*

Chloe, Yakima, 2004

Tom's horse shied and he looked perplexed, but he pulled up on the reins and looked around. He didn't see anything, but he could feel the bay's nervousness. Chloe came up beside him, her small pinto still appearing enormous beneath her tiny frame. "It's the rattlesnake past that fallen pine log, Wheezer." She didn't even try to call him Tom anymore, and he'd stopped caring about the nickname.

He studied her for a moment. Her hair was long, already to her waist, jet black and straight. Her face was still girlish, but he knew that in a few years she would be lovely. Her body was awkward now, arms and legs growing faster than her torso, but he imagined men would fight over her by the time she was eighteen. "Okay, let's head this way, then." He pulled the reins and the two walked their horses over a small knoll and into a copse of trees, startling a doe, which leapt and bolted.

"Call her to you, Chloe."

"What?"

"Call her to you."

"Uh…here, deer, c'mon deer." She giggled like a…*well, like a teenage girl*. Tom sighed.

"Quickly, Chloe, with the charm. Hurry or she'll be too far away."

***

Chloe dismounted and walked to where the doe had stood. She reached onto the ground and took a handful of dirt, sifting it through her fingers. She began to mumble the words Tom had taught her under her breath. They were singsong words, melodic and sweet—nothing like the harsh or guttural phrases for the fire charms or the binding charms.

She felt the words flowing out of her and imagined them as butterflies gathering around her. When she finished, she blew out a long breath and pictured them fluttering after the doe, pictured them reaching it and landing on her. She pushed her mind outward and tried to follow the words. She couldn't.

"I can't do it."

"Concentrate, Chloe. Be patient."

Chloe tried again, breathing the soft, slow breaths as she'd been taught. She reached out with her mind, trying to picture the word butterflies, trying to see through them to find the deer. She heard their wings, buffeting the air in tiny blasts around them. In her mind's eye she saw them, each word with delicate wings in shades of blue and yellow and red. They flew with purpose, but she couldn't see the doe.

Chloe shook her head and looked back at Tom. He sat on his horse, leaning over the saddle horn, smiling.

"But I couldn't call her."

He still smiled. "Look behind you, Chloe."

She turned and felt the doe's breath on her face before she saw it. She reached out and threw her arms around its neck as it nuzzled her.

CHAPTER NINE

Gathering

Chloe, Seattle

Chloe watched Amber rush away and sighed. She drained her mug and stood to follow her, but the ringing of the phone stopped her. She looked at her watch. 5:45 a.m. *Who calls this early?* She stepped over to the counter and pulled the handset out of the cradle. "Hello."

"Why hello there, favorite child."

"Becca. Hi. Is everything okay?"

"You tell me. Mom's in a bit of a panic over you. She sensed something and asked me to call you and check in. What's up?"

"God, Becca. You aren't going to believe this. Remember the prodigy the museum hired?"

"The genius from New York?"

"Yeah." Chloe walked to the table, got her mug, and walked back to the counter. With the handset balanced between her ear and shoulder, she poured herself another cup of coffee. "Her name's Amber...there's definitely some weird stuff going on with her."

Becca assumed her older sister voice. "So, a twenty-one year old genius who went to college at what—twelve?"

"Sixteen, Becca, and —"

"Went to college at sixteen has some personality quirks. Should I call in the press? Wait! This calls for something more. A screwed up overachiever — hell, we should call the army. We should convene the coven. We should —"

"Listen, Becca. She has these nightmares about wolves and vampires. In them, she's not quite a witch or one of them, even. But there's something about the dreams. She's in the bathroom crying now. You...." She trailed off, realizing she hadn't the faintest idea at all what she wanted Becca to do.

The line was silent for a moment, and then the Older Sister voice was back in full force. "Whoa, Chloe! Are you saying that a woman is dreaming about vampires and witches and werewolves? My God! That just doesn't make any sense. It's not as if there are eighteen million movies out about those subjects or anything. This is totally unique. We better get right on this!"

"Becca, she described the charm of flames."

The line was silent.

"Did you hear me, Becca? She —"

"I heard you. Tell me what she said."

"She had a dream about wolves and a man calling her some kind of prophecy fulfillment. Then, she kept drifting in and out with me. One of the times she was in, she talked about floating in fire and streaming it from her fingers."

"I know you're Ms. Super Special Sight and all that, but lots of people wish they could shoot fire from their hands, Chloe."

"She didn't say *shoot*, Becca. She said *stream*. She said she *called* the fire." Chloe realized she was shaking and felt her hand burn as coffee spilled out of the mug. She let go, and it shattered on the floor. "Damn!"

"Chloe! Are you okay? What was that? Chloe? Chloe!"

"Relax, Becca, I just dropped a coffee cup. Look, Amber didn't use general terms. She used charm words, just not in the right order."

Becca's voice wasn't sarcastic anymore. "Okay, there could be something to what you're saying. Of course, Mom is going to freak out when she hears this. You'll have to talk to her right now. In the meantime, make sure you light some sage and some rosemary and run your protection circles two...no, three times. You need —"

Chloe rolled her eyes. "I got this, Becca." *When will they realize I can handle my own life?* "Look Becca, I gotta go. Tell Mom I'll call her later. I'm fine and Amber needs me now."

"Don't you think you should talk to Mom?"

"I'll call her later, bye." Chloe could hear Becca talking as she put the phone back on the cradle. She swept up the broken cup and mopped up the floor with a dishtowel. Then she started for the bathroom, but she stopped.

Damn it, Becca, I would have done this on my own. She walked back to the kitchen, pulled out a small brass incense burner, and crushed some rosemary and sage from the spice rack into it. She struck a match and winced as the pungent odor filled the kitchen. *Maybe Becca's right. What kind of a witch hates the smell of sage?*

She cleared her head and exhaled. *Maybe it's okay with pork chops, but god, couldn't vanilla sanctify a place?* She began murmuring her protection circles in soft whispers and felt the power begin to seep into her from the smoke. When she finished the charm a second time, she decided a third wouldn't be necessary and distanced herself from the essence of the magic. Already her senses had changed.

With her charmed eyes, it seemed that the air in the apartment was thickening, unusual elements overpowering the air. *Okay, something more than oxygen and nitrogen at work here*. Chloe concentrated on listening. She heard the Mannings in the apartment next door. Timmy was in the bath and Charles and Megan were making love in the master bedroom, trying to keep the noise down so Timmy couldn't hear. *School bus comes in a couple of hours, Meg; hang on until then and you can scream instead of whimpering.* She heard the other neighbors as well, but she pushed them to the background and focused on the apartment.

She could hear the static noise that came whenever something extra-natural was present, but there was something else. Something was out of sync, discordant with time, like an echo coexisting with a present sound. Chloe couldn't make much sense of it. She could hear Amber sobbing softly in the restroom. It was her voice, but another was present as well, the echo. Chloe cast her perception throughout the apartment, but she felt resistance at the bathroom door. *Won't stop me, sweetie.* Chloe pulled more energy from the smoke and her circles and focused it on the door, but the damned thing was like a force field and she couldn't make any progress. She knew there was a charm of opening, but she hadn't had need to learn it before, and she didn't want to release the circles to go to the bedroom and search her books. Finally, she gathered strength and prepared to hit the barrier full force. She could hear the static noise growing as the energy coalesced within her. *Okay, here goes, babe. Three, two, one, blast –*

The apartment was normal again. The only noise came from Chloe herself. She released the charms and felt the power dissipating as the door opened and Amber emerged. She stared at Chloe. Her face was streaked with tears. *God, Amber, even pathetic you look hot…bitch.* Amber's lips started to tremble and Chloe felt a stab of guilt for the jealousy. *Oh God, the poor girl doesn't know what to believe anymore.*

Amber didn't cry. Instead, her lips parted and she breathed out a sad, soft whisper. "Help me." Chloe stepped forward, but wasn't able to catch her as Amber collapsed to the floor.

Michael, Rome, 1802

Michael enjoyed the ruins. Often, he would climb to the top of the Coliseum and stare over the enormous place. Kabos had told him an earthquake had felled a giant piece of the wall, and his maker had known the architect who used some of the marble for construction of St. Peter's Basilica. Of course, Kabos—Jacob—had said it in passing. He rarely spoke of his maker. Tonight, Kabos was gone again, meeting with his daylight agents and hearing of the various business enterprises they ran for him. Michael felt a light breeze against his skin and set out for the.... *What did Kabos call it? The Flavius Arena.*

He heard their voices before he saw them, three men surrounding another. They were trying to take a cloth pouch from him and he was struggling. Michael watched silently. The victim was holding his own surprisingly well. Still, fists tended to fail against steel, and when one of the attackers drew a knife, Michael intervened.

He landed on the nearest assaulter and snapped his neck before leaping to the next. His teeth tore into the man's throat, past grime and dirt to taste his blood. He fed on it for just a moment and remembered he still had a third to contend with. He bit down, severing the man's spinal cord, and threw himself at the one with the knife.

The man fell backwards and Michael relished the terror in his eyes as he lowered his head to the brigand's neck and began to feed. The man was dirty, sweat and mud caking his flesh, but his blood was rich and salty and tasted of the fish he must have eaten for dinner. He drank slowly, enjoying the robber's feeble efforts to stop him, to beat him away, hitting his back with fists no more effective than a thimble in the face of floodwaters.

The struggles grew fainter and Michael heard the heartbeat grow dimmer, until finally the man lay limp beneath him. Reluctantly, he stood, flushed with the strength of the blood, drunk in the way he always was for a moment or two after feeding. He reached down and lifted the man's cloak to his mouth, wiping away the blood and in the process making the body hang like some kind of child's rag doll.

It was after he dropped it that he remembered the fourth man. He glanced at him and cursed. The knife had found its mark before he'd acted, and it was buried to the hilt in the man's chest. Michael knelt beside him. The man was handsome, with thick brown hair, and there was something about him; he was —

Michael leapt backwards nearly fifteen feet as the man jumped up and swung. His eyes were wide and angry. He reached to his chest and pulled out the knife. Michael stared at him — the wound was closing…he could see the flesh coming together.

"You have stolen my prey!" The man looked at the bodies on the ground. "Is there nothing left?"

"I only drained this one, but the blood will be cold by now."

The man ignored him and fell to the ground on top of one of the others. Michael watched him feeding until finally he stood again, reeling a bit and then wiping his mouth with the back of his hand.

"I am Marcus." He extended his hand. "I thought I was alone in Rome."

Michael studied him then took the offered hand.

"Machiel...uh, Michael. My maker and I have been here for several decades now. Where is your maker?"

Marcus sighed. "She is dead. She was hunted like an animal and killed. She...." He shook his head. "She hadn't finished teaching me what I was to do. I am less than a decade this way, and only a few weeks in Rome."

"Well, then. You must come and meet Kabos. We'll have to look after you."

Amber, Seattle

Amber stood in the woods, but this time she wasn't naked, and there were no flames. She stood wearing her jogging suit, feeling strange and out of place. The wolves were there and the man was there, his face still obscured, and she tried to concentrate on it, to picture him.

"Ilyris, my queen. Come to me." She felt her legs moving. She tried to stop but couldn't, and almost immediately stood before him. "Dear Ilyris, don't fight what you are. Awake, my queen. Awake and let the prophecy come to pass."

He laughed then, a deep and hollow sound, and she saw his mouth clearly. Long, white teeth extended into points, and thick, red blood dripped from them. Amber couldn't move. She couldn't speak. The wolves moved, and the enormous black dog attacked the man. Amber watched as his jaws locked on the man's arm, tearing into the man's flesh. He didn't stop laughing. Instead, he simply placed his hand over the wolf and the black behemoth grew limp.

Amber screamed. The sound melted the other figures into nothingness and a white glare filled the woods. It grew, blinding her eyes until Amber had no more voice and she opened her eyes. She was in Chloe's apartment, and Chloe was looking down on her, a worried expression painting her face. Amber was almost mechanical in her motions, but she extended her arms as Chloe reached out to hold her.

CHAPTER TEN

Awakening

Amber, Seattle

Amber kept to the hotel for the next few days, making polite excuses to Chloe when she tried to invite her to dinner, lunch, or drinks. She busied herself with the arrangements with the moving company and looked forward to starting at the museum. She called cabs and saw Seattle, taking in the Space Needle and the coffee shops that seemed to be on every corner. On Monday night, she ate at Dick's Drive-in on Queen Anne Avenue and spent less than five dollars for a burger and fries.

On Tuesday morning, she arranged for a cab to take her to her new apartment so she could wait on her things, laid out jeans and an old t-shirt, and stepped into the shower. She screamed as the water streamed down on her, freezing cold rather than warm, but as she started to back away, she found herself transfixed by the nozzle, which was even now sending out an endless stream of icy darts against her breasts and her belly.

"You'll catch your death of cold," her husband said. "Why are you out in rain like this?"

"It's to find you I've come outside, love." Amber looked

at her husband, his shaggy brown hair shading his brow, his strong back bare and glistening from the rain.

Wait — not rain. Not.

"My darling, all of Illyria marching as one could not keep me from finding you. You are my Dessaro, my princess, my love." He smiled at her and winked.

"You flatter me, my lord, my Illyrius. Do we attack Greece then?"

"Who can tell? The talk of politicians is like this rain; it comes and goes and soaks everything with…with…." He shook his head. "I'm afraid I am not a poet, Bircenna."

Bircenna laughed, shook rain from her hands, and reached to her husband.

Wait. No, not Bircenna. Not rain. Not.

"Domator, you are all the poet I need, my love."

The two turned back to their door.

No! I am Amber! This is not rain!

Amber and Chloe, Seattle

Chloe stood at the hotel door. Amber had avoided her since that first night, but she couldn't avoid her today if she wanted the museum staff car. She lifted her hand to knock at the door.

"No! I am Amber! This is not rain!" The scream came from within the room, and Chloe knocked hard at the door.

No response.

"Amber, it's Chloe. Let me in."

Only silence. Chloe pushed on the door, but it was secure. Sighing, she looked around the hallway and spotted a rhododendron plant on one of those imitation sixteenth century Georgian tables the hotel seemed to like. She ran to it, plucked a few leaves, and returned to the door. She began to speak the charm of opening while crushing the leaves in the palm of her hand. A click, a flash of green light, and the door was ajar.

Chloe pushed it open. The bathroom door was open, and she could hear the shower. Amber wasn't yelling anymore, just sobbing in a strange, keening way. Chloe rushed through the door and saw her lying in the tub. Drops of water bounced on her. *Oh, great. She's even gorgeous naked.* Chloe shook her head, but stopped when she noticed Amber's lips were almost purple and even her nipples had a bluish tinge. She reached forward, wincing as icy water splashed her arm, and turned the faucet off.

"Amber, can you hear me?" She reached down and grabbed her under her arms. *Jesus! She's ice.* "Come on, sweetie, come on." She half lifted and half dragged the redhead to the bed and called room service for coffee. She tried to remember the charm of warmth, but she was panicking and the words wouldn't come. Instead, she rushed to the restroom, grabbed towels, and set about drying Amber. *Some super genius you turned out to be.*

When the girl was dry, Chloe began rubbing warmth into her, starting at her fingers and arms and moving up to her shoulders. Chloe sighed. The words finally came to her and she felt warmth flowing from her, watched color returning to Amber, her lips, fingers, toes, nipples, and face gradually becoming pink again.

Amber's eyes opened and Chloe smiled down at her, went to the bathroom, and retrieved one of the hotel robes. Amber took it, looked confused for a moment, and said, "I'm naked."

"They teach observational skills like that in genius school?"

"I was taking a shower, but the water was cold. I tried to turn it off, but...I was somewhere else. Oh God, Chloe. It was like the dreams, but different; it was like I was someone else. What the fuck is happening to me?" Amber nearly jumped when a knock sounded at the door.

"Relax, it's just the coffee I ordered." Chloe stepped over to the door, and a young man pushed a room service cart inside. The aroma of the coffee was powerful, and wonderful. The man lifted his head and noticed Amber, his eyes growing wide.

Chloe rolled her eyes. "Don't worry, sugar. My girlfriend and I were just trying out your wonderful bed." To Amber, she said, "You might want to put that robe on, sweetheart."

Amber turned white, and then red. She pulled the robe around her and wouldn't return the young man's gaze as she signed the check and Chloe ushered him out. She was still red with embarrassment as she took a cup from the tray and poured coffee into it.

Chloe took a cup of her own and said, "Look. I know it's confusing for you. Still, you'd better let me help you. I mean, of course, if you don't want to end up like some Playboy centerfold Popsicle."

Michael and Marcus, Rome, 1802

Kabos didn't rise when the two entered the inn's room. Back still to them, he said, "Ah, Michael. I see you have found Eliza's spawn."

Marcus froze. "You knew her?"

Kabos turned, and Michael was surprised to see a strange and wistful expression in the older one's face. He stared at Marcus for a moment and then gestured at the table, where two glasses of wine had already been poured. Kabos reached for the bottle, poured a glass for himself, and took a sip. "I knew her. We hunted together in Flanders for a few years before the canals filled and she moved on to Iberia—you'd call that Spain. She was a fine companion." What was that in his eyes? *He loved her*, Michael thought.

Kabos blinked twice and shook his head. The old man was back, his expression normal again. He turned to Marcus. "You're new. How long?"

"About nine years, now; but she's been dead for —"

"Seven." Kabos sighed. "I heard about it."

"What happened?" Michael asked the question and sat down at the table, taking a glass and draining the wine in a single drink. It was sour, but that gave it taste, and Michael liked it.

"Eliza was a peasant girl from Catalon. About two hundred years ago, I think it was, she died in childbirth — that is, she was about to die in childbirth. A rash and new one of our kind saw her and made her rather than to let her die. He was new and didn't understand the responsibility involved." Kabos shook his head. "He was foolish in every way, actually. Couldn't accept the loss of his humanity and tried to live among humans in the night. Eventually he was killed in his sleep by Church officials."

Marcus sat down, took the last glass, and sipped it. "What of Eliza?"

Kabos turned to him. "What is your name?"

"Marcus."

"Eliza was not two days old when her maker was killed. I found her and took her home to Flanders and taught her what I could. She told me about you, you know. You're the clock maker's apprentice, right?"

"I was. My master died of the palsy and the banker cast me out on the street. She found me one night, nearly dead with cold, and took me in." Marcus sighed. "I loved her."

"There was not much about her that could keep one from loving her, Marcus." Kabos smiled at him. "And now the hunter has taken her from you."

"She was hunted like an animal. She was cornered and killed by a scarred man." Contempt filled Marcus's voice as he said the words.

Kabos nodded. "Valentine. Scarred from eye to chin by his own sword."

"Who is Valentine, Kabos?" Michael leaned forward as he asked the question. "Have I not heard you say that name before?"

Kabos shrugged. "I may have, in passing. Valentine the Hunter. He was created in much the same way Eliza was, by the stupid, unthinking young."

"What do you mean?" Marcus stared at Kabos, studying the old man.

"The young of our kind have always lacked discretion. Valentine's wife, Mary, was drained in front of him, along with his infant son. The idiots. Instead of just taking them, they deceived him, told him they were doctors of a sort, and then made him watch when they killed the ones he loved. It changed him, of course, and now he hunts us."

"What are we?" Marcus looked at Kabos. "Are we the *strigoi*? Eliza told me we were the gypsy's *strigoi*."

"I suppose we are, Marcus." Kabos poured another glass of wine and took a sip. "We're also the *vyrkolokas*, in Athens, the *lilitu* in Babylon, and the *vitali* in India." He stood and poured the rest of the wine into their glasses. "We may have been the *lamia* when Greece was new."

"But what do we call ourselves?"

"There is a word for us in the old tongue, but nobody speaks it any longer. Our historians are pretty sure it only meant Old Ones, though, and many of us call ourselves by that name. Some of the young use the new name the daylighters have given us."

"Vampire." Michael breathed the word softly.

Kabos smiled. "Not Valentine, though. He calls us by one name alone, no matter the word he uses."

Marcus spoke. "When I kill him, I would like to use that name."

"It will be ironic, Marcus." Kabos drained his glass. "He calls us *prey*."

CHAPTER ELEVEN

Arriving

Amber, Seattle, Present Day

The day was almost a blur. Amber agreed that she needed Chloe's help, but the two of them had to rush to get to Amber's apartment in order to meet the movers. On the other hand, the museum staff car was nice, a hybrid sedan and the first new car Amber had ever owned. After a few hours of watching impossibly overweight men struggle with her furniture, the two rushed to the museum for Amber's first afternoon of work. There they parted ways, Chloe to her tribal art and Amber to the human resources department to complete paperwork.

The hours seemed to drag on and on, and just as she thought the paperwork and orientation videos were over, a new stack would arrive. Finally, Amber found time to make a trip to Chloe's office. She wandered the unfamiliar lower halls of the museum and was surprised to see her name on one of the doors. AMBER STONE, CURATOR, MACEDONIAN COLLECTION. She tried the door, but no luck. *Curator…makes me sound old, but it could be hot, in a sexy bookworm kind of way.*

A few doors down, she saw Chloe's nameplate. *Tudor? I'll start calling her Queen Chloe.* She heard the rustling of paper and knocked. She heard Chloe's voice shout, "Come in!" and took a deep breath before opening the door.

Chloe sat behind a desk littered with wooden, stone, and cloth dolls. Her face was hidden behind a strange wooden form that looked like a pregnant woman with the head of a lizard. She had stacked paperwork on the floor next to her desk.

"Hi, Chloe. You said you can help, and I said I'd let you. About this morning, I don't know what came over me. It was all messed up the first night I got here, and my dreams are getting worse."

Chloe put her pen down and looked at Amber. "I under—"

"No, listen. This is so weird that if I don't just get it done, I won't have the guts to do it. Can we go out for a couple of drinks and just talk? Something's going on with me, and I don't know what it is. If you're...." Amber rolled her eyes. "I can't believe I'm saying this. If you're a real witch, or even if you just think you are, maybe you can help. I don't understand any of what's going on, but...."

Chloe smiled and nodded. "Okay, so I'll spend the night getting you drunk and trying to convince you you're not crazy and I'm not crazier. Still, Amber, I've got to push you back until tonight. Meet me at my place around seven. I have to get back to this. Sorry, but super genius babysitting put me behind, and I have a six o'clock deadline."

"Tonight's fine. I like deadlines! They're easy to understand." She left Chloe's office and felt a strange uneasiness that gave way to a wave of nausea. She made her way back up to the HR department, but she felt weak, lightheaded. *Oh, God. I haven't eaten a damn thing today. How to start a new job. Step one: Go crazy. Step Two: Freeze yourself. Step Three: Starve yourself.*

In an hour, she was rushing down to the museum café and falling madly in love with Mr. Hershey, all Three Musketeers, and whoever came up with the idea of putting chicken breast on a Caesar salad.

Michael and Marcus, Rome, 1802

"Eliza is gone, and you are a danger to all of us. There are ways to hunt without being seen, ways to live without notice. You've never been taught." Kabos studied Marcus, who had tensed at his words and stood.

"I will trouble you no more, then." Marcus started for the door, but Michael stepped in front of him.

"Both of you sit down. This impulsiveness is exactly what I mean." Kabos walked to the chest in the corner of the room, opened it, and pulled out another bottle of wine. Both men stood in place.

"I said sit!" Kabos's eyes seemed to flare with a red tinge. Michael felt a strange gust about him, almost like wind, but not quite. It was as though the old man's voice itself was tangible — palpable and present in the room.

The two men sat. Kabos slowly and methodically poured wine into each of their glasses and slowly delivered them. He took a long slow sip. "I cannot train you, Marcus. I must attend to my daylight enterprises and prepare them for Michael. I — "

"Kabos, why...?" Michael's voice trailed off as Kabos shot him a warning glance.

"I will be consolidating my network of agents and estates. I'll retain a few for myself, but the majority will be yours. It's more extensive than you imagine, and it means that I cannot take responsibility for our young friend." Kabos sighed deeply. "I'm leaving tonight."

"Leaving?" Michael's voice was plaintive.

"You must meet me in Bruges soon. Let us say...." Kabos closed his eyes, nodded for a moment, and looked again at Michael. "...forty years. That should give ample time for me to make the arrangements and for you to make progress in your destiny."

"But Father! You are part of my destiny! I don't want your businesses; I want you!" Michael stood up, placed his hands over his head and ran his fingers through his hair.

"I will be arranging them for you, Michael. We all have a role to play, and it appears that your role is more important than mine is. There is something I must show you, but first," he turned his attention to Marcus, "we must address the issue of Marcus."

Kabos finished his wine and stared at the young man. Marcus shifted uncomfortably. Finally, the old one spoke. "You have no maker. Michael is now your father."

"What?" The two had both leapt to their feet, but a stern glance from Kabos and the memory of his voice gradually pushed them back down.

"Michael can teach you our ways, and you can help him on his journey." From within his cloak, Kabos pulled a rolled parchment. "And your journey, Michael, appears to be more than the ravings of a mad gypsy."

Chloe, Ellensburg, 2007

Chloe walked over the steps up to the information booth. She wasn't sure if she liked the idea of Central Washington instead of Seattle University in Seattle, but she'd promised her mother she'd apply to at least two schools, and here she was on a stupid student scholastic night. Two boring hours of all the benefits of a college education. If her mother wasn't waiting in the car...*I'd find a bookstore and read for two hours.*

A hawk-faced woman stood behind the booth.

"Hi, Mrs. Ellen. I'm here for the prospective student night."

The woman looked confused. "Do I know you?"

"Oh, I'm Chloe. I'm here for the student tour night."

"But how do you know my name?"

Uh oh. Good thing I didn't tell her nine cats is too many to keep in a two bedroom apartment with creaking floors, poor heating, lime green wallpaper, and furniture that should have stayed in the seventies.

"Um, I think I heard you introduce yourself to another girl a while ago, but I had to run to find the ladies' room. Did I pronounce it wrong? I'm dreadfully embarrassed." Chloe felt stupid, but she batted her eyelids like a complete ditz.

The woman's face change immediately and she smiled. "Oh no, sweetie. You just caught me off guard." She pulled out a red folder and a blue *Hello, my name is*_____ sticker. "You just go through the double doors at the end of this hallway and the girls at the table will help you."

"Thanks!" Chloe took the folder and started away.

"Don't forget your sticker, honey!" Chloe forced a smile as the woman peeled it from its backing and put it on her shirt. "And by the way, Maryanne at the table is the president of one of the best sororities here. Make sure to introduce yourself to her. A pretty girl like you is always a welcome addition."

"Well, thank you for the tip." Chloe smiled. Eight thousand stampeding elk couldn't drive her to join a sorority.

Chloe walked to the double doors and stopped. Something was wrong. Something was very wrong. Noise was everywhere. It was as though the ground, the air, the trees, even the bricks in the building were shouting out at her. She hadn't lost control of her sight in years, but the noise was growing, overwhelming her. Breathing deeply, Chloe tried to quiet the voices and focus, but nothing worked. She was spinning. No, the world was spinning. The trees, the buildings were hurtling around her, and she felt herself falling.

Her mother caught her. "Come on, Chloe. Help me here." The world came into focus for a moment and then out as she held on to her mother's waist and stumbled with her to the car. She sat, almost paralyzed in the seat, but she was vaguely aware of the car starting and the sensation of movement beneath the seat. *What is...? I....*

She heard her mother chanting, but she didn't know the charm. Waves of calm flowed over her. Her heart slowed and she felt the panic subsiding, her breath returning to normal. Still, the noise didn't subside. Everything yelled or spoke or even screamed.

"I just need to give you distance, baby. Hold on." Chloe stared at her mother. She was gripping the steering wheel so tightly that her knuckles were white. Chloe lifted her hand and tried to turn on the radio, but something was still wrong with her depth perception.

"Mom. Music." The voice was barely a whisper, and Chloe wasn't sure she had even spoken aloud, but her mother pressed the button and classic rock filled the car. Chloe tried to focus on the music and to exclude the rest. It took fifteen minutes before she realized the noise was gone. Steve Miller was on the radio and his was the only voice she heard.

"I'm okay now, Mom. What happened to me?"

"Tom and I were a little afraid of what your sight would do to you if this ever happened. We can all sense them, and they make us all nervous, like some *Star Trek* red alert." Her mom looked at her. "You're really okay now?"

"I'm fine now, Mom. What does it? What makes us all nervous?"

"Vampires."

Michael, Denver, Present Day

Michael felt hands lifting the coffin and knew he was being transferred to the plane to Seattle. He reached for the clasp and made sure it was secure. Four inches of wood and copper. That was all that separated him from the sun and burning.

Kabos, I wish you were here. Why hadn't he waited just a few more years? All of their years of planning were reaching an end. There was only Marcus now. He had no idea if the two of them would be enough. He was sure it was the right girl, but if Kabos was right about the prophecy....

I don't have your wisdom, Father. I never have had it.

He felt himself being lowered onto a cart and felt the movement of the wheels on the tarmac until he was lifted again. *Soon now.*

He heard the workers loading other bags and boxes. The engines roared to life a short while later and he felt the liftoff. *Soon now, Father.* He slept.

CHAPTER TWELVE

Converging

Amber, Seattle, Present Day

Amber turned off the shower and stepped out. She approached the steamed mirror, wiped away some of the moisture, and looked at her face for a moment. As usual, the contrast between her red hair and green eyes stood out first. She smiled at herself. *Not a freckle in sight, you sexy thing.* Even with the water dripping from her hair, she was still beautiful, and she knew it. Her long neck, full lips...*any guy gets lost in these eyes.*

She wrapped a towel around her hair and walked to her room. Boxes lay everywhere, still unpacked, but she located a suitcase and pulled out a pair of black slacks and a green silk shirt. *Tonight, I'm sexy. Crazy, but sexy.* She gathered the rest of her outfit and returned to the restroom, where she dried her hair and got dressed. She clasped a patent leather belt around her waist and returned to the bedroom, searching through the boxes until she located her thigh-high boots. She pulled them on and returned to the mirror.

Almost. She located her travel bag and pulled out a crimson lipstick, applied it to her lips, and blotted them with tissue. *There we go. Dressed to kill.*

A stray hair hung down over her forehead, blown by the breeze, and she brushed it away. The men were coming, and she knew before they arrived that they bore bad news. She recognized the taller man as one of King Monunius's guards, but the other was a typical and nameless young boy, a boy soldier. The boy carried a shield.

She felt the bile rising in her throat but swallowed hard and stood without wavering.

"Bircenna, I have come with Domator's shield. I come also to tell you he died honorably and took enemies with him. He behaved as a man of Dardania should. He was a credit to all Illyria. The king mourns his loss."

Numbly, she reached….

No, I am not Bircenna! I am Amber!

Numbly, she reached for the shield and….

I am not Bircenna!

Numbly, she reached for the shield and took it in….

I!

…her hands. A tear fell from one eye. "Oh, Dom….

AM!

…ator, my love."

AMBER!

She was back in the bathroom, and a cat was shrieking nearby. Amber's breath came heavily and she tried to slow her heartbeat, but the damn cat wouldn't stop yelling. She cried out, "Quiet kitty!" and it came out louder than she'd intended.

There was no response from the cat. Her apartment was quiet. She shook her head and stepped out into the living room. Boxes littered the floor, but the movers had placed her old, oversized plush sofa in one corner and the large rocking chair on the other side. *Well, maybe the furniture isn't sexy, but it's home.* She remembered when her father had delivered the furniture from the family home to her apartment in New York. Suddenly, and surprisingly, she realized that she missed her adopted parents greatly. *Maybe I'm more connected to them than I thought.*

She shook her head again and exhaled a long, calming sigh. *I need to get drunk and laid tonight.* She locked the front door behind her and headed to Chloe's apartment.

Michael and Marcus, Paris, 1803

"Tell me about Kabos, Michael." Marcus sat across from Michael on a carved wooden chair on the small bistro patio. Michael studied him for a moment. His dark eyes were deep set above his thick Roman nose, while his hair, thick and brown, hung an inch or so over his forehead. His hands...Michael looked at his own. They were delicate...long fingers, straight nails. Marcus, by contrast, had worker's hands...strong, thick fingers on heavy palms. Two of them held a cigarette, and Michael watched as Marcus brought it to his lips and smoked.

"I don't think I worked a day in my life before I met Kabos." He reached to the pouch and began to roll his own. He shook his head. "It's funny, isn't it, Marcus? There is no joy left in these things, or beer, or — or even wine, really. Still, we smoke and we drink, and we remember." The young waitress returned to the table with wine, fruit, and thick slabs of creamy white cheese streaked with blue veins. Michael smiled at her and she smiled suggestively, looking up and down his face.

When she left them, Michael poured the wine and sliced an apple with his knife. "I can almost taste fruit, Marcus." He cut a portion of the cheese and spread it on the apple. "Sometimes I can." He took a bite, closed his eyes, and put the rest of the slice back on the plate. "Not tonight, though."

He sighed, reached for the votive, and lit his cigarette. The smoke was tasteless, but it burned pleasantly, and Michael sighed.

"Kabos, Michael?" Marcus sipped his wine.

"His family controlled the dried fruit in Bruges. In Flanders, we use it for beer, so the family was very wealthy. Certain of our kind thought the wealth would be useful and decided on a family member as a protégé. Kabos managed the family's accounts, so he was the natural choice." Michael sipped his wine and smiled as the waitress returned. She was a slight girl, with dark hair and the perpetual pout that all of the girls in Paris seemed to wear. Marcus shook his head as she began to flirt with Michael, eyes batting, head bowing, hands clasping behind her back.

"When will you be finished here, my dear?" Michael smiled up at her and sipped his wine.

"Eleven o'clock, monsieur."

"Well, then. I suppose I will have to return then." He reached forward and pulled her to him, sitting her on his lap and squeezing her thigh. The girl squealed, laughed, and kissed him on the cheek.

"Michael, tell me of Kabos." Marcus poured more wine.

"All right, my dear. I'm afraid I may only taste the wine and cheese until later...when I will taste my little angel!" The girl jumped up, giggling, and walked away. Over her shoulder, she blew Michael a kiss as she walked into the bistro.

"It appears Kabos was more involved in the affairs of...what was the new word? Oh yes...us *vampires*." Michael smiled and drained his cup. "There is a group that calls itself the *Avalani*. Don't ask me why or what it means. Who the hell knows? Anyway, he is evidently somewhat high in their ranks, responsible for a great deal of Europe."

"But…well, why did he make you? Were you rich?"

"Oh, my family was rich enough, but he didn't turn me for our assets, Marcus."

"Why then?"

Michael laughed. He leaned back and called into the bistro. "Do you have any lambic beer in there?" Then, he refilled the wine glass. "I was at a bar. Two idiots from Italy were making stupid comments about Flanders and its beers. I was already drunk, so I evidently attacked them. I don't remember a bit of this, mind you, I'm just retelling Kabos's story. He was in the tavern, remembering Flanders in all of its glory before the canals all jammed."

The girl was back. "I'm afraid we have no beer from Flanders, sir. The politics prevent export. Maybe I can be sour and sweet for you?"

Michael laughed. "Not until tonight, my dear. Not until tonight. Still, bring another bottle of wine, something red and dark and strong." The girl curtsied and left.

"So, you were at an inn, Michael?"

"Yes. I was Machiel back then, a rich, pampered brat. Anyway, some fools complained about Flanders and its beer and I challenged them to a fight. They beat the hell out of me, and Kabos decided to make me one of us rather than let me die in the gutter."

"But now, why does he leave?"

"Oh, I don't know. Kabos has strange ideas about honor and destiny. Ever since the gypsy hag said I was to find the queen…." The word seemed strange on his lips, and Michael paused. "Kabos has talked of the prophecy."

"The prophecy of the queen?"

"Yes, the one who is to come and change everything."

Marcus smiled at the waitress as she brought the wine. "The one who will change our lives, our destinies, our goddamned wine glasses?"

"I know it sounds stupid, Marcus, but look at us. We survive on the blood of people we once loved. Is it too much to believe in more?"

"I suppose it isn't."

"This queen will do more than change us, Marcus. She will change the *loup garou*, the—"

"The wolf people? Are they real?"

"Don't interrupt, Marcus." Michael set his glass on the table. "Yes, they are real. I killed one in Flanders as Kabos and I left the city. It was a wolf that attacked me and a man that lay dead on the ground when I was done. But that is not the point. The queen will change us, the *loup garou*, the *wörterbuch*, the—"

"*Wörterbuch*? Do you mean the sorcerers?"

"Jesus, Marcus! Stop interrupting. The wicca, the witches, the wise-women, the warlocks, the fucking spell-casting humans. The queen will change them all." Michael reached for the wine bottle but didn't pour. Instead, he left his hand on the neck of the bottle. "And I have to find her, Marcus. I have to find her and make her one of us."

"That's what that parchment was saying?"

"No." Michael finally poured the wine. "The parchment doesn't mention me in that way. It talks about the queen's consort, and I guess that will be me. The parchment talks about the death of the queen and her return."

"I don't understand any of this, Michael."

"Well," Michael said, glancing toward the bistro door, "tonight I only understand our dear—what was her name? Oh yes, Monique. Our dear, lovely Monique." He looked at Marcus. "Run along home now. I'll be in later."

Amber and Chloe, Seattle, Present Day

"Tonight, we're just having fun and getting tipsy." Amber was smiling as Chloe opened the door. "I think I have the problem licked." Chloe tried to pay attention as Amber told her about the vision at the mirror and how it ended, but she focused instead on her outfit.

When Amber finished, Chloe had her sit down. "Let's not say, 'licked,' Amber. It reminds me of just how tasty you look compared to me." Both chuckled, but Chloe became serious for a moment. "Sweetie, I'm a witch. That's not the same as a religion, or not exactly. I don't *practice* witchcraft, I *am* a witch. It's not something you can learn how to do. Wait, that's not exactly right. You have to learn how to control your power, but not everyone has the power in the first place, nothing to learn how to use."

"I don't understand, Chloe." Amber sat at the kitchen table and shook her head. "I thought it was a religion. I thought anyone could practice witchcraft."

"Oh, anyone can say the charms and do the rituals, but that's not the same thing. If I spoke the — oh wait, look." She walked to the counter, filled two clear glasses with water, and placed them on the table. "Okay, pay close attention to the words." She spoke strange, guttural syllables slowly twice. "Okay, now you."

They repeated the words three or four times, and Chloe was amazed at how quickly Amber caught on. Finally she reached out and gently touched one of the glasses. "Okay, now. I'm concentrating on heat, okay?" Chloe gathered her power and began to chant the charm. In just a few seconds, bubbles formed in the water, and a moment or two later, the water was boiling. Amber touched the glass.

"Ouch! Jesus!" She put her forefinger in her mouth and sucked at the tip, a sour look on her face.

Chloe laughed. "Okay, now, take the other glass,

concentrate on heat, and you say the words." *God, anything to get that out of your mouth.* "And by the way, thanks for getting all dressed up for me."

"Yeah, yeah. Like you didn't dress to the nines tonight. Okay, here goes." She reached out with her hand and lightly touched the glass. Then, she began chanting. She kept it up for two to three minutes, but nothing happened. "All right, Chloe, I get it."

"It was weird, though, Amber. For a moment there, I thought I felt power in you. Anyway, you get my point. The words can be used by anyone, but without the power, they're just mantras." She chanted again and touched the boiling cup. The steam stopped rising immediately, and she raised the glass to her lips and took a sip. "You know, some of our historians think it was us that gave rise to stories of elves and faeries and sprites, and all of those fun forest creatures. Nobody really knows. We're pretty certain we're human, we're just human with a special power."

"Chloe, I can't argue with what you say, but I just don't believe in all of these myths and fairy tales." She paused for a moment. "I guess with what's been happening, I have to admit there have to be some parts that are true."

Typical human thinking, genius. Chloe smiled, a little indulgently, and finally said, "Look Amber, I made some calls today. When you told me you were ready for help, I asked my coven leader about vampires and prophecy. He didn't know anything about it, but the eldest witch among us called back and told me something that I have to share with you. It's not going to be easy to hear, but you need to listen to me tell the story. Promise not to interrupt, okay?"

"Okay. I will listen all the way through, Witch Girl. Still, I think it's all academic now. I stopped the vision."

"That might not matter much at all, Amber; I mean other

than making it more peaceful for you now; but listen. She told me that vampires came to the U.S. during the major European immigration waves. Witches and vampires don't get along, but they sent emissaries to express hopes that they might exist in peace. We've had an uneasy truce with them on this side of the Atlantic ever since."

Chloe took another sip of the water and paused. Amber looked desperate to interrupt, but she held her tongue. Chloe continued. "However, they've existed far longer than that. Some centuries ago, there was a young lord — well, he looked young; he could have been a thousand years old, I guess — named Michael, who was king. He had many names before that though. We lost track in the years. Anyway, he had a queen named Ilyria or Illyris, something like that. He wasn't loved, but he ruled the vampires with an iron fist. Anyway, he treated humans like meals and werewolves like servants until — "

"You're not serious about werewolves."

"Amber, you promised. Now, shut up!" She pointed her finger. "Don't make me point my finger and boil your eyeballs. Anyway, the werewolves eventually rebelled and so many were killed that the old witch is pretty sure they're now extinct.

"Okay, here's the part that matters to you. Evidently, there was an old prophecy about the queen that foretold her birth. She was supposed to unite the wolves with the vampires and even the witches, and when the king figured out Illy-whatever wasn't just a pretty fang-face, he paid some sorcerer to destroy her. Anyway, the wizard wasn't sure that it worked, said it's really probable that he'd just delayed the prophecy and someday she'd be back."

***

Amber waited for Chloe to continue, but she didn't.

"That's it, Amber. That's what she told me, but listen...all of your dreams are filled with images that make sense with the prophecy."

"Chloe, do you really think — and I'm not saying I believe any of this — do you really think some orphan girl would be the child of prophecy?" She rolled her eyes and shook her head. "You know, before I was adopted, I would dream that my real parents were a king and a queen, or super spies, or rich tycoons. We all did. That's what orphans do. But let me tell you something. Most of us never even get adopted, and we're not special; we're just unlucky kids."

She remembered the orphanage as clearly as she remembered yesterday. The bitch in charge was never nice to her, never nice to anyone. In fact, Amber had known that Mrs. Brown couldn't wait to be rid of her. When a childless couple came in wanting a girl, Amber hid in the hallway and listened. They were humble, and timid, and Amber wondered what they were like. Mrs. Brown mentioned Amber, but called her a *redhead* like it was a curse word, told them Amber never spoke to anyone but the janitor, and trouble followed her around. Still, they had taken her in with open arms. She loved them, but she never felt that connection she'd dreamed of, the one all of the orphans dreamed about.

"Anyway, I guess it doesn't matter, right? If werewolves are extinct, the prophecy couldn't happen anyway, so we're off the hook. Let's go drink more than we should and hope we get lucky." She looked at Chloe, softness returning to her eyes.

Chloe stood up. "Okay, grab your purse. I think you understand why I had to say that, but right now we'll just let loose and have some fun, Vampire Prophecy Girl."

CHAPTER THIRTEEN
Engagement

Marcus, St. Petersburg, 1871

Marcus stood in front of the chest, breathing shallowly. Was this a random fancy? He knew that he could hope for no understanding from Michael if he were caught. It was horrible misconduct at best, utter betrayal at worst. He sighed. *Michael saved my life on the Dunbar Sands. If he hadn't arrived, I would have died on that shoal.*

He sighed. A knock sounded at the door and he opened it to find the innkeeper's daughter with the tray of wine and food. He smiled at her and took it. There was something about her face, heavy eyes and slightly off-balance facial features, that gave her the look of one of the — *what did we call them back in Rome?* — the god-touched, the idiots. She wasn't though. She was bright and cheerful, and three days in Russia at this inn had convinced him that she was the reason the inn survived. While her father sat with the guests, drinking potato spirits in the dining room, she constantly moved, cleaning this, lifting that, helping one guest after another.

"Anastasiya, will you take some wine with me?" He smiled at her, and she smiled back. Her body was quite attractive, slender and curvy all at once. But her face...she wasn't beautiful, not even pretty. *Face it, Marcus; it would be kind to call her homely.* Still, there was something alluring about her, something...*special.*

"*Spasiba.* You much are kind, *dorogaya moya,* but you would not enjoy to spend an evening such as this night drinking wine with a girl as me. Beside, *ya ne piyu* – uh, I not drink wine." She smiled up at him, produced a corkscrew from her apron, and opened the bottle.

Marcus reached forward and touched her hand. "How do you say 'please' in Russian, Ana?"

She laughed, pushed his hand away, and began to pour the wine. "*Pozhalujsta.* This is please how say Russian, *Gospodin* Marcus. But I not drink wine tonight. But you drink wine." She smiled and handed him the full glass.

Marcus took the glass, smiled, and shook his head sadly. She smiled at him, walked to the door, and closed it, but remained in the room. He watched her as she reached to the floor and picked up a small spider. "*Preevyet,* little *pahook.* Not home for you." She crossed to the window, opened it, and gently set it outside of the pane.

Marcus stared at her. "Not say not staying, *dorogaya moya,* just not drink wine." She reached forward and touched his cheek. "I stay," she said as she pulled his face down to her and kissed him. As her tongue flicked gently against his lips and teeth, he felt an almost electric thrill. *My God.* A little light-headed, he wondered for a moment if the wine had affected him before remembering that it was impossible now. *I'm not drunk. Oh Jesus, eighty years. I haven't been with a woman since before.*

He took her in his arms, and she pushed against him until he fell back onto the bed. She smiled as she reached behind her back to unclasp her dress and let it fall to the floor. She was naked beneath. What her face lacked, her legs and neck and...*she's beautiful.*

Then she was on him, pulling at his shirt and his trousers, pulling off his underclothes. She moved above him with urgency and a frenetic passion that amazed him. He kissed her, moved, and tried to keep up, but she was a master of misdirection, reaching with her hand but instead using her mouth, or straddling him but then flipping him over on top of her. Her lips, her arms, her legs were everywhere, and he finally grasped her at the waist to still her and pushed his mouth to hers.

She laughed through his kisses, moving with purpose beneath him, and grasped his shoulders, at last crying out *"Milaya moya! Ty takaya chudesnaya!"* He felt her shuddering beneath him, felt the great rush of warmth around him, heard the blood rushing through her body. The blood! The sound of it coursing from her heart and down to where he pushed into her was overwhelming. He pushed a final time and cried out against her, overwhelmed by her. As she buried her lips in the crook of his neck, her throat pushed against his chin, and Marcus could see the pulse of blood through her jugular. He opened his mouth, still reeling and feeling her.

"Ty takaya chudesnaya, Marcus. You are wonderful." The breeze of her breath accompanied the whisper, soft against his ear, and he inhaled sharply and retracted his fangs. He kissed her cheek and disengaged himself, stepping backwards to put distance between himself and her blood.

"I'm sorry. I...I need you to leave. I...."

Marcus expected tears and hurt, but she smiled. She walked to the table and lifted a hard biscuit from the wine tray. "Please, Ana, you must leave." She ignored him and took up a sharp paring knife. "Ana, I need you to leave! I don't need to eat!"

"But you do, Marcus. You need eat." She took the knife

and cut a furrow under her breast, putting the biscuit against the flow of blood until it was soaked. She handed it to him. "Eat, Marcus my *upyr*, sweet my *upyr*."

He took the biscuit and put it to his mouth. The blood was sweet and strong, and he cast the biscuit aside and pushed his face to the cut she had made. She stroked his hair as he fed, cooing softly over him. "Marcus, you more just *upyr*. Special are you. *Milaya moya*, angel my. I dream of you and dream. You prophecy." He lifted his head and stared at her.

"Prophecy? What prophecy, Anastasiya?" She smiled as she directed his mouth back to beneath her breast.

"*Koral, korolyeva, vedma, volk*, and you, my sweet."

Marcus pulled away and wiped his mouth, feeling the blood-drunkenness come upon him. "I have fed, Ana."

She stood, tore a long strip from the bed linens, and tied it around her chest beneath her breasts, covering her wound. Then, she pulled on her dress as Marcus sat on the chair next to the table, still reeling. She smiled at him. "Good dreams, Marcus, sweet."

He looked at her. "What were those words you said?"

"Which said?"

"I know *volk*, wolf. But *Koral, Koralee….*"

"King and queen." She giggled at him and started for the door, but he called out to her and she turned back, smiling.

"Wait, Ana. *Vett — vet?*"

"*Vedma*, Marcus. The one sees, the seeing one woman. Uh…the witch. Now, have other guests and no time left."

He watched the door close behind her, then reached into the little box on the table, withdrew a cigarette, and lit it with a candle. Finally, he stood, walked to the chest, and opened it. The tube lay beneath Michael's cloak. He opened it, pulled out the parchment, and began to read.

Amber and Chloe, Seattle, Present Day

The two walked into the bar and made a beeline for a table in a far corner. Amber was concerned that they'd not be able to get the bartender's attention. Chloe solved the problem by ordering a full bottle of tequila and a bowl of lemons. "Okay." Amber poured two shots out as she spoke. "I may have underestimated you."

Two shots of tequila, two lemon wedges, and about a half teaspoon of salt later, Amber stood up. "Okay, I'm loose enough to dance now." She brushed by two frat boys, who looked her up and down and tried a couple of cliché lines, but gave up as she walked away. A tall blond man in a business suit was slightly more interesting, but he fumbled with what to say and she smiled and kept walking.

By the time she got to the dance floor, the up-tempo neo-disco number had ended and Amber closed her eyes as the Beatles' "Oh Darling" came on.

Oh Darling! Please believe me.

Amber closed her eyes, moving softly, swaying to the music.

I'll never do you no harm.

She smiled and let the bluesy voice wash over her.

Believe me when I tell you, I'll never do you no harm.

She could feel the tequila warming her belly, making her just a touch lightheaded, and she smiled as she continued to dance.

Oh Darling! If you leave me, I'll never make it alone.

As she swayed, she felt the stress of the move and the visions and the new job slowly dripping off and away.

Believe me when I beg you — ooooooh — don't ever leave me alone.

***

Back at the table, Chloe sipped her tequila and watched

Amber dance. She smiled as she watched two or three different guys consider approaching her and give up. The tequila was good, smooth, but still hot against her throat as it travelled down.

When you told me –

She heard the tables crying out first, and the shock of it paralyzed her for a moment, so that before she could react, the walls were screaming as well.

You didn't need me anymore.

Chloe took a deep breath and spoke the charm her mother had taught her, concentrating on focus and centering her power on herself.

Well you know, I nearly broke down and cried.

She felt the power entering her, quieting the walls, the table, and even the tequila itself. The noise dimmed, but she felt her hands tingling and actually saw miniscule blue sparks at the ends of her fingertips.

When you told me –

She chanted for a moment more, and she felt the power centering her and removing the distractions.

You didn't need me anymore.

***

Completely unaware of Chloe, or for that matter, anyone else, Amber continued to move, feeling the song and enjoying it. She swayed as she tried to remember if John Lennon or Paul McCartney was singing.

Well you know I nearly broke down and died.

As the long note faded, she felt a tap on her shoulder. She opened them and saw an attractive man who looked to be in his late twenties.

Oh Darling, if you leave me.

He smiled, but the smile couldn't hide a sadness lurking behind the strange, light blue eyes that occupied deep-set sockets over a somewhat sharp nose. She found him breathtaking.

I'll never make it alone.

There was something about him that captivated Amber. She didn't usually like the aristocratic kind of look he displayed, the blue-blood manicured grooming and a casual red silk shirt that cost enough to buy everyone in the bar two rounds. He brushed a strand of sandy blond hair from his forehead as he spoke. "Hello. May I buy you a drink?"

Believe me when I tell you.

His smile was disarming, and Amber smiled at him.

I'll never do you no harm.

"My name is Michael."

CHAPTER FOURTEEN

Storming

Michael, Rome, 1802

Michael watched the door close behind Marcus and turned eagerly back to Kabos. "Come now, Father. Tell me."

Kabos smiled. "How did you know?"

"There was nothing in that parchment that I didn't already know. There was nothing new there." Michael pointed at the document, still on the table and weighted at three corners with a wine glass. The wine bottle held the other. "There's coming a queen in the time of the wolf, and she's the key to everyone's survival. Tell me Kabos, how is that different from what the old woman said?"

Kabos smiled. "All right, Machiel. Perhaps there was a little play acting there for Marcus's sake."

"There's play acting now, old man. You may have wanted Marcus along for the journey, but nothing there explains transferring to me what you've spent centuries building. Nothing there explains why you're leaving."

"The translation is incorrect, Machiel. Come, look." Kabos pointed at writing in the middle of the parchment. "This is written in the language of the Phoenicians, probably from an old settlement in Sidon, where the Avalani were first formed.

125

Look here." He touched a few scraggly lines in the margin. "This is where a scribe indicates that he's copying from an original. It's probably from hundreds of years after the original was written."

"But what does this have to do with the translation? Did the original mistranslate? What are you — ?"

Kabos pointed to symbols and runes at the top of the page. "This is the old tongue. This is the language we spoke millennia ago. Some ancients believe everyone spoke it...us, humans, wolves, everyone. Somewhere along the way, the races of beings separated. Nobody really knows why, but there are theories. In any case, whether we alone spoke it or whether we alone continued to use it, the old tongue is all but lost now. The man who transcribed this document didn't know it."

"How can you tell?"

"First, the writing is too perfect. He copied the symbols as individual pieces of art, exact replicas."

"Come on, Kabos. He could just be attentive to detail."

"No, his Phoenician is not near the quality. He copied it, Machiel. Besides, the real reason I know this is because the translation is wrong — well, incomplete. What is written there is only about half of the prophecy. And that is all that I have translated below," he pointed to newer writing at the very bottom of the page, "into Flemish."

"What is the missing part?"

"The missing part, Machiel, is your destiny."

"Stop the cryptic, mysterious statements, Kabos. If I am to continue without you there is no more time for riddles!" Kabos smiled up at Michael, who softened his tone. "Please, Father. Come with me. Help me."

Kabos placed a forefinger in the middle of the strange characters and trailed along as he read. "The consort of queen will enamored of power — forgive me Machiel, the language is not structured as is ours; I will read it as is, though — and purposeful power will make strong." He looked up. "That means that your ambition and your single-minded determination is your strength."

"It's been due to be recognized for some time."

Kabos chuckled and continued to read. "When the day of the wolf comes, the queen rise, but consort must sacrifice for all. The queen will end separate ways wolf, oracle, and — uh, there's nobody left who knows how this word was pronounced, but it was the old tongue's word for us, the uh, vampires. Betrayers lurk for queen and wolf and oracle. Only consort stops betrayers to protect all."

"What does that mean, Father?"

"Get me some wine, Machiel." Kabos waited for the glass before continuing. "There's more to read, but it's more of the same. It means, my son, that you are the key to the whole thing. The queen will have enemies. You can only imagine what uniting us with the wolves and the oracles will do. You hold the key to seeing the prophecy to the end."

"What are the oracles?"

"The hags, the witches." Kabos sipped his wine.

"Like the gypsy woman?"

"I suppose a bit like her."

Michael studied the parchment for a while. Finally, he poured a glass of wine for himself. "Father, how am I to do all of this?"

Kabos smiled sadly at him. "I don't know. That, you must discover on your own."

Amber and Chloe, Seattle, Present Day

Chloe loved obscure words. Growing with the Sight had left her aware of everything at all times in a way that kept life constantly moving and shifting around her. At twelve, she had discovered Webster's Unabridged Dictionary and lost herself in the definitions. As necklaces and cars and rocks and people cried out to her, she comforted herself by finding definitions to attach to the circumstances.

Perspicacity. That was the definition for what her Sight was doing to her now. "Latin," she said aloud. "Keenness of perception, insight, mental awareness. Archaic: Keen Vision." Every aspect of her energy was focused and aware. There was a vampire here. She knew it as plainly as she knew that the agave grown on a small Mexican farm outside of Oaxaca to make the tequila she sipped came from a family who had lost their eldest daughter in a freak accident with the electric tiller the family had saved for six years to buy.

She scanned the bar and saw the tall blond man with the red silk shirt. It was him, and he was talking to Amber. She listened and could feel his mind reaching out to Amber, directing her. As Amber turned to walk with the vampire to the bar, a group of college kids began a wild, loud, and bacchanalian dance, jerky movements and silly antics completely out of step to the music. They obscured sight of Amber, and Chloe cursed inwardly at their chicanery.

She breathed deeply and began to chant under her breath. In a moment, the students stopped dancing, looked around as if dazed, and then one by one returned to their table. Amber and the blond had almost reached the bar. Chloe began a second chant, and the dim blue sparks at her fingertips grew brighter. She reached out and felt first surprise and then resistance. The vampire looked around, and Chloe quickly put her hands under the table and turned her head as though she were looking at the DJ. She felt Amber's presence, but not her mind, and she realized that she had yet to read anything about her; not her clothes, not her things, not even the antique crystal necklace she wore. In fact, Amber was probably the only person she'd ever encountered who gave no information to her at all.

The vampire turned back to Amber, and Chloe felt his mind straining and concentrating to a greater degree. *You can't have her, you son of a bitch.* Chloe focused harder, called upon the voices of the tables, the chairs, the glasses, the grain farmers, the distillers, and even the contractors who had built the bar, and lashed out with all the strength she could muster.

***

Amber turned to Michael and smiled at him. "You know, Michael, I just remembered I'm here with my friend. I'd better get back to her, but I'll give you a rain check on that drink if you'll give me your number."

Michael frowned, but quickly smiled. "Ah, I'm afraid I've just arrived in Seattle and I don't yet know my number. Perhaps...." He looked at her, and Amber thought about how he looked boyish, eager, and insecure now.

"I work at the museum. If you call there, you can ask for me, Amber Stone."

"Well, I regret that we cannot share a drink now, but I will call on you at the museum. My advisors and I were considering an endowment there, so the timing is perfect."

Amber smiled at him and walked away from the bar, fully aware that Michael was studying the way her rear moved as she did. *Play your cards right next time, and I'll show you what it can do.*

Amber walked towards the table but Chloe met her halfway. "Amber, this place isn't working for me, too many college kids. Want to hit a couple of dive bars like total sluts?"

Amber nodded. "Okay, but no promises afterward. I was hoping to meet someone tonight, but now I'll wait for him to call me."

Amber saw that Chloe smiled at her strangely but didn't think any more of it as the two walked out. But when Chloe kept her hands in her pockets until they reached the car, Amber thought it was totally strange.

***

Chloe saw that the sparks were gone but wondered at Amber's flirting with the vampire. She waited for her friend to say something, but Amber was slightly buzzed as they drove to the next bar. Chloe realized that her friend was beautiful and sexy. She was definitely attracted to Amber, but knew that was just a sign of curiosity. Chloe had been with many women before, but none were as innocent as Amber.

Deep down, Chloe knew that her power had saved Amber this time, but what about the next time?

CHAPTER FIFTEEN

Reaching

Amber and Chloe, Seattle, Present Day

The smell of coffee and frying bacon stirred Amber from her sleep. She stretched and opened her eyes. The accountant next to her was still sleeping. She smiled and kissed his cheek before she got out of the bed and pulled on her clothes. He mumbled something incoherent and turned over. He'd been fine last night...not spectacular, just fine. And that was just fine with Amber. She was used to doing most of the work with encounters like this anyway. His body was there, and that was pretty much all she wanted.

She pulled her blouse around her and buttoned it, staring at the man on the bed. He was attractive enough in his way, but not the kind of man she usually picked up. *I must have hit the tequila a little too hard.* Still, he'd been exactly what she wanted last night. She imagined she'd give him a repeat performance some time if he wanted one. She sat on the edge of the bed and pulled her boots on. His room shouted "Man!" in a deep, booming, action hero voice. The white walls were bare except for an old Led Zeppelin poster. A computer sat on a metal desk, a spreadsheet up on the monitor. A big-screen television was on the wall, complete with two—no, three—

different game consoles attached, their wires curling from behind the screen to their boxes.

He had about four hundred DVDs in a bookcase — *probably keeps his porn in the closet* — and an iPod in a cradle next to impossibly large speakers. She shook her head, smiled, and leaned down to kiss his cheek another time. Another mumble and another turn.

She stretched again and followed the smells to the kitchen, where Chloe was frying bacon with a very tall man with spiked hair and almost Asian features. They didn't hear her coming, but she heard the man say, "...and now you are making breakfast like last night was the best night we ever had." Chloe was dressed in one of the man's t-shirts, and it hung down just below her waist. It was long enough to conceal her, except when she moved. She moved as the man tickled her at the waist, and Amber got a glimpse of her tiny panties.

She cleared her throat. The two turned and smiled at her. "Is Andy up yet?" Amber was confused for a minute before she realized that Andy must be the accountant's name.

"Sleeping like a baby." She took an exaggerated breath through her nose. "I think I smell heaven in here."

"Come get some coffee." Chloe turned to the man. "Where do you guys keep the cups?"

"Second cabinet on the right. I'm going to jump in the shower and come back for the grub." He leaned forward and kissed Chloe's cheek, mumbling something in her ear.

"You'll have to play your cards right for that one, Bub." He turned and walked away, but not before Chloe smacked his rear.

Amber reached to the cabinet and pulled out two mugs. She poured a cup for herself and one for Chloe, and opened the refrigerator. "These guys have any milk?"

"It's already out for the pancakes. Did you have a good time last night?"

Amber added some milk to her cup. "I had two or three good times last night. It's weird, though, I never go for, uhm...Andy's type. Still, he did the trick. How about you, Ms. Almost Naked in the Kitchen?"

"Oh, Bobby and I get together every month or two. He's a software guy. He and Andy built a program to catalog some Internet thing in college and sold it for a bunch of money to Microsoft. The guys have lived together since the dorm, and they're building their second tech company." She took a sip of her coffee and smiled as it warmed her. "Truth is, I was happy as hell to see them at the dive yesterday, because the pickings were getting slim."

"They had to be. I never pick guys like Andy. Still, I remember when you dared me to do the shot with him," she laughed. Chloe smiled. Amber had lain on a table, a lemon wedge in her mouth, salt on the base of her throat. Andy downed a shot, licked the salt off her throat, and put his mouth to hers. "You know, the moment his tongue hit my neck, I had to have him. That never happens to me. Well, not with an accountant, anyway."

***

Chloe smiled. "You're just a slut, Amber." *At least you're a slut when I have to charm you to get you to forget about the fucking vampire.* Chloe felt a stab of guilt. Strictly speaking, a lust charm was only to be used on yourself, to get yourself into the mood or to heighten the pleasure of the experience. It was morally questionable to use it on a willing participant, and absolutely unethical to use it on an unaware subject.

"No, I'm serious, Chloe. I don't go for guys like him. He wasn't even very good, but somehow it was the best sex I've had in six months." The guilt was coming full force now.

Chloe took a gulp of her coffee.

"Well, then, aren't you glad you gave the number cruncher a chance? Come help me mix the pancake batter." *It was worth it, though*, she decided. Until the charm, Amber hadn't stopped talking about the vampire. Everything was about Michael. *I just did what I had to do.*

"I guess you're right, Chloe. Maybe I'll try another run at him in a few weeks, find out if it was just stress release from the move."

What I had to do. God, I'm a bitch — a witch bitch.

Michael, France, 1893

The woman lay still beneath him, and Michael rose. Her blood had been thin, diluted by the endless stream of wine she drank, wine supplied by her sales of orphan children to rich men who used them to satisfy their darker desires. He'd learned of her just yesterday, when he'd walked the rooftops and chanced upon a fat banker moving atop a ten or eleven year old girl as she alternately cried and screamed. He'd pulled the man off and held him by his throat over the side of the roof until he learned of the woman. The girl he'd wrapped in the fat man's cloak and left her at the steps of a convent house. He had systematically broken the man's legs, arms, feet, and hands before draining him. And now, the woman was drained as well. A wolf howled in the distance. *Whore*. He spat on her. Her blood made the spittle red.

He was tempted to leave the body where it was, but Kabos had trained him too well. He took a blanket from the woman's bed and wrapped her in it. Hefting her over a shoulder, he lifted her window pane and climbed upward to her roof. A series of jumps brought him to a copse of trees, and he threw the body from the rooftop and followed it, lightly landing beside her.

Two hundred yards south was an abandoned well. He'd seen it that morning, and he lifted her body over his shoulder and began to walk. "Last walk, bitch," he said, and hit her through the blanket with his free hand, feeling foolish, but still enjoying himself.

As he walked, he heard panting in the trees. A soft whine confirmed for him that a dog was near, and he contemplated feeding her to it. *She's dead, fool. Nothing more can be done.* He kept his pace and arrived at the well, dropping her in. When he didn't hear her drop he looked and saw that the body was wedged about three feet below the top of the well.

"Damn." He leaned over, put one leg in the well, and began to kick at the body. It was wedged firmly, and he kicked over and over, hearing her bones break as he did. Finally, he kicked with all of his might and she fell, but it left him unbalanced, and he ended up splayed out on the ground next to the well. "Shit!" He lifted his head and stared into the eyes of a large black wolf.

He felt his fangs and nails extending as he leapt to his feet, but the wolf didn't attack. Instead, it stood on its hind legs and began to change. It reminded Michael of the way he'd seen potters in Flanders work clay...lumpy blobs giving way to discernable shapes. The snout retreated, the paws grew smaller, the body grew longer, thinner. In twenty seconds or so, a man stood, a shaggy black beard and thick eyebrows the only hint of wolf remaining.

"We have no quarrel, Machiel of Bruges. Your prophecy and our prophecy are the same."

Marcus, Seattle, Present Day

"Yes, about two million." Marcus sat at the desk, the phone propped between head and shoulder as he typed at his computer. "Take it from the Caymans account, and place it with a local charitable trust. Authorization is on its way now." He tapped the keyboard a final time and reached to his shoulder for the phone. "Whatever department Amber Stone curates. That's where the endowment goes. Yes…uh huh…. Okay. Let me know when it's done."

He put the phone down and walked to the window. It was a cool night, and the needles on the pine trees swayed softly in the breeze. Michael was in Syria, or more appropriately, was on his way to Syria. Something had kept him from controlling the girl last night, and he wanted to find out what it was. In the meantime — well, there was nothing in the meantime. He would stay at the estate, feed on the servants, and try to learn what he could about this queen.

If Michael can't control her now, how the hell does he expect he'll be able to when she's turned? He chuckled a little at the thought. Michael didn't like it when he didn't get his way. He didn't like it at all.

CHAPTER SIXTEEN
Propinquity

Weeks passed and Chloe noted with satisfaction that Amber hadn't spoken of Michael again. She had, however, had another date with Andy, and when she stepped into Chloe's office the next day she seemed so disappointed that Chloe felt the guilt rise up again and wash over her. Worse, when she mentioned in passing that she had to grab a hotel for a week while her landlord laid new copper piping in the apartment, Amber insisted on Chloe staying at her place.

Aw hell, all I did was make it good for her. But that was a lie. *Jesus, it's no different than slipping her Rohypnol.* She smiled up at Amber and swallowed the guilt. "Okay, but no crying and no chick flicks."

"Not even a little crying? Maybe we get some ice cream and cry at the way we women are so misunderstood? Get some french fries and get over all the men who have hurt us?"

"Amber, I'm pretty sure there's a joke lurking somewhere in all of that, but it wouldn't be all that funny even if you knew how to deliver it."

"Okay, fine then. No chick stuff. You want to come with me to meet the museum's newest patron saint?"

"What do you mean? Actually...." Chloe stood and stretched her neck, rolling her head in a circle. "I don't care what you mean. I've been at this desk for too long today." She looked at her watch; it was nearly eight o'clock. "God, the museum's almost closed."

"The director has ordered me to his office. Evidently someone donated a bunch of money to the Macedonian collection's care, so I have to go brownnose."

"You think he'll mind if I come?"

"There are a few fetishes in the first dig, so I'm planning on acting like I'll need your help with the work." She winked at Chloe. "Besides, I'm the super genius, so I can get away with anything."

Chloe rolled her eyes, but she followed Amber through the office door, into the hallway, and to the elevator. "I've been here two years and I've never even met the director. When did you two get to be pals?"

"I've never met him before either. I just got the phone call from his secretary a half hour ago. Come up to the fifth floor, reception desk is on the left." The elevator opened, and the two stepped inside. "You know Chloe, I've been thinking about Andy." Chloe felt her heart sinking. "I really needed that night with him. I'd been so stressed and the dreams were so scary, I think it was so good because I really needed it. I didn't need it last night, and it was...well, it was sex with an accountant. Still, I really needed it that first time." She turned and pulled Chloe into her arms. "Thanks for taking me out."

Chloe felt a little better, just a twinge of guilt, but she noticed Amber's eyes were wet. "What's wrong, Amber?"

Amber shook her head. "Oh, it's just the damn dreams. They're back and they're as weird as ever. I don't know, I just want to sleep once in a while, you know? Just sleep, no images, no noise. Just sleep."

"I'll see if I can help you do it tonight."

Amber rolled her eyes. "Eye of newt? Dragon scale? Sweat from a horse's ass?"

Chloe started to reply, but instead she ended up giggling like a school girl. Amber laughed along until she finally blurted out that they had to get to the meeting. Chloe pressed the button for the fifth floor, but not before quipping that too much horse's ass sweat would make Amber sleep for a week.

Marcus, Twenty-Nine Palms, 1982

The desert air was cool on his face, and Marcus stood at the top of the Joshua Tree National Monument Visitor's Center, a one story tourist building overlooking the Oasis of Mara. He heard the soft bubbling of water and smiled, although he knew it was a pump moving the water now and not a natural spring. The location was remote, but he'd already decided against locating an estate here. Michael had been born into wealth nearly three hundred years before, and Marcus doubted he could create an estate that would maintain the lifestyle his father had come to expect.

He heard a soft rustling on the roof next to him and turned to see two yellow eyes glaring at him from across the roof. *He's finally found me.* Marcus had seen the signs of the bobcat the first night he'd come here to the roof. Now, he reached out with his mind tentatively, drawing the cat to him. It walked to him and pushed its head against Marcus's knee. Marcus reached down and scratched its ear softly. "I think I shall keep you." The cat purred a strange growling purr against him, and Marcus smiled. "Well, my friend, you're male. I can't very well call you 'Mara.' How about 'Mojave' or…no. I'll call you 'Joshua.' That'll work." Joshua looked up at him, then promptly sat and began cleaning himself with his tongue.

Marcus stood and looked over the desert night. The lights from the small town dotted the landscape; not as many as a few hours ago, but the streetlights and the occasional window light still shone. To the north, he saw the lights of the Marine Corps Air Ground Combat Center, and there was still a small trickle of cars leaving the city toward the main gate, marines heading home now that the bars had closed.

He ducked down as he saw headlights entering the parking lot. The car pulled to a space next to the center entrance and Marcus prepared to jump down to the parking lot. When the door opened, however, it wasn't the man he expected. Instead, a young man in a green and white letterman's jacket stepped out of the driver's door. He was followed by another, also in a jacket, from the rear. The passenger reached into the car and pulled out a six pack of generic beer. He lifted up his head and howled.

"Stop it, Tommy! Somebody will hear." It wasn't the driver who spoke. Instead, the admonition, tinged with a bit of childlike enthusiasm, had come from a teenage girl climbing out of the rear of the car. She was dressed in the jeans that ended three inches above the ankle that the teenagers seemed to favor these days.

The front passenger door opened and another girl stepped out. "Oh relax, nobody's around. Besides, what're they gonna do, tell us to leave?"

Tommy lifted his head again and howled. "Beat Yuck-ahhh!"

Marcus squinted. The boy must have meant Yucca Valley High School. *God, why did I set this up on a fucking football night?* He looked south and saw no headlights, but the man would be there within the hour. Marcus hoped the kids would leave by then, but when the driver turned and said, "Hey, grab that other six pack, too," he realized they'd be hours.

He sat on the roof and considered the situation. Joshua came to him, and as the cat nuzzled his chest he absently petted it. *He'll kill them.* The man he was meeting would allow for no witnesses. *No, worse. I'll have to kill him.*

The four young people had already crossed through the little courtyard and climbed the short adobe wall to the oasis proper. Tommy was holding onto one girl's waist, letting his hands occasionally cup a buttock. Marcus watched them, uneasiness growing, until finally it rose to panic as he saw lights a mile or so to the south. "Jesus, Joshua. This wasn't the night I wanted."

For a moment he thought he may have been wrong, that the car would pass the visitor's center, but instead it slowed at the last minute and pulled in. He leapt from the roof and landed lightly on the sidewalk by the teenagers' vehicle. The other car pulled beside it and the driver turned off the engine. He left the lights on, and they cast a surreal glow over Marcus's feet. The door opened, and the man exited the vehicle, leaving the door wide.

"You said you'd be on foot." Suspicion dripped from the man's tone. He stepped into the light, glaring at Marcus. "I don't like changes."

"Let it go." Marcus eyed the man with a glare he hoped was intimidating.

"No changes. Never. Every word must be accurate."

"It's not my car. I am afoot. Now, to business."

"Whose car is it?" The man was looking to the left and right now.

"I said to let it go. Did you bring it?"

"Goddamn it, whose car is this?" The man screamed the words, pointing his finger at the car while advancing on Marcus.

Goddamn it is right. The man didn't even see the movement as he was knocked to the ground. In fact, it took three or four seconds before he realized the mouth on his neck had ripped through his flesh. It took three or four more before he understood that he wouldn't be getting back up. His body took a little more time, and it was still jerking spasmodically a minute later when Marcus stood, reeling from the blood drunkenness.

When his head cleared, he went to the man's car and popped the trunk with a latch beneath the driver's seat. He took a briefcase from the trunk and then leaned down and lifted the man. He had to bend the body nearly in half to make it fit, but he finally closed the trunk over him. *Well, I've eaten and saved a few thousand dollars as well. Damn it.*

He took the briefcase, placed it on top of the hood, and opened it. Inside was a stack of twenty or thirty old pieces of parchment and a small leather journal. He sighed softly and looked toward the closed trunk. "I'm sorry, Javier. I would like to have used you again."

He looked up at the roof. The wildcat was on the edge, peering down on him. "Well come on then, Joshua. It's time to go." He watched the cat leap from the roof onto one of the trees that had given him his name and climb down to the sidewalk. Marcus gestured to the car door and the cat jumped in over the driver's seat and settled in the back, first stretching and then curling up on the back seat.

Marcus smiled, got into the car, and drove away.

Amber and Chloe, Seattle, Present Day

The office was much as a museum director's office should be. An old oak desk sat in front of an equally antique, and not quite matching, credenza. A hutch above the credenza held an eclectic collection of what in a normal office might be called knick knacks. Their placement here, though, suggested that they were most certainly artifacts or representative folk and high art. Wood paneling covered the bottom half of the walls, and the top was adorned with cream-colored wallpaper with barely discernible flower patterns.

Amber didn't notice any of it. The moment she and Chloe walked inside the office, her eyes were drawn only to the man behind the desk. He sat in a charcoal three piece suit with a muted maroon tie. He smiled as she entered, and the thick sideburns she'd first seen jogging next to her in New York rose with his cheeks. "Miss Stone? I'm Malakai Ridgewater. It's good to meet you finally...I mean formally." He stood from the desk. "And, uh, you are Miss...Miss Tudor, right?" He extended his hand in their general direction.

Chloe nodded. "There are a few pieces from the Macedonian digs that fit my area of expertise, and Amber asked me to join in the meeting...if that's okay with you, of course."

"Of course, that will be fine. I'm glad to see you're already getting into the collection, Miss Stone." Amber realized he still had his hand out and took it in hers, feeling foolish and a little clumsy. "Ah, I can see you're a little put off by it being me in this chair. I have to admit I was a little surprised to see you walk through the door as well." He motioned for them to sit. "I travelled to New York to see a collection at the MOMA that they were thinking of locating here. It seems one of their patrons collected a great many anthropological pieces as well as art. Of course, they wanted the Pollacks and the Picassos, but they weren't all that interested with the drums or the baskets." He reached forward and pressed a button on his phone. "Anne? Would you be so kind as to bring some coffee?" He looked at Amber and Chloe. "Can I get you anything other than coffee?" They shook their heads and he released the intercom. "Anyway, I stopped by your house hoping to introduce myself to you, but you had already left for Seattle. I wish I had known it was you I passed jogging on the trail, and I think I saw you on the plane as well."

"That was me. I saw you too." Amber smiled at him. *To think I was running a mental commentary about your muscles.* "Did we acquire the collection?"

"No. It was all mid-century tourist goods from northeastern tribes, Lenni Lenape mostly. He even had a copy of the Wallum Olam. He—"

"That was discredited a few years back, right?" Chloe had blurted the question without thinking, and she felt a little embarrassed. This was Amber's meeting. If she had any reason to be, the others gave no indication.

"Well, no. That is, the Wallum Olam is a genuine manuscript, dates back centuries. It was the translation that was discredited." Ridgewater lifted his head and smiled as the receptionist brought in coffee. "Thank you, Anne. When Mr. Reyns arrives, please show him right in."

When the receptionist left, he turned his attention back to Chloe and Amber. "Michael Reyns has created an endowment for your collection, Miss Stone."

"Please, call me Amber."

"Very well, Amber. The endowment is just shy of two million dollars, and will produce an annual budget influx of about one-hundred and sixty thousand. We already fully funded your salary, the contributions to the interns, and the storage of the collection. How should we spend the new money?" He stood and poured coffee into three cups while Amber answered.

"Mr. Ridgewater, I—"

"Ah, my turn. Call me Malakai, please."

Amber blushed for a moment. "Okay, Malakai. I think we could hire a photographer to catalog some of the more fragile pieces before we begin their preservation process. I'd also like to see about a laser scanner that will integrate with a CAD modeling program. It might help me digitally reconstruct some of the fragments so we can determine their original purposes. I imagine the endowment income would cover the equipment lease."

"You just found out about this meeting a few hours ago and you've already figured out what to do with the money." Malakai chuckled and drained his cup. "I see we made the right decision hiring you, Amber." Everyone laughed a little awkwardly. Finally, the director looked at Chloe. "You know, Miss Tudor, we've never had anyone who could catalog as quickly and accurately as you. There's a rumor going around among the directors that you've sold your soul to the devil."

Chloe smiled. "Well, I'm not going to let Amber have you call her by her first name and keep up formalities myself, so please, call me Chloe. As for selling my soul, my soul's worth just a bit more to me than being able to distinguish a Zuni spearhead from an Incan arrowhead."

The director stared at her for a moment. "Perhaps the rumors would end if you stopped dressing like a character out of the *Rocky Horror Picture Show*?" Chloe sat mortified, but Malakai's face broke and he began to laugh, and Chloe felt her cheeks burning a little in embarrassment. "Dress like Little Bo Peep if you want to Chloe, just keep up the good work."

Just then, the door opened.

CHAPTER SEVENTEEN
Determinations

Michael, Sidon, 1911

The room was small. That was what first cried out to be noticed, the tiny size of the damned place. Seven others were there, vampires. That was the word now. *Vampires.* The rest of the words had gradually slipped into obscurity, and the new one, the one Polidori and Stoker had used, was accepted not only among the mortals but among all of his kind as well. For a while, he'd worn a crucifix and sipped holy water in a capricious rebellion against the glamorization of his kind by the day dwellers. *Well, they got the sunlight right.*

Only one chair at the table that filled the room was empty, and all waited for the one who would fill it. Michael shifted impatiently in his seat. "When will he be here?"

A vampire sat two chairs down. He looked old, and Michael wondered how old he had been when he was turned. "Mr...Reyns, right?"

"Call me Michael."

"Thank you, Michael. I believe the chancellor will be here soon. He asked you to meet with us because he believes there is some urgency to your prophecy. I can't say more, he hasn't shared everything with any one of us. This meeting is a gathering of the minds of sorts, a way for us to pool our knowledge and ensure the prophecy doesn't—"

"Oh, shut up, Pyotr. We owe this youth...." She almost spat "youth" out of her mouth. "...no explanation and no discussion." It was a tall woman with straw-blonde hair, who looked to be nineteen or twenty, that had turned her eyes on him. She wasn't really young. In fact, Michael was pretty sure she was older than Kabos. "The Avalani doesn't wait on your pleasure, Michael. You await ours."

Michael stared at her for a few seconds. He wondered how different, if any, she looked now than when she was, what? A farm girl? She had the build for it. She was pretty, maybe almost beautiful, but if she'd lived she would have gained the features of a farm woman, the work accentuating her large bones, her wide face. A lady in waiting? That would explain her haughtiness. He'd seen it at his father's estate back in Bruges. *Nothing makes a woman without title more arrogant than when she acquires it by association, that's what Dad said.* A whore? *Ah, one can only hope.* He gave up and simply said, "Tell me, were you this much of a bitch when you were alive?"

Her eyes flashed and filled with the half-yellow, half-red color that always came with the hunt. Michael yawned, making a show of it, and the woman bared her fangs. Her voice was quiet, but a river of malice ran beneath the surface. "You insolent insect. I don't care if you're Kabos's whelp...you will pay for your flippancy, child."

Michael stood and calmly reached for his wine. "Oh no, the really scary vampire woman is angry with me. Whatever will I do?" He sipped his wine. "Perhaps I'll cower in the corner and pray she forgets me. Perhaps I'll run away." He turned his eyes back to the fuming woman. "Or perhaps I'll ignore the already irrelevant woman from the increasingly irrelevant ancient," he rolled his eyes as he said this word, "organization and get on with my life. That is, of course, unless you'd like to feel how a Flemish man pleases a woman."

She leapt over the table at him, a blur of movement, her claws outstretched. Michael was surprised at how easily he tracked her movement. He'd heard that she was faster than any other. He reached his right arm out, trying to appear nonchalant, and caught her by her throat mid-jump. He held her that way for a moment, never looking at her, and she hung in shock. He kept his eyes on his wine glass and lifted it with his left arm to take a sip.

"You upstart!" She clawed at his arm, and it took a great deal of effort to keep from looking at her. *I bet she looks like an angry cat.* "You are an insub—"

"Well. It appears that Kabos wasn't exaggerating." The voice that spoke was rich and sonorous, and Michael inclined his head to see the tall vampire in black robes who spoke. *So this is Gerard.* He had been turned late, Michael concluded, because his crow's feet surrounded his eyes and heavy, wrinkled jowls hung from his face. "Stronger than most, perhaps all; and rash as a boar surprised by a hunter." The man pulled out the chair that had been left vacant for him and sat. He reached for the wine bottle and began to pour his glass. "Michael, I would consider it a favor if you would return Isabella to her seat."

Michael flicked his arm, almost imperceptibly, and the woman flew across the room, crashing against the wall that stood only a foot or so behind her chair. She screamed and prepared to leap at Michael, who had already returned to his seat.

"Take your seat Isabella. You've been humiliated once, no need to make it twice." Gerard said it dismissively, but

Isabella stood, her eyes open wide, claws and fangs extended. "Isabella, sit now or I will give Michael leave to drain you and leave the husk on the roof to greet the sun."

Slowly, reluctantly, she took her seat. Gerard turned his eyes to Michael and said, "Well, now. It appears that the queen we've awaited for so long has chosen you to find her. We have a great deal of work to do."

Chloe, Lake Washington, 2008

The cool water enveloped her, and Chloe felt the strange mix of invigoration and relaxation that came with swimming in the moonlight. She opened her eyes, watching silvery ribbons swimming away from her and then tentatively returning to swim beside her. *Little trout inside the stream, little fishies, little dreams.* Where had she heard that nursery rhyme? Had Tom told her that one? Her mother?

She flipped over and let herself float to the surface, feeling the night air against her face and her breasts as the water flowed off. She stroked slowly backwards and saw a raven flying above her, and smiled. The bird looking down at her would see her body, but also her hair fanning out in the water like some kind of giant fish creature. She imagined some of the boys in college looking at her now, flying like the raven and looking down to see her naked in the water like some kind of water nymph. It was a little strange coming to the college. Because of her unique situation, Thomas and her mother had homeschooled Chloe. Sometimes she thought Tom just wanted an excuse to move in and be closer to her mom. She imagined the two would marry someday, but they'd lived together, slept in the same bed, and raised the same child for fifteen or sixteen years, and there wasn't a ring in sight. Still, the two of them loved her and taught her and made her what she was.

That's the problem, guys. What she was…. She was smarter than the boys at the college, and a hell of a lot more self-assured. They fumbled about, playing games or simply losing any coherent ability to communicate when they got close. Sex was hilarious at best, tragic at worst. The coven had been open and extremely unrestrictive when it came to sex. She felt like the entire university was repressed, even as boys downed beer by the gallons and screwed their sorority girls in an unending stream of debauchery on Fraternity Row. Above all, they put so much significance in the act it was sad, really.

She knew someday she'd meet someone she'd love and want in all ways, exclusively. Until then, the act was just that, an action. Hell, entertainment. *A whole lot cheaper than the opera, too.* She giggled a little at herself, and the trout that had paced her ducked deeper into the water. She smiled as she turned back over and headed to shore, where she'd placed her clothes next to a small juniper. *You guys don't get stressed over it, do you? Just swim and eat and —*

She saw them standing on the shore. There were three of them, frat boys from the university. As she saw them, images of football games and beer bongs and clumsy episodes with virgin cheerleaders washed over her. One of them, a pretty boy with straight black hair, was holding her panties in his hands.

She stopped moving forward and treaded water about ten feet from the shoreline. "What's the matter, buddy? Is that the first pair of panties you've held that didn't come from a drunk seventeen year old freshman?"

The three started and looked down at the water. Pretty Boy sneered at her. "Well, look at the little fish we caught, boys. Anybody hungry for fish tonight?" The other two laughed a little nervously. "I don't know about you two, but I'm feeling mighty comfortable right here. I think we could hang out an hour, two, maybe three. At some point little fishy is going to have to get out of the water." The boys laughed again, nervousness fading as Pretty Boy took control.

"I'll tell you what, bucko. Put my panties down and walk away. You'll save yourself a whole lot of grief, and I won't have to look at you anymore."

"Oh no! I'm so terribly frightened of the naked girl in the water. Listen, Fishy. You better watch your mouth because I'm starting to feel like a little more than just a look. In fact, I'm downright hungry for fish now."

"Oh really? I'm afraid you don't know how to cook this fish, sweetie. I'm afraid you'll just end up burning yourself or cutting your pretty little fingers." Chloe eyed the panties, muttering under her breath. Pretty Boy glanced down at them, a confused look on his face, and suddenly dropped them. Before they reached the ground, they had begun to smoke. The smoke became fire, and the boys began stomping on them.

"Jesus, Tobe! What the hell did you do?" It was one of the hangers-on that spoke, but Pretty Boy just shrugged.

"Jesus, that's weird." He turned his attention back to Chloe. "You can't stay in there all night."

Chloe smiled. "Oh, I'm not staying in," she said. She spoke softly again and felt her power growing. Slowly, she rose. Three mouths opened in unison as she stood naked in front of them. "She's fuckin' hot, she's…." The boy trailed off as he realized she was standing on top of the water. She stepped forward, one step then another. The three stood transfixed, and she smiled.

Suddenly, Pretty Boy grabbed at his crotch. The other two stared at him, and one after the other grabbed their own. "Well boys, it appears your underwear has the same problem." She walked forward.

Pretty Boy bolted first, grabbing at himself and running until he leapt into the water about thirty feet away. She leveled her gaze at the others, and they joined him.

She walked slowly to shore and reached for her towel. "Don't worry boys. As long as you stay in there for an hour or two, you'll be okay. Come out any earlier, and I can't promise your panties won't ignite, too." She made a show of drying her body, trying to make sure they all got a clear look at her from every angle they could. She even lingered at her ass and her breasts. *I'm such a bitch.* In truth, though, the levitation had taken a great deal of power, and she needed the time to recover. Finally, she pulled her dress over her head, slipped on her shoes, and walked slowly away. *Maybe I should tell them I never completed the charm and their little shorts won't even stay warm for very long.* She giggled a little, and continued to walk.

Michael, Seattle, Present Day

She sat in front of the desk with the friend he'd seen her leave the bar with. *My God, she is so beautiful.* He smiled at the director and extended his hand. "Mr. Ridgewater? I am very pleased to meet you. Thank you for accommodating an eccentric man and meeting me in the evening."

"Well, Mr. Reyns, I must confess that a donation of two million dollars makes me more flexible than I might otherwise be. May I get you some coffee?" He pressed the intercom, but Michael waved him away.

"No, thank you, I've had enough today to last me two lifetimes." He turned to Amber. "Well, we meet again. It's uh...Amber, right?"

Amber seemed to glow a little. "Yes it is. And you're Michael, if I remember correctly. When I told you to reach me at the museum, I didn't anticipate this."

Michael nodded. "I'm pleased to hear that the brilliant curator everyone has told me about is also the lovely girl I thought I'd missed my opportunity with." His eyes turned to the other woman. There was something about her. She radiated some kind of—not completely unlike when he extended his mind to a horse or even a servant, more focused, maybe. "Are you working on the same collection?"

She stood and extended her hand. "Chloe Tudor, Mr. Reyns. I specialize in tribal artifacts, and I'll assist Ms. Stone with some of the pieces included." Michael took her offered hand and felt a strange warmth, not a pleasant one. He looked into the girl's eyes, a vague remembrance of something Kabos had taught him beginning to gel. *A witch. That's what happened at the bar. Well, she knows then.* He released her hand.

"Well, it appears my money will be well spent, then. No—not my money any more, but the museum's." He glanced at his watch. "I'm afraid I'm otherwise engaged, but I wonder if I might impose upon you for dinner, Amber? I had intended to call you tomorrow, here at the museum, but I had no idea you were handling the endowment. Still, it's fortuitous, isn't it?"

"You're very charming, Mr. Reyns, I'm sure." She hesitated, and Michael could feel the eyes of the witch burning into him. He turned to her, smiling brightly.

"Actually, Ms. Tudor, perhaps you could join us. Marcus is a family friend, and he administers my estate. Perhaps we could all have dinner, not tomorrow night but the following. If there is no joy in our company, at least we will be able to turn to matters of business instead."

Amber smiled at him. "Well, Michael, I would be glad to join you for dinner." She looked at Chloe. "And Chloe wouldn't miss it for all the world."

Michael had an idea that Amber was correct about that.

Chapter Eighteen

Juxtaposition

Amber and Chloe, Seattle, Present Day

Twenty minutes later, the two women pulled out of the museum parking lot in Amber's car. Chloe sat in the passenger seat, trying to determine how to approach her about the vampire. She didn't notice they weren't going to her apartment until Amber pulled up to a mall. "We only have an hour, Chloe, but I'm getting a new outfit for the date." Chloe sighed and followed her into the mall, where Amber chose a black designer dress and Italian black heels. Chloe picked out a coffee colored pants suit, but didn't miss the opportunity to remark that she was supposed to be the one who wore black.

They drove away from the mall in silence until Amber finally said, "Don't you like your outfit, Chloe? I think you'll look sexy as hell in it."

"Oh, no. I like it a lot."

"Then what's up? I haven't ever seen you quiet for more than sixty seconds, and it's been an hour and half with you."

Well, you got a date with a vampire, idiot! "I'm just thinking, Amber. We really need to talk tonight."

"Sure, but I've got a box of stuff from the dig I was going

to go through tonight. Maybe we can talk while you help me sort it."

Back at the apartment, Chloe rooted around in Amber's kitchen until she found tea, and she set about making a pot. Amber had finished unpacking, and the only evidence she'd just moved in was a row of empty boxes lining the front hallway. When the kettle whistled, Chloe poured the water into the teapot and called for Amber. "Tea's ready!"

"Coming." The word came out as a grunt, and Chloe looked around the kitchen counter to see Amber dragging a large wooden box, a crate really, into the living room. Along the side was stenciled Dalmatia, location 14A. Once she got it to the center of the room, she stretched and walked to the kitchen.

Chloe poured a cup of tea for her and offered cream. "That the box from the dig?" Amber nodded, and Chloe poured her own tea. "Amber, we need to talk. Your dreams are getting worse, right?" Amber was silent. "Are the dreams more than what you've told me about? What happens? We never really finished talking about them, or what they might mean. I've done some more research with the coven, and our leader has located a few writings from the sixteen-hundreds, writings brought from Europe when our group first came to America. The man in your dream said you were a ruler, right?"

Amber sighed. "I don't believe any of this, Chloe." She saw Chloe's face and sighed again. "Okay, he called me his queen, his queen of prophecy, or something like that."

"I remember. I wanted to make you say it. According to what Emily — that's our coven elder — found, there is a queen that the vampires await. Here's the crazy part — we have a prophecy about her too, and so do the wolves...the werewolves."

"I thought you said they were extinct."

"I said nobody has seen one for a long time. We don't know that they're extinct. Anyway, this queen is supposed to have a mark that will identify her to the races, but nobody knows if she starts out with it or if she gets it when she becomes queen."

Amber shifted uncomfortably, her hand involuntarily reaching for her neck.

"Wait, Amber. What's there?"

Amber smiled. "What's where Chloe?" but her friend reached across the table and brushed her hair from her shoulder. She stood, took Amber's hand, and led her to the bathroom. "Chloe, stop."

"Just walk, Amber." She led her to the mirror and pulled her hair back. The mark stood out in deep red contrast to her pale skin. Amber stared furiously at Chloe's reflection in the mirror, but Chloe ignored her, pointing at a curved sickle shape in the center of the mark. "This is a moon, Amber. It's the symbol of the wolves." Amber felt her heart pounding. "And this," she felt Chloe's forefinger tracing the mark on her skin, "is the symbol of the witch." Amber felt weak. Fear was rapidly replacing anger, and she turned to look at Chloe, but her friend cupped her chin and turned her face back to the mirror. "This part," she said, pointing to the strange, glyphic piece surrounding the other two. "I don't know, but I can only guess it's the mark of the vampire."

Chloe released Amber's chin. Amber turned to look at her. "This is too crazy, Chloe."

Chloe sighed, shook her head, and said, "I know it must seem crazy to you. Still, do you really believe most people have the same dreams over and over? If you're not the queen in these prophecies, it doesn't mean you don't have to deal with them. Come back to the table." Amber followed Chloe back mutely, and they sat. Amber took a sip of her tea, but it was cold.

"Amber, Michael is a vampire. He's fixated on you somehow."

"Vampire?" Amber stood up. "Chloe, it's getting harder and harder to be your friend. I like you, I really do, but I want to live a nice normal life, okay? When we're together, can you forget all the Halloween stuff for a while?" She turned and headed for her bedroom, and Chloe sighed yet again. She set about washing the dishes and the teapot. When they were dripping in the dish rack, she walked back to Amber's room. Amber's eyes were as red as her hair.

"Chloe, it's so bizarre. I...I would have thought you were crazy before the shower and the mirror, but now...." She sniffled and finally, softly, asked, "What if you're right?"

"Amber, I'm not trying to hurt you. There are witches. There are, or at least were, werewolves. There are also vampires. Michael is one of them. I just don't know what he has up his sleeve. I don't know for sure what he wants with you."

"Oh, God. I just don't know what to believe at all." Amber sighed. "There's a bottle of Patron in the cabinet. I need a drink."

"Look, I can't read his mind. But I know the prophecies, at least as much as the writings say, and it seems strange for him to show up now, right? I don't want him to turn you or have you for a meal. I don't know if he is planning to use you somehow. We didn't make much progress on the prophecy. I'm sorry. I really am."

Amber nodded. "I know you are. I just don't know what's real anymore. It's just ridiculous that I could be this queen. Tell you what. Let's just go on this date and you do your spooky stuff and let's figure it out then. If you're wrong about him, you'll be able to tell, right?"

I'm not wrong. "Okay, Amber, but you need to let me try to help you with your dreams, okay? Let me come in while you sleep and see if I can figure anything out."

"Okay, deal."

Marcus and Michael, Seattle, Present Day

"Would you please keep your damn cat out of my study?" Michael was brushing hairs from the velvet chair behind the desk, shaking his head.

"It was my study for fourteen years before you came to America, Michael. It's hard to retrain him."

"How old is the beast, anyway?" Michael sighed and sat down.

"I think he was about seven when I found him, so he's something in the neighborhood of thirty-five to forty."

"They don't live that long, Marcus."

"Ah, well, every week or so, I mix a bit of my blood into his food, and it seems to have helped his vitality a bit."

Michael opened his mouth, but instead of speaking, he sat silently agape for a while until he finally burst into laughter. "I think you're more man than vampire: no — more boy than vampire. It doesn't matter. Bring some wine. We're celebrating."

"Celebrating what, Michael?"

"We're celebrating the birth of our queen, Marcus. The time has come."

CHAPTER NINETEEN

Juxtaposition

Michael, Beirut, 1911

As Kabos stepped into the room, Michael gestured to a full wine glass on the counter built into the south wall. He looked at his progeny. "You're back a little sooner than expected."

"Believe me, Father, they wanted this done as quickly as possible. The reputation you've created for me preceded my arrival."

"Which did you kill?" Kabos sat down, crossed his legs, and sipped his wine.

"I got out of that one. I made an ass of myself until a cute little blonde girl named Isabella attacked me. I was planning on snapping her neck, but Gerard walked in and diffused the situation."

The old man's eyes narrowed. "They must believe you are ruthless, Michael."

"Father, I may not have killed her, but that does not mean I left her, or for that matter, a great deal of furniture, unscathed. Your plan is very much in order."

"Our plan, Michael. I may not live to see it through."

"I think you shall live long after me, long after Gerard,

163

and long after this queen of ours has left this world."

"Perhaps, Michael, but perhaps I will die tomorrow. Still, do you believe they are convinced?" The old man leaned forward, and despite the years that should have made him immune, Michael still shuddered beneath his gaze.

"Father, they believe exactly what we wish them to believe. I am powerful, probably more powerful than any other. I am rash and violent. Most importantly to Gerard, I believe, I am malleable, an easy target to control and manipulate."

"So he has instructed you, then?"

"Oh yes, Father. I have received the charge you told me I would, almost word for word." Michael drained his glass, stood, and set it on the counter.

For quite a while the two sat in silence. Finally, Kabos spoke. "Well, if the gypsy was correct, we have about seventy or eighty years left in which we can engineer your rise and fall. Still, Michael, you will need to kill one of them soon."

"Well, I rather like the blonde, Father. Perhaps one of the fat ones?"

Kabos shook his head. "In a decade or so. You'll have to take offense at something said. Fat or thin, I don't care, but nobody 'rather likes' Isabella for long, Michael. Not for long at all."

Chloe, Seattle, Present Day

"God, it's almost ten o'clock." Amber stepped up from the bed. "Did you eat dinner yet?"

"No, I was just working, then the meeting happened, and then we got here. Now that you mention it, though, I'm starving." Chloe stood as well. "I wonder what delivers this late. Well, I know there's a pizza place somewhere, but I don't know, there's got to be something else, right? Maybe Chinese or Indian deliveries around here somewhere...."

"There's a Chinese place just down the block. I've been meaning to try them anyway. You want me to call?"

Chloe nodded and Amber walked out of the room. Chloe slowly followed her to the kitchen. *I can't believe I just agreed to let her date the bloodsucker.* Amber grabbed a flyer from a drawer next to the refrigerator and picked up the phone. Meanwhile, Chloe searched the cabinets for the bottle of tequila and found it next to a bottle of lime juice. By the time Amber had ordered, two water glasses held two kamikazes. *About three drinks in a bar, but what the hell? We'll drink them slow.*

Amber took the glass, smiled, and took a long sip. "Thanks, Chloe. I needed that." She reached under the sink and took out a claw hammer. "We better get to that box. Most of the stuff was sorted and pre-cataloged in Greece before it was shipped here, but there are seven crates just like this one, and they're full of odds and ends all packed together. I wanted to get everything in this one sorted by tomorrow."

They took their drinks to the living room and set them on the coffee table. Then, Amber set to work on the crate, and in a few moments she'd pulled off the lid. Crinkly strips of cardboard packaging paper filled it. Rummaging through the paper, Amber pulled out a vase, two pots, a surprisingly ornate dagger, and then struggled with a larger item.

"This damn thing's heavy." Her hair formed a little pile over the packing material as her shoulders disappeared into the box. Chloe heard her groan with the effort until she finally pulled up, holding a disk of some sort, wrapped in paper of its own. The package was about three and a half feet in diameter and about two inches thick. Amber brought it to the couch. "It's not that heavy, it was just wedged in there."

Chloe watched as Amber stripped away the paper,

revealing some kind of wood with occasional metal studs. Gradually, it revealed itself to be a shield. Amber pulled the last strip of paper away and looked down at it. "Oh, Domator," she whispered, and Chloe saw tears falling from her face.

"Amber?" No response. "Amber?" Chloe shouted a little louder now, but on the couch, Anber just held the shield and wept.

Chloe walked over and sat next to her. "Amber, honey, it's okay. I'm here." She put her arm over Amber's shoulders, but there was still no response. She reached out and put her hand over Amber's, and when she did, her fingertips brushed against the wood. With one hand on Amber and one on the shield, she felt the Sight coursing through her.

"Oh, Domator," Amber said again, letting the tears flow freely now that the men had left. Chloe watched as she held the shield to her, only now she was dressed in a flowing muslin shift and sitting on a bare dirt floor in some kind of hut or tent or something.

"Amber?" She showed no sign at all of recognizing her friend, or even noticing that she was there. Chloe thought she must have cried for an hour, and every "Amber" and every "Can you hear me" and even a shouted, "Listen to me!" got no response.

Finally, Amber stood and placed the shield on a peg on the wall. The wall. It was a building and not a tent after all. She wiped her eyes and walked to the bed in the corner of the room. From beneath it, she pulled a short knife. "God Amber, no!" Chloe screamed as Amber put the knife to her breast, but as before, her friend gave no indication that she heard.

"Bircenna!" The voice, a man's voice, came from the door.

For a moment, Amber looked indecisive, but she finally took the knife from her breast and put it back under the bed.

She walked to the door and opened it. A tall man walked in, his face shrouded by the hood of his cloak, and Chloe felt the noise around her grow. She felt the blue sparks at her fingertips. The man smiled, at least he seemed to, but shadows still covered his face. "Bircenna, I can bring you joy again. I can bring you happiness again."

"Amber! He's a vampire. Run away!" Chloe was again unheard.

"You will bring Domator back?" Amber whispered the words.

"That is beyond me, Bircenna, but I can make you forget your pain." The vampire's voice was thin, but compelling. Even Chloe almost believed him. She shook her head. *Damn it Amber, resist him!*

But she wasn't resisting. Instead, she stepped forward. The tall man pushed back his hood. Chloe was surprised to see his face didn't belong to Michael at all. It was scarred and ugly. He pulled Amber close and pushed her hair to one side, holding her head at an angle. "No!" Chloe screamed and gathered her power, lashing out at the man with all of her strength, but the power flowed past them and away as though they weren't there. Helpless, she watched the man lower his mouth to Amber's throat and bite down.

It's Amber's dream. I'm just seeing her dream. Chloe was comforted for a moment, but something nagged at her. She couldn't frame it in words, couldn't grasp it. She watched as Amber's body grew limp, and then the man stopped. He smiled, a red, blood-stained grimace of a smile, and ran a nail across his wrist until a crimson stream flowed from it. Grasping Amber's head, he pushed her mouth to his wrist, and Chloe could see her sucking at him, watched as color returned to her face. After a moment she stood straight again.

"What...I...what happ—?"

"Shhh." The man placed a finger against her lips and then tilted her neck and drank again. Chloe watched, horrified. The man again drank until she grew limp, again made her drink. Twice more he repeated the cycle. *It's not Amber's dream. It's the Sight. It's the shield — and Amber's having the same vision.*

Four times, maybe five, the vampire drained her and fed her. Finally, she stood before him a final time. He caressed her cheek and smiled softly. Without warning, he smacked her face with his hand, and the sound of it made Chloe jump. Amber's eyes grew wide, and as Chloe watched they grew richer, lighter, until they were the yellow of cat's eyes. She opened her mouth, and her incisors had grown to two or three inches.

The vampire reached out and softly stroked her face. "Oh Bircenna, my Bircenna. I watched you for months, and now you are here with me. Now, my sweet Bircenna, you and I may love one another forever." He pulled her into his arms, and turned a little so that Chloe's perspective changed. She saw Amber's head on his shoulder, her lips brushing his neck. "My sweet Bircenna."

Chloe watched as Amber smiled. "No. Not Bircenna. Bircenna was filled with the grief of Domator. Now, I am filled with the grief of all of the women of Illyria. I am Illyris now. I am not Bircenna." Chloe watched as she suddenly tightened her hands around the man's shoulders and bit down heavily at his neck. His struggling was violent, but she held him tightly until finally he grew limp in her arms.

Amber released him, and he crumpled to the floor. She looked down at him. "And I am no longer sweet."

The doorbell rang, and Chloe and Amber looked together toward the apartment door. Chloe turned back to Amber. She was breathing hard, and Chloe realized that she was breathing hard herself. Finally, Amber said, "I think our food is here."

CHAPTER TWENTY

Extrapolation

Michael, The Médoc, 1974

The moon was bright, illuminating the rows of vines in an almost phosphorescent glow. Crouching behind the cover of a mature vine, now lush with green and fat with thick purple grapes, Michael cursed. Sperchek looked over at him and asked what was wrong. He was squat, almost fat, and extraordinarily ugly. Worse, he was utterly inept at all but the most basic tasks, and even those required constant supervision in order to ensure anything close to the desired effect. Michael wondered, not for the first time, what had possessed whoever it was who made him.

"Be quiet, Sperchek." That was Jean, the smarter of the pair, although that wasn't much of a distinction. *Like saying a slug is smarter than a rock.* "Master Michael is thinking."

"I'm not thinking, Jean. I'm concerned about the light."

"Oh!" Sperchek's voice was loud and delighted. "Because somebody could see us!" Occasionally, when a glimmer of understanding hit him, the fat one was uncontrollably excited. "I understand. You don't want—"

"Be silent, Sperchek." Michael spoke in barely a whisper, but the authority behind the command was in no way understated. Michael glanced at the small cottage on the south side of the estate. A soft glow came from within. *She's awake at least. Two hundred yards.*

"Oh! Because someone will hear us!" Sperchek was delighted again. Michael shook his head and sighed.

"Sperchek." Again just a whisper. "If you don't shut your mouth, I will taste your blood tonight and use your body to fertilize the grapes." He looked up to the sky and saw that clouds were approaching the moon. "Both of you, when I run, you run." The clouds grew closer, closer, and finally Michael jumped to his feet and dashed toward the cottage.

Sperchek and Jean leapt after him and followed. Fifty yards, one-hundred. He could almost feel the moonlight following them, trying to shine on them before they reached the place. One-fifty. He felt as though eyes were on him, but he knew it was his mind alone and he shrugged it off. There. He crouched beneath the window through which he had seen the light moments before and waited. The others had kept pace, at least, and they joined him beneath the window. Gingerly, he reached up, pushed the window open, and climbed inside.

"I knew you would come, night walker." An old woman sat in a rocking chair, a glass of wine in her hand.

Sperchek and Jean had climbed through the window as well. "How did she know we would come, Jean?"

"Shut up, Sperchek." Jean looked smug. "Sorry, Master."

Michael looked at the woman. She gestured to a divan beside the rocking chair with a withered hand. He sat and studied her. The woman looked nearly dead, a husk. She was thin enough and frail enough that Michael wondered that she could even lift the glass.

"You wish to know of your queen, no?" The woman sipped the wine, licking her lips in a strange and almost lascivious manner. When Michael nodded, she smiled. "She is yet to be born. You have something to give?"

"I am prepared."

The woman laughed, a cackling and piercing laugh, and Michael shuddered. He heard Sperchek ask, "Why is she laughing?" and heard Jean tell him to shut up.

"I don't want to see the baron dead, Machiel of Brugges!" She was still laughing. "You are so eager to kill, to prove that you would do all for her. I don't want that. I want only a taste of blood, something to give me another decade in this cottage among my grapes."

"Done."

"Very well. Your plan is working even now."

"What plan?"

"Shut up, Sperchek!"

"Gerard does not suspect."

"What doesn't—?" Sperchek's question hung in the air, but Michael was already at his throat. Michael held him against his struggles, looking over his shoulder at Jean, whose eyes opened in fear. Jean turned and leaped for the window, but Michael had already dropped Sperchek and caught his ankle, dragging him back to the floor.

"No! Master, please, I—" Michael lifted him by his ankle. Jean wept.

"I'm sorry, Jean." With a twist of his wrist, he rotated Jean's body and pushed his mouth onto his neck. When he had finished, Jean, too, lay on the floor.

The old woman looked at him. "I take it they were not part of your plan with the Brewer of Bruges?"

He shook his head. "Sadly, no. I didn't know that you would be or I mightn't have brought them here."

"Oh well. As I said, the queen is not yet born, but her mother plays with toys in her cradle."

Michael smiled. "Then you must tell me about her mother."

Amber and Chloe, Seattle, Present Day

Amber stood in front of the mirror; the black bra and black thong panties stood out in dramatic contrast to her pale skin. For a minute she considered changing to red, but it was already getting too close to the time when she and Chloe would have to leave. She pulled the new black dress out of its box and let it slide over her. "Chloe! Come zip me up."

Of course Chloe had gotten all spooky over last night. They had eaten Chinese food in silence until her friend had finally said, "That vision you had tonight wasn't a dream. It all happened. I saw it all." She'd provided details about this Bircenna woman until Amber had to admit Chloe had seen the same thing that Amber had. "The good news is that it happened a long time ago. When do you figure that shield was made?" Amber had estimated something in the neighborhood of 750 BC, and Chloe nodded. "I don't get everything, but it seems you've got something like the sight in you. I didn't get the vision from you, I got the history from the shield. Maybe your dreams are like my gift…maybe we're okay."

The bottom line, tonight she wasn't going to worry about vampires, witches, or anything supernatural. All Amber cared about was how good she was going to look for Michael.

***

Chloe walked in. She looked stunning in the pantsuit. "For someone who doesn't want me to go out with the hot bloodsucker, you're sure all dolled up."

Chloe shook her head and found the zipper on Amber's back, pulling it up. "Laugh it up, but don't for a minute drop your guard tonight."

The dress was absolutely stunning. She looked twice in the mirror, turned around a few times, and remarked that it perfectly showcased her legs and her butt. "And my boobs, Chloe. It works for my boobs, too."

"Okay, okay—you're the picture of hot elegance. I have a bottle of chardonnay on the table with our names on it." She turned Amber by her shoulders and pushed her toward the door, but a flash caught her eye. "Hey, that's a nice necklace."

"It belonged to my birth parents. There hasn't been a day in my life that I haven't worn it. What do you think, inside or outside?"

"Outside. People should see it."

The two walked to the table and Chloe poured the wine into glasses. She sipped hers, but Amber downed a glass in just a few seconds. "Slow down, Amber. We've got a night ahead of us, and you need to be on your toes." *I should ask to hold the necklace.* "Amber, I should—" The alarm on Amber's cell phone sounded.

"Time to go!" Amber grabbed her little designer purse and started for the door. Chloe sighed and followed.

***

The two began the three block walk to the same bar at which Amber had first met Michael. As she walked, Amber felt strange. She was actually sweating. *I never do that. Am I nervous about meeting him again?* No. Amber never really felt nervous about men, and Michael was no different. Still, her palms were sweaty and they hadn't even made it to the bar yet.

When they got there, they spotted Michael and his friend at a table in a somewhat secluded corner. Chloe whispered to Amber that the new one was just as good looking as Michael, but that she still had to gather her power to dull the overwhelming noise that told her they were both vampires.

Michael waved them over to the table. They both stood as the girls arrived, and Michael smiled and introduced his friend. "This is my estate manager and a dear friend, Marcus."

Amber doubled over, a sharp pain suddenly erupting in her stomach, and she caught the table to keep herself from falling. Chloe reached for her, but suddenly Marcus stood in front of her, fangs bared. "Back, witch."

**

Michael caught Amber in his arms and lifted her to a chair. "Sit down, Marcus. Amber's hands are freezing." In the general direction of the bar, he yelled, "Brandy!" Amber mumbled something about being okay, but then she screamed and collapsed, maintaining the seat but falling forward so that her head rested on the table.

Thankfully, the music had taken most of the volume from her scream, but a group a table down looked over at them. When the bartender came, a snifter of brandy in his hand, one of the group stopped him and pointed at the table.

He brought the cup warily, and Michael took it. "There is no need for a doctor. She just fainted." The bartender stood, dumbly, and Michael looked intently at him. "There is no need for a doctor. She just fainted."

The man smiled. "I hope the brandy helps. She doesn't need a doctor if she just fainted." He walked back to the bar, already teaming with customers wanting drinks.

Michael looked up and noticed that Marcus still stood in front of Chloe. "Ms. Tudor, your friend is more important than Marcus's bluster. Marcus, this woman is important to me. Both of you sit down." He reached to Amber, brushed the hair from her forehead, and recoiled. "Ach! She burns!"

**

Chloe reached around Marcus and managed to whisper a charm of soothing over Amber, and over the table for good

176

measure. Amber grew still and her eyes opened. She looked at the company and smiled.

"I'm sorry. I didn't eat anything today; it must be the wine."

"Think nothing of it, my dear. That we can fix easily." He turned to Marcus. "Settle our business here, please." He stood and looked at Chloe. "Shall we get your friend some food?"

Chloe nodded, and together they helped Amber to the front door and out. She gulped down the night air and finally said that she felt fine. Marcus joined them and Michael took Amber's arm. He glared at Marcus, who finally shook his head and offered his arm to Chloe. She smiled.

"Believe me, Bub, it's no picnic for me either."

Michael smiled and the two couples left the bar to walk the three blocks to the restaurant. "I have not been in Seattle long," Michael said, "but Marcus assures me that the food here is more than adequate."

When they arrived, Marcus moved quickly to the podium, and Chloe saw a bill pass to the man there. In a few moments, they were seated. A server walked up, but Michael waved the menus away and ordered the prix fixe menu and a bottle of 1974 Chateau Mouton Rothschild.

"Very good, monsieur. If I may, sir, uh…there are many who believe that vintage is past its prime. Perhaps a 1978."

"Ah, thank you. I visited the vineyard some time ago, and I have a special weakness for the vintage. Decant it for me, and while we wait have the chef choose aperitifs that will complement the first course."

The waiter left but soon returned with sweet liqueurs and oysters with shaved horseradish and spices served on ice. As they ate, Chloe warmed to the date but still found it hard to keep from staring at Amber.

When Amber placed the last empty shell back on the ice,

the waiter was back, placing small round plates filled with exotic greens, walnuts, dried fruit, and gorgonzola. Amber took a bite. "Oh. This is heavenly." She saw Chloe nod in assent, but noticed the men hadn't touched the salad at all.

"Michael, why aren't you eating? The salad is delicious."

"I don't care much—"

"The guys are vampires, Amber. They're blood-sucking, blood-lusting creatures of the night. They're bat-changing, blood-eating, neck-biting—"

Marcus laughed out loud, cutting her off. He looked at Chloe and smiled. "For a witch, you're a pretty fun date." He turned to Amber. "Tell me, Amber—stop glaring, Michael— tell me, Amber, what has Chloe told you about our kind?"

Amber shifted uncomfortably, but Chloe responded instead. "Amber, we witches don't really get along with vampires, but we have you in common."

Amber rolled her eyes. "Oh yes, there's something about me and an old prophecy, but nobody knows what it is. I'm not sure I believe it, and I'm not all that worried about getting holes in my neck, no matter what Chloe might tell me."

Michael cleared his throat. "I…well, there's something to what Ms. Tudor says, Amber. We believe you are, or rather will be, the queen. I…Amber, what's wrong?"

Amber had moved from pale to flushed in seconds. She clenched her hands into fists next to her plate. Her eyes rolled to the back of her head and she began to speak in a strange guttural series of words and clicks and groans.

Michael looked at Marcus. "That is the old tongue."

Chloe put her arm around Amber and said, "Calm down, honey, I'm here."

Amber gave no indication she heard her, but instead opened her hands, extended her fingers, and kept speaking. Her fingernails, freshly painted just hours ago, gained a deeper shade of red, and blue sparks began to spray from her hands. Marcus covered them with one of the maroon linen napkins the waiter had brought with the oysters.

"Is this your doing?" It took a moment for Chloe to realize Marcus was speaking to her.

"No. I...I don't know what's happening." Chloe tried the soothing charm again, but she couldn't even call upon her power.

"...no matter what Chloe might tell me." It was Amber's voice again, and the three looked at her, dumbfounded. "What? Isn't that what you've said, Chloe?" She reached for the salad fork and took another bite. "Vampires or not, you two don't know what you're missing."

***

The rest of the meal was quiet, and Amber wondered what had changed the mood. When dessert was served, Michael turned to Chloe. "Perhaps we could continue this evening at my estate. We have much to discuss."

Oh, that was brilliant. Like Chloe wants me anywhere near you. Amber took a bite of her crème brûlée and sighed. *So much for a nice evening.*

Chloe looked at Michael and surprised her. "I think that would be lovely, Michael."

CHAPTER TWENTY-ONE
Transformation

Marcus, Big Bear, 2006

The wind blew softly, and Marcus lifted the cell phone to his ear. "Yes, Father."

"She's in America, Marcus. Or, at least she will be. The crone was adamant."

"Where did you find this one, Father?" Marcus absently reached down to scratch Joshua, who had padded out from the cabin onto the porch. "A carnival in Prague?"

"Leave the sarcasm alone. Who is P.T. Barnum?"

"What?" Joshua looked up and growled at the exclamation.

"P.T. Barnum, who is he?"

"I think he started a circus or something. What's going on, Michael?"

"Find out when he was born."

"Look, I don't understand, what do—?"

"Find out when he was born, damn you!"

Marcus pulled the phone from his ear and sighed. Finally, he breathed out a long sigh and put it back to his ear. "Give me a moment, Father." He stood and walked back into the cabin, Joshua following. When he reached the den, he sat in front of the computer. "Almost, Michael." He tapped a few keys and waited, and then he tapped a few more.

"PT Barnum was a showman, a circus promot—"

"I just need to know when he was born." Michael sounded impatient. Michael always sounded impatient. Marcus saw the date on the screen but still counted ten seconds.

"1810. July 5, 1810. He died on—"

"I don't care when he died, Marcus. 1810—we're only a few years away, Marcus."

"I'm not following you." Something was strange about Joshua's stance. Marcus could see the hairs of the bobcat's neck standing on end.

"Two hundred years from Barnum's birth. Right around then is when the queen will come." Marcus could hear his excitement. "Are the estates ready?"

"All but New Orleans, but if we have four years yet, we'll be fine."

"Five years. I'll be there in five. The hag said *after* two hundred years, so five years. I'll call you in a few weeks."

"But why—?" The line was already dead. *Jesus, P.T. Barnum?*

He heard Joshua's roar before he saw the man. He jumped to the side as the sword crashed into the computer screen. A scraggly man in black pants, black shirt, and a black ski mask held the sword. The man pulled the sword free and screamed. "Die, demon!"

Marcus braced himself for another attack, but he'd dropped his cell phone and his left foot fell upon it, causing him to stumble as the man lunged at him. He watched the man leap forward, sword raised. The man screamed, "For Valentine!" as he brought the sword down. Marcus closed his eyes. *Goodbye, Michael.* The blow never came.

Marcus opened his eyes. Joshua had leapt upon the man. The sword dragged upon the floor until the man finally released it to push at Joshua. Joshua's paw swept across the man's face and red furrows appeared from his brow to his chin. He finally pushed the cat off and reeled backward. He reached for the sword, but Marcus reached him first.

Who the hell is Valentine? Marcus felt the blood filling him and felt the man growing limp. When he finished, he backed into the recliner built from an old pine stump and tried to gain control of the blood drunkenness. Joshua was at his side, nuzzling his palm.

"*Optime*, Joshua." Marcus thought his voice sounded distant. "You probably don't understand English either Joshua, but well done. Well done."

Michael, Edinburgh, 1985

"Are you sure this is necessary, Kabos?" Michael sat on the roof of the castle, the night breeze and a soft misty rain alternately cooling and irritating his face. Kabos sat a few feet away, leaning on what Michael assumed was a chimney.

"The king will be our greatest challenge...your greatest challenge, Machiel. He banished the queen once before, and he will want to do so again."

"But why must I do this? It's a strange witchcraft, I...." He paused and shook his head. "I may not have the best mind, Kabos, but I don't know that I want to let anyone else's memories into it."

Kabos stood, and as his cloak rippled in the wind and rain, Michael thought once again that it was amazing that the old vampire still commanded attention in any situation. There was a presence about him that made him somehow more relevant than anyone else, no matter who else might be there.

"It's the fifty years of life, Machiel." Kabos smiled at him. "Most of our kind enter this life before they are twenty-five. I don't care if you live to be two thousand years old. When you are one of us, you don't face the trials and hardships that truly breed wisdom." He looked down at Michael, still smiling. "You think me special only because I lived so long as a man." Kabos gestured for Michael to follow and leapt down.

The two began a quick descent, first from the castle, and then from the steep green cliffs that surrounded it. Kabos finally stopped in front of an ornate fountain. He stepped onto the lip and dipped a hand into the water, agitating it idly as he sat.

"Kabos, I want an answer. Do we have to do this?"

"Machiel, if we fail, perhaps all fail. You heard the hag."

"But this, I...." He couldn't frame the objection, and so the two sat for a while in silence. "Father, I just don't like the idea of being anyone other than me."

Kabos snorted. "You're being dramatic, Machiel. This ritual will only give you some of the king's memories. It will not make you the king. Would you rather he found her?"

"No, of course not, I—"

"Then we will speak no more of this." It was Kabos's command voice, and Michael sighed.

"As you wish, Father."

They heard her before they saw her, her shoes echoing on the paving stones. She hobbled into view, and Michael had to suppress a laugh when he noticed her wearing a necklace of garlic bulbs. Kabos, however, recoiled and spat out, "What treachery is this, hag? Take that off!"

"You would ask me to come unprotected into your company?"

Now Kabos laughed. He walked up to the woman, pulled

a bulb from the string, and placed it whole in his mouth. "Yes," he said as he chewed.

The woman turned to run, but Kabos took her shoulder and stopped her. "You have nothing to fear from us. Are you prepared?"

"Did you bring the materials I requested?" The woman was still shaking. Kabos reached beneath his cloak and pulled a vial of something thick and red from within. He handed it to her and she shook her head.

"I don't know how you got this, but for all of our sakes, I hope he never finds out."

"Let us begin." It was the command voice again.

The woman produced a small bowl from her pocket and poured the contents of the vial into it. She scooped up a bit of the water from the fountain and added it. Then, she spit in the bowl and began to chant. Slowly, wisps of orange smoke snaked up from the bowl. Finally, she said, "Drink it," handing the bowl to Kabos.

"Not me. Him." The hag extended the bowl to Michael, and though he wanted to cast it aside, he lifted it to his mouth and drank.

Illyris stood before him. Michael roared at her. "You cannot continue to treat the wolves like us. They are slaves, damn it!"

"They will be your end, my lord." Illyris smiled one of her vicious smiles and turned to walk away. Michael reached out and grasped her arm.

He intended to say, "You are not leaving!" but he only got so far as the word "you" before Illyris turned on him, and with an amount of effort that seemed no more than a child might use to step on an ant, she sent him flying across the antechamber to bounce heavily from the wall onto the floor. He heard Illyris laughing as she left the room.

You'll not laugh when the wizard arrives, bitch. Michael the king waited until he could no longer hear her footsteps. Then, he stood and walked from the room.

Cold water splashed his face and he was back with Kabos. The hag was speaking, "...and the memories will be less intense but more like his own. He will need to learn how to distinguish the difference."

"Or what?" Michael croaked out.

"You'll either go mad," the woman's voice was almost gleeful, "or become the king."

Amber and Michael, Seattle, Present Day

The parlor was decorated like some Victorian sitting room, dark oak divans with cream upholstery embroidered with ornate flowers and leaves and high-backed chairs with warm-colored cloth cushions. Plants were arranged on shelves and tables throughout the room. Amber sat silently on a red crushed-velvet couch and watched as Michael actually pulled a bell-rope for a servant. Chloe was listening raptly as Marcus pointed out some of the pictures, especially a large portrait of a beautiful woman hanging above the fireplace.

A servant dressed in a black tuxedo entered, received whispered instructions from Michael, and left. *There's something more going on here, and no one is telling me anything.* Chloe was giggling and Marcus had his palm on the small of her back as he pointed to a brass sculpture of a man on horseback. Marcus wasn't certain about its authenticity. Amber heard Chloe talk about Earl Erik Heikka and the W.A. Clark foundry.

"You're very quiet, Amber. Are you unwell?" Michael was beside her. She was startled, but she masked her reaction and turned to look at him.

No, nothing's wrong. My friend over there is flirting like a teenager with a guy she says is a vampire, which is no big deal I guess, since the ass his hand keeps grabbing evidently belongs to a witch. "Shouldn't this be some kind of a Gothic castle?" *Oh, brilliant line, Amber.*

Michael laughed. "I'm afraid real estate prices in Seattle are such that moving the castle from Transylvania was not economically feasible." He smiled, and Amber felt a soft flutter of excitement at the way his eyes narrowed and crinkled at the raising of the corners of his mouth.

"So what's next, Michael? Is there where you—?" She was interrupted by the return of the servant, who held a tray with bottles and glasses. Michael stood, took the tray from him, and dismissed him with a gesture. Amber sat on the couch alone again, watching Michael take ice cubes from a bucket in the tray and fix drinks. *The worst part about all this is? Even if this guy's a vampire, I wish Chloe and Marcus would go get some privacy so he could get on top of me.* She watched Michael deliver a highball glass to Marcus and a martini glass filled with a clear red drink to Chloe. He returned to the tray and in moments was bringing two glasses to the couch.

"I'm not the best bartender—"

"Even with a couple of centuries of practice?" *God, I am brilliant tonight.*

"Not even with the practice." He handed a martini glass to her. A strawberry floated in liquid the color of a rose wine. She took a sip, tasted cranberry juice, lime, and vodka. "Still, when I first learned, my instructor pointed out that it was difficult to make a poor Cosmopolitan." He raised his eyebrows and looked at her.

"It's very good, Michael." *Now get over here and do me.*

"Amber, you know something, don't you? We are all here in the privacy of my parlor to talk. I have to tell you that I would ordinarily be able to read your mind." He sipped from his highball glass then lifted it to the light. "What do you think of the single malt, Marcus?"

"I can taste it."

"Yes, me too. Can we order a number of cases?"

"They only have six left, and they're not selling."

"Then be persuasive." He looked back to Amber. "Stop playing games and let's really talk about this. You know all of this is real, but you continue to pretend to yourself it's not."

She studied his face. He was still smiling. She took a sip of her drink, swallowed it, and slowly exhaled a long, soft sigh. Michael lifted the scotch to his lips again. "All right, Michael." *What I wouldn't give to be that glass right now.* "I suppose I'm coming to believe in vampires and witches. I do know that the pictures I keep seeing in my head are somehow connected to all of us. I also know that I am tired of not knowing the full story." Michael smiled at her and she reached forward, using her thumb to push a dribble of scotch from the corner of his mouth. "I don't want to keep hearing cryptic bullshit, and I don't think I could take it if you start trying to explain that the creature from the black lagoon is really my second cousin. And," she drained her glass, "I'm ready for another drink."

***

Michael took the glass and walked to the tray. *I will not let you control me. You will not unite us with the wolves, little queen.* He bit into his lower lip until he tasted blood. The king's memories came unbidden to the surface far too often now. *I wonder where you are now, my king. Do you speak only through Gerard? Has he drained you in his little Phoenician clubhouse?*

***

He returned and handed the drink to Amber. She stared up at him. "So, someone better tell me about this prophecy

188

and why it connects you to me. Either tell me now or I am going home and want nothing more to do with this." *And you better tell me, because I'm looking forward to tearing those clothes off you, and it will be a little awkward to make a scene and then come back. Uh, excuse me, I'm still pissed, but aren't we supposed to hit the bedroom?*

Chloe called out to her and asked her to join her in the restroom. Amber smiled at Michael. "You're not off the hook yet, Michael. I want answers when I get back." She walked to Chloe, drink in hand, and took her arm.

"To the right, Chloe, and then it's the third door on the left." Amber could feel Chloe shudder at the sound of Marcus's voice. *God, you're as much of a slut as I am.*

As they walked, Chloe whispered softly. "I need to tell you something about them. I don't have to go."

"What? Two girls heading to the restroom together for anything other than normal biological processes? I'm shocked, Chloe." They pushed open a large brass door and gasped as they crossed the threshold. "This bathroom is bigger than my living room. Hell, it's probably bigger than my whole goddamn apartment! And who puts plush carpet in a bathroom, anyway?"

Chloe walked to the floor-length mirror. "At least he's got money."

"Seriously, Chloe. Money isn't everything. Let's not forget he kills people by sucking their blood, blah, blah, blah."

"Okay, Amber. Laugh it up. Seriously, though, you should know that vampires would never have survived for thousands of years without certain qualities. The only one I want you to be aware of tonight is an almost constant charm."

"Oh no! You mean these guys are charming? We better run away right now."

"I didn't say charming, I said charm. It's like the spell we did for the water. Vampires, though, have a constant charm that makes a mortal want them. I mean, throw them on the floor, rip off their clothes, want them. It's the kind of thing that could make you want...." She almost said *an accountant* but caught herself. "A forty year old fat man who lives with his mother."

"Hey, I think I have that charm. Maybe I *am* the queen."

"Just be aware of it, and see if you go a minute and a half straight without thinking of the two of you in bed." Chloe walked out the brass door and Amber followed her back to the parlor.

***

Michael and Marcus sat on the couch sipping their drinks. Michael smiled at them as they returned, but it was Marcus that stood, pulled two of the high-backed chairs closer to the sofa, and spoke. "Please sit down, Amber. Michael and I have spoken. This is all too strange to us. There are many humans who know what we are. In fact, the whole damned house is filled with servants who do. It's hard to have a human who knows of us but doesn't understand any of it. For more than two-hundred years Michael and I have prepared for the day that we would find you. There are parts of the prophecy we don't understand. I think we thought you might be the one to fill in the gaps."

Michael stood. "Amber, I have waited lifetimes for you, and I have waited lifetimes for answers to questions that you now ask. The prophecies are unclear. We know that you will end the enmity between our kind and Chloe's kind. The wolves as well." He felt his hand clenching into a fist. *You will never unite the wolves, bitch! You will never control me. I will....* He forced himself to unclench his hand. *Oh, Father, if I ever meet that Scottish hag, I think I will torture her before I drain her.*

"I wish I could offer more, but most of what I've learned has been about how to find you, not what to do with you once you were found."

CHAPTER TWENTY-TWO

Alteration

Michael, Sidon, 1994

The girl was struggling as he drank, and Michael watched as blood dripped from her neck and onto the white robes Gerard wore. He'd taken to white robes lately, as had the rest of the Avalani. He slurped as he drank, making wet bubbling noises. Michael gestured to the short woman who stood nearby and she came to him. He took her hand and bit into her wrist, closing his eyes as the blood filled his mouth. He drank softly for a moment or two before he released her, kissing her wrist as he did. The woman looked nervous, her eyes darting left and right before she finally curtsied and left the room.

He turned back to Gerard. He was still drinking and the girl's struggles were growing feebler. Finally he released her, and she crumpled to the floor. Gerard raised a fat forearm to his face and wiped the blood away with his sleeve. "The time grows nearer now, Michael. The king is certain of it. He wishes for me to remind you that you will be well rewarded for your efforts."

"The king is most generous," Michael said. *He will kill me within moments of giving her to you, you disgusting, fat bastard.*

"But why does he think the time grows near?"

"He has inklings of her presence. She's not fully of this world yet, but he is certain the mortal who carries her soul is born." The girl on the floor stirred and weakly lifted her head. Gerard ignored her. "You will find her, as has been foretold, and you must turn her and bring her here."

"Of course, Gerard." *Not for all of the beer in Bruges.* "I could do nothing else."

"Michael, there are some who question your loyalty. There are some who wonder if you won't take advantage of this…situation for your own benefit. I tell them they are mistaken."

"They are. Our arrangement is clear. We cannot allow the queen to ascend." Michael looked down at the girl, who was slowly crawling to the door.

"I'm glad to hear you say that." Gerard stood and walked to the girl. "Remember, Michael." He reached down, took a handful of her hair, and lifted her to her feet. "It may be that no one other than the king is stronger than you, but you would have a difficult time contending with all of us at once." The girls eyes grew wide as Gerard bit into her neck, closing his eyes as he drank what little remained. Michael watched the blood drunkenness come upon him and averted his eyes.

"Then it is good that none will have a reason to question my loyalty."

Gerard smiled at him. He removed his robe, threw it on the girl's body, opened the door, and shouted for another. Michael found himself grateful that he wore linen pants and a t-shirt beneath the robe. "Michael, if you fail, nothing will be the same. We may never recover."

"I understand, Gerard." *I've heard that for two centuries.*

Amber and Michael, Seattle, Present Day

194

"But, the night grows late, so whatever it is we'll do with you will have to wait for later. Perhaps Marcus and I should escort you ladies home. It is, after all, a most dangerous night. Isn't it, Chloe?"

Chloe looked at the men and then at her friend. She nodded, and took Amber's hand in hers. A quick squeeze, and then she stood and held her hand out to Marcus, who smiled and took it. At the door, the same tuxedo-clad servant met them with their coats, and Michael helped Amber into hers as Marcus did the same for Chloe. The door opened, and the quartet stepped out. Another servant had driven the car to the front, and Marcus opened the door for Chloe, who stepped in, smiling.

"You know, Amber, it's a beautiful night. Why don't we let them take the car and we can walk? It's only a mile or so to the restaurant, and I believe you said only a few blocks to your apartment from there. What do you say?"

"I think that would be lovely, Michael."

Michael nodded at Marcus, who took his place next to Chloe and gestured to the driver. Amber didn't notice the look of concern on Chloe's face.

Michael extended his hand and Amber took it. His skin was cool to the touch, but not the cold she was expecting. "Michael, tell me about vampires. Do you sleep in a coffin? Do you get burned by holy water? Do you ever fall in love? Do vampires marry each other and have little vampire babies?"

Michael laughed and smiled at her. He placed a finger under her chin and tilted her face so that their lips could touch. After the briefest of kisses, he started walking, holding her hand softly.

"We usually use a coffin when we fly, but I sleep on a bed. I can drink holy water, eat garlic, wear a crucifix, and dance the conga line." She chuckled. "And I have loved. Before I was what I am now, I loved a servant girl at my father's estate."

"What happened?"

He turned her to face him again and looked at her. His face seemed wistful to Amber, something deeper than sadness. Was there anger there as well? "I'm afraid we were not able to continue the relationship when I was turned. We do indeed love, Amber, but there is no future for one of us and a human."

They were still on the grounds of his estate. Amber looked at the trees lining the long road that led to the manor and sighed. "I wish that wasn't so, Michael."

He stopped moving and pulled her to him, pushing his lips against hers. She put her arms around his neck and moaned softly. He kissed her again, and Amber opened her mouth to him but pulled away. "Wait, Michael. Does this mean we can have only now, only tonight?"

"What do you mean, *amour*?"

"I mean, if you can't be with a human, what can...how do we? I...."

He cupped her cheeks in his hands and tilted her head as he leaned forward to kiss her, and Amber realized she longed for more than the "charm" Chloe wouldn't shut up about. Suddenly, the release a single evening offered wasn't much of an offer at all. She pulled back a little. "I'd rather have nothing than to have just one night, Michael."

Still holding her, he smiled. "Relax, *amour*, I have no intention of entering a relationship with a human." With that, he pushed her face to the side and kissed her neck. She felt herself giving in, but raised her hands to push at his chest. He was unyielding. "No intention at all," he said, and she felt his teeth at her neck.

"Wait!" She'd intended it as a scream, but as she felt the skin break above her shoulder, she realized no sound had come. She struggled, but Michael's grip was firm, and she could feel her strength leaving with her blood. *Chloe.*

***

She was alert again, eating. She felt strength returning to her and opened her eyes to see Michael looking down at her. His hand covered her mouth. No, not his hand...his wrist. She sat up, feeling stronger, and looked at him. "What happened? I—"

"Shhh, *amour.*" Michael leaned down, and Amber felt his mouth at her neck again.

CHAPTER TWENTY-THREE
Marking

Chloe, Pasco, 1994

It was hot, and dusty, and Chloe wanted to go home. She shifted in her seat, looked out the window at the men and women fishing from the banks of the Columbia River, and sighed loudly. Her mother, in the front passenger seat, didn't respond. Wheezer, who was driving, ignored her as well. She turned to Emily, in the back seat opposite her, but the old lady was staring off in the other direction. "Can't we just go home, Mommy?"

"We can't—" Both Whezer and her mother spoke at the same time. Her mom smiled and mouthed "Go ahead."

"We can't, sweetie. You are a special little girl, and we need to make sure you're safe."

"But I'm safe at home, Whee...uh, Tom. I want to go home."

Emily put her hand on Chloe's head and stroked her hair. "Your hair is growing very long now, Chloe. You must work very hard to keep it beautiful."

"Mommy makes me brush it every day." She smiled at Emily but then scowled. "And I still want to go home."

"You're smart, too, Chloe. Tom isn't talking about the

same kind of safe as not getting hurt or sick or anything like that. You have more inside of you than an ordinary little girl, and sometimes that can be too hard for a person. We're taking you to a special place so that you can be strong."

"But I don't want to go to a special place! I want to live at home with Mommy and Rebecca!"

The adults laughed. Chloe felt tears welling up. Her mother turned to look back at her. "Oh, sweetheart, you're not going there to live. We'll be back home tonight."

"But I heard Wheezer say he was giving me a new residence, and I know what that means!"

"Chloe." It was Tom. "I said we were giving you a new resonance. It's not the same thing, honey." She wasn't convinced, and sat on the seat and pouted. The car continued to move, and when it turned up and away from the river, she mumbled about going home, but knew the grousing was useless.

Twenty minutes later, the car pulled into the driveway of a small house. Tom parked and opened the door for Emily. Chloe sighed as her mother opened her door, took her hand, and started to walk her to the house. "Chloe, have I ever lied to you before?"

"No."

"We'll be home tonight."

"Okay."

Tom reached the door and rapped on it. By the time the rest reached the doorstep, it was opened by a small, fat, motherly woman who smiled at all of them. "Come in, come in. I've been waiting for you. I've been cooking all morning."

She had been cooking. Chloe could smell it. She closed her eyes. There was soup or stew, something with beef and carrots and celery. The woman had also crafted a banana trifle, or something like that. Chloe smelled the thick cream and the touch of allspice she'd added. In the oven, some kind of meat she'd never eaten before, never smelled, was braising with herbed broth. There was grape juice on the counter, along with weak iced tea and strong iced coffee.

"Come in, sweetheart." The woman was looking at her, and Chloe realized she was the only one left on the porch. "Would you like something to drink?"

"I'll have some of the grape juice, please." The woman gave her a startled look that turned into a half smile and extended her hand. Chloe took it and they walked into the house. Mother and Tom were sitting at a small kitchen table. Mother was already dishing out bowls of the stew. She smiled at Chloe.

"This is my Aunt Astrid. That would make her your great auntie." She took a loaf of bread, tore off a piece, and dipped it into the stew. She put it in her mouth and her eyes seemed to glaze over for a moment. "Oh, Auntie As, I forgot how you cook. This is wonderful."

"I have lamb braising in the oven, too." She held a cup out to Chloe. "Here's your juice, sweetie."

"Thank you, Great Auntie."

Emily walked into the room. "Well, Astrid, I looked it all over, but let's just face it, you've always been far better than me at this sort of thing, so we'll have to trust that you've done it right."

Chloe watched Astrid chuckle. "Oh, sit down, Em. There's plenty of food to eat and I worked all morning on it. Besides, I was building the cairns before you were born."

Emily shook her head. "Only if you were building them at three years old." She still sat and took the bowl Mother handed her. Chloe took a chair next to her mother, who handed her a bowl as well. Emily looked at her. "Child, do you know why we're here?"

"To get a new resonance."

"Yes, but do you know what that means?" When Chloe shook her head, Emily said, "All of us, all of us can hear the animals speak, the trees speak, the water speak. All of us can do that sometimes, Chloe. You can do it all the time. Is that right?" She nodded. "Sometimes they give you pictures, too, right?"

"Pictures and movies. Sometimes they're things that are going to happen, and sometimes it's stuff that has already happened." Chloe tasted the stew. It was very rich and there was a sweetness beneath the surface. She closed her eyes and saw Great Auntie Astrid pouring molasses into it.

"Yes. Very few of our people ever see the movies, Chloe, and most of them don't see the pictures very often at all. But all of us can sometimes hear when the rivers and the forests speak to us. But you, Chloe. You never don't hear, do you?"

"I don't have to listen."

"What I mean, sweetie—you hear the trees and animals all the time, don't you?"

"Trees, animals, spoons, doorbells, tables." Emily waved her hand and Chloe was silent.

"It is very rare and very special that you can hear things like tables or spoons, Chloe. But it's also very dangerous. Today, we are going to make sure you have a resonance, a frequency for—uh, I have no idea how to explain this to her."

"It's like music, Chloe." It was Tom speaking. "Like the piano scales you're learning. We're going to tune your power to a specific pitch. It will keep your power from just banging on the keys and making a mess of the music. You see, listening to tables is different than listening to trees or rivers. We want to make sure that it's in harmony."

"Like a chord?" Tom nodded and Chloe shrugged. "Okay." She got down from her chair and walked into the kitchen, and then through the back door to the back yard. She found the pile of stones Astrid had built that morning and sat beside it.

"What is she doing?" It was Emily's voice.

"She saw me, Em. She saw me build it this morning. She saw the instructions in my head. She saw it all." Astrid smiled. "I guess we do this first and eat later."

The four stepped into the back yard. Tom was about to tell Chloe to put her hand on the cairn, but she had already done it. Chloe looked at Astrid. "I'm sorry about Nanook, Great Auntie." Astrid cocked her head but said nothing.

Tom and Mother began placing leaves and branches around them.

"Nanook?" Emily said the words in a whisper.

"It's the dog. He was hit by a car on Tuesday. He's buried back here."

Tom and Mother joined hands and gestured for the others. Chloe remained in the middle as the four began to chant. Chloe felt a tingling at her hand where she touched the stones. It was warm now. No, it was cold. No, warm again. The rock wasn't sure what to be. Chloe felt the warmth and the cold coming over her in waves. She felt her hair blowing around her, and the noise was growing. Soon it was deafening. Everything in the back was shouting at her. *Everything except poor Nanook, who's just whimpering.* Shouting, yelling, cold, warm. Too much. Too much. *Poor Nanook.*

She opened her mouth and screamed. The others stopped chanting and stared at her. It was suddenly silent. Chloe stood and ran to her mother, who lifted her up and held her, stroking her hair to soothe her.

"Are we done?" It was Wheezer's voice.

"I don't know, Tom." Astrid replied.

"I think we're done." Emily suggested. Chloe lifted her

head to look at her, but Emily wasn't watching Chloe. Instead, her eyes were fixed on a small patch of ground beside the fence. Dirt was pushed away, forming a small hole, and a malamute, dirty but healthy, stood there whining softly, it's pink tongue a startling contrast to the greys and whites that made up its dirt-caked fur.

Chloe and Marcus, Seattle, Present Day

As the car pulled out, Chloe watched Amber and the vampire disappear behind them and turned to Marcus with a scowl. "What the hell is this? Why did we leave them?"

"Apparently they wanted some privacy, Chloe. Let it go." Marcus pressed a button on his door and a privacy shield began to rise between the rear and front seats. "In the meantime, can I make you a drink?" He reached to the mini-bar built into the center and took a tumbler. As he reached for the ice, Chloe took his hand, and he felt her power coursing into his arm like electric pins.

"What the hell do you think you're doing?" he growled.

Chloe smiled. "Oh, am I interfering with your plans? I want my friend back and I know something's not right here."

Marcus took her wrist with his free hand and pulled her away. The electric feeling disappeared. "You give me too much credit, witch. Michael isn't in the habit of sharing his plans with me." Chloe glared at him, and he spoke a little softer. "Listen, Chloe. He has searched for that girl for more than two centuries. Harming her is the farthest thing from his mind. Neither Michael nor Amber need us to interfere."

"I don't believe you." Chloe twisted her arm to grasp the hand holding her wrist. Her voice was low, and her chant was harsh, "Powers that be —" The slap was unexpected. Her cheek stung with the impact and her eyes filled with water. She looked up at Marcus in shock. "How dare you? How...?

I...I can't believe you would—"

"You put your hand on me and channeled your power. Don't sit there like some innocent little schoolgirl who just got abused, Chloe. What I did was defensive. What you did was an invasion—damn you, it wasn't but a step or two from rape."

"Rape? Listen, Marcus, you—"

"No, you listen, Chloe. Do you think it's right to use your power on people whenever it's convenient? Jesus! How the hell do you sleep at night?"

Chloe stared at him, visions of accountants dancing in her head. She almost gave in to the guilt, but instead said viciously, "What does a vampire know about channeling power?"

"Let me tell you something. You witches think you have all the wisdom. You're the holy fucking guardians of knowledge, right? There are eleven-hundred books back at that house, give or take, and I've read every damn one of them." His arm was still tingling, and he shook it violently. "That's one of the beautiful things about living for centuries; everything eventually loses its charm, everything except for knowledge. There are another three or four thousand books in our manor in New York. I once killed a man for one of the books at the estate in New Orleans. I may not know everything there is to know about you, Chloe, but I bet I know a hell of lot more than you do. I offered you a drink, goddamn it, now what'll you have?"

Chloe sat in shock, then found herself unable to keep from smiling. "Gin and tonic, you bastard."

Marcus poured the gin and added a splash of tonic from a small Schweppes bottle. He handed it to Chloe, and she took a long sip. "You have an estate in New Orleans, huh?"

"Actually, Joseph—that's the driver—just arrived from

New Orleans with four of our cars. The last time I sat in this seat was for Mardi Gras a few years back."

"I went there once for Mardi Gras." She took another sip. "No way in hell I'm gonna tell you what I did for beads."

Marcus looked at her for a moment and then pressed the intercom button. "Pull over, Joseph." When the car was on the side of the road, he looked at Chloe. "I'll be right back." She heard the trunk open, and in a few seconds, Marcus climbed back in. As the car pulled back onto the road, he smiled at her and lifted his hand. In it, he held a loop of green and blue beads. He raised his eyebrows, slipped the string over her head, and left them hanging from her neck.

She sat in silence for a moment and then leaned forward and kissed him. The kiss was soft and sweet, but in moments, he was grasping her hair and pulling her tightly to him. She fumbled with his tie and tore buttons from his shirt as she pulled it off him.

He pulled off her jacket, tore off her blouse and ripped her bra from her. She gripped his shoulders as she kissed him. He pushed her off for a moment, unbuttoned his slacks, and dropped them to his ankles. She reached for him, taking his length in her hands. "Oh my," she whispered. He was warm, even hot. *I thought you'd be cold, no heat.* She stroked him softly, and he groaned. He reached forward and pushed her hair out of the way so he could lean down and kiss her shoulder. He never got to it; Chloe was already out of reach as she leaned over and kissed him below and then above her hands. Marcus leaned back with a husky sigh as she opened her mouth and took him in, still moving her hand softly. He felt her hair fall against his thighs and his lower abdomen, felt it over her mouth and hands. He gathered it and pulled it away from her face, marveling at how heavy it was.

His hands found her back, stroking her skin from her

shoulder blades to her lower back. She pushed her head farther now, taking him deeply, one hand moving to his thigh and the other to cup him beneath her mouth. "Oh, God. Chloe, I...." He finally pushed her away and she struggled with her pants, trying to find room to remove them in the cramped quarters, until he impatiently pulled her to him.

As she kissed him, she felt his teeth grow and she backed up. He lifted his hands, and she watched his fingernails jut out an inch or so. He reached down, and she felt his hands on her rear and then heard his nails ripping the seat of her pants out of the way. She kissed him again as he eased her on top of him. His hands found the tiny thong panties she wore, and she felt a brief pain as he tore them from her.

She pushed her mouth onto his and felt his teeth retracting. As he pushed against her, she could feel his fingertips soft on her breast. *He isn't cold at all, goddamn it!* In fact, he was rather hotter than she'd ever felt before, and as he entered her gently, she grasped his shoulders and pushed down hard upon him. She moved quickly, feeling the vibrations of the car and the urgency of his movements.

He thrust upward, and Chloe saw him with his first woman in Rome, in a storeroom closet at fourteen while the thirty-two year old shopkeeper's wife moved on top of him. She saw him at seventeen in the blonde prostitute's apartment, holding her head as she knelt in front of him, moving and sucking eagerly, and Chloe felt him at the back of her throat. Then, he was eighteen in his parents' bed, pushing into the neighbor girl, who bit at his ear and whispered Italian words to him, words Chloe spoke softly now, not knowing what they meant. She sat atop him in St. Petersburg, feeling him push inside of her, moving her hips frenetically, knowing he would drink from her when he finished. Finally, she felt him in an alley in New Orleans as she leaned forward over the boxes and he grasped her hair, pushing furiously while costumed revelers paraded in the streets, never knowing what was happening just a few yards away in the shadows.

He was holding her waist tightly now, pulling her down to meet him with each movement. She felt his urgency, knew it was close, and pushed down hard again and again. She screamed as she was overcome and put her lips to his neck as she finished, crying out against him. A moment later he finished as well, one hand holding the arc of her lower back and pulling her down as he pushed impossibly deeply into her. She heard him cry out as he did, the hand on her back instantly stopping both their movements. His other hand was clasping her breast firmly and almost painfully. As he held her, she felt herself gripping him, and she was still overcome with the climax. She screamed into his neck as he yelled out as well.

Suddenly, she felt heat on her lips and cried out at a burning pain on her breast. The two both recoiled, Chloe ending up on the floor in front of him. His neck was smoking at the base of his throat, and Chloe stared at him and then at her breast. Smoke rose from there as well.

Marcus looked at her, reached forward, and traced the mark on her breast. Chloe looked at his neck. "Oh, Marcus. I didn't mean to, I...I've branded you." She studied the mark, the witch's symbol she'd pointed out to Amber just hours before. Marcus shook his head. "I've...I...." He closed his eyes tightly, opened them again, and finally stammered, "I've done it to you, too." Chloe nodded and looked at her breast. There, beneath the nipple, was another mark, one of the ones she'd shown Amber, the one she assumed was the symbol of the vampire.

CHAPTER TWENTY-FOUR

Praxis

Michael, Hong Kong, 2009

Gerard sat at the head of the table, and he ceremoniously cleared his throat. The murmured conversation around the table came to an end and those seated fixed their eyes upon him. There were seven there, Michael and two other vampires, a man and two women he didn't recognize, and Gerard. Gerard stared at them all for a moment, reveling in the authority he thought he had. Michael almost sighed impatiently before he caught himself.

"I want to take a moment before we begin to...." The inappropriate dramatic pauses were beginning to wear on Michael. "...thank our guests." He gestured to the man and the two women. "For those who have yet to meet him, the man to my left is Machiel of Bruges." The others at the table nodded toward Michael. "As you know, we have discovered that he is connected to the prophecy. In fact, we have confirmation from a number of seers that he is to be the one who finds the queen."

"I still don't understand why we don't just kill the woman before she's turned." It was one of the women who spoke with a strange accent Michael couldn't place. She looked to be in her mid-thirties and trim, like she worked hard to fight time's effects with her course brown hair pulled back into a severe bun. "The risks of turning her appear too great."

"The king desires that she be brought to him." The woman started to interrupt, but Gerard lifted his hand and she stopped. "We know the prophecy. If she is not turned, it is possible the queen will simply be born elsewhere. Machiel will find her and turn her. Then, she will be brought here while she has yet to come into her power, and we will destroy her."

"The covenant is very concerned about the possibility that we will lose her." It was bun-woman again. "There are large factions in North America that don't agree with the rest of us. Even in death she could become a — how do you say the word?"

"A figurehead." It was the other woman who spoke. "We are concerned that the covens in America have become corrupted with ideas about the mixing of kinds. Even if she were dead, they could unite behind her."

Gerard growled. "Then we will hunt them down and eradicate them as we did the wolves."

The woman dismissed him with a wave of her hand. "And how do we know we can trust this…Machiel of Bruges? How do we know he'll not keep the queen whore for himself?"

Michael was across the table before she finished the word, and he lifted her in the air by her hair. The woman turned red, grasped at his arm, and kicked at him. Bun woman was chanting something under her breath, and Michael began to feel warm, but he didn't release the grip. "If you don't shut your mouth I will feed on your blood and vomit it over your children."

"Enough." It was the man, who stood. "Machiel of Brugges, I would very much appreciate your release of Joanna. She spoke out of turn, but she is valuable to me and to the covenant."

Michael relaxed his grip but didn't release her. He turned to the man. He hadn't thought about it before, but the man was interesting. He had spoken with a soft French accent, wore a tailored Italian suit that probably cost two thousand dollars, and was groomed impeccably. His jet black hair was cut business-like, and his face was professional, impassive. "I'm not in the habit of doing favors for people I don't know."

The man smiled. "My name is Jean-Pierre. As for me, I am not in the habit of asking for anything twice."

Michael smiled and released the woman. He nodded at Jean-Pierre and returned to his seat. "My loyalty is not an issue here. When she is turned, I will bring her here. I want her unity no more than the rest of us."

Amber, Seattle, Present Day

Illyris stood on the dais in the chamber she'd recently acquired as a throne room. It belonged at one point to a pharaoh or a king from centuries before, but earthquakes or floods or other events had buried it twenty feet beneath the soil, and she'd only chanced upon it when one of her wolves discovered the cave-like ruins while chasing a rabbit into a burrow. She wore a white silk robe a witch from the east had presented to her the previous evening. It was light on her body and she enjoyed the strange feel of nakedness while clothed.

Giorgos stood in front of her. She smiled at him, noting again how strange it was to see such a bristly beard on a man from Greece. The country's men had developed a more manicured look a century or so before. Still, she knew the hair on his face, or for that matter, on his neck and probably his entire body, had less to do with grooming and more to do with his dual nature. He knelt and held out a small box. "My queen, perhaps you would do me the honor of taking this gift. My daughter found it and crafted the thing that holds it."

Illyris took the box. "Rise, Giorgos. There will be no more kneeling of your kind to mine. That is why you call me your queen, and that is why you will stand in my presence." She unlatched the small brass catch on the box and opened it. Within was a dusty piece of quartz, a slight rose color to it. A small leather string wrapped around one corner and formed a necklace of sorts. "Oh, Giorgos, you must tell your daughter that it is lovely and I will wear it always." She slipped the cord around her neck and smiled.

A tall woman entered...Brenwhynn, who had arrived yesterday. She smiled as she entered. "My queen, the remnants of the druid—uh, the witches—in Hibernia await your command." She curtsied, and Illyris though it a little odd of a gesture in the woman, who must have been close to ninety. The age wasn't the centuries of some of her associates, or even Illyris herself, but it seemed girlish and a little out of place. Still, she smiled.

"Then the three are joined and none can stop them. The millennia of oppression has seen the first days of its end. Shall we drink together?" She gestured to a small stone table at the side of the room. Her servants hadn't completely removed the rubble, and only three sides were available for use, but the three nonetheless made their way to the seats. Illyris took the pitcher that sat on the table and poured inky red wine into clay cups. She handed one to Giorgos and one to Brenwhynn and raised the third to her lips.

"I'm afraid there will be no joining of the races, Illyris." The voice came from the chamber entrance, and she turned to stare coolly at Gerard. "This has gone on for far too long."

Illyris laughed. "And the king has sent his lap dog to stop me? Go home, Gerard, or I will fill this pitcher with your blood and drink it with my wine."

"He is not alone." It was a tall man who spoke, thin and dressed in a dark green robe, his face obscured by the hood. He stepped from the passageway, as did four others…three of the old ones, including Gerard, and two in the robes, probably rogue witches. "The races will not be joined."

"There is nothing you can do about the covenant we have created here." It was Giorgos who spoke. She could hear the growl in his voice as he did.

"Shut up, wolf. Even an animal such as you should know better than to address your betters when unbidden." Gerard's eyes flashed red over his flaccid jowls. "But it is an interesting choice of terms, for we have created just that. A society, if you will, to ensure that we are all kept pure."

The tall man spoke again. "The Covenant." He reached to his hood and pulled it down. He was somewhere in middle age, his bald head streaked with blue tattoos, a hook nose over a nearly lipless mouth. His eyes were black, with yellowing whites.

"You do not speak for the old race, Gerard," Illyris sneered. "In fact, you do not speak at all unless the king provides you with words."

"But you are wrong, my queen." He pronounced the word disdainfully, mocking her. "In the Covenant, I now speak for us."

"As I speak for the witches." The tall man smiled.

"You speak for none of us, Mailik." Brenwhynn rose to stand beside Illyris. "Your darkness is not the way of the *draoidh*."

He laughed. "Ah, but it will be *bana-bhuidseach*. It will

be." He began a low chant, guttural harsh words that he seemed almost to spit out. Yellow sparks appeared around his eyes as he spoke.

Giorgos was in the air in seconds. His body transformed as he leapt, arms disappearing into forelegs, his face elongating into a snout. He was fully changed when he hit the first vampire, locking his jaws on the neck. Illyris was on the second, who had stepped in front of the sorcerer. She grabbed his hair and sank her other hand, nails first, into his throat. His eyes opened wide for a moment, terror bright within them. She kept pushing until she grasped where his spine met his skull. Then, she pulled bone and blood and flesh out, dropping the lifeless body and the gore on the ground.

Giorgos was already on the man in blue. His mouth closed over his face, and Illyris heard bones break, but not before she heard the man croak out, "Too late! Too late!" She watched him crumple to the floor, watched Giorgos lift his head and howl. Gerard was already gone, and the other sorcerer was in flames, writhing on the floor. Illyris turned and saw Brenwhynn chanting.

She walked up to Giorgos and stroked the fur on his neck. "Thank you, my friend." The wolf turned, blood covering its muzzle, and she smiled at him. In a few seconds, Giorgos stood human before her again. "They will never stop, my queen. They mean to kill you."

Brenwhynn stopped her chant. The man on the floor was a charred husk, still smoking, but the flames stopped. "That spell he cast was not to kill, Giorgos. That was a banish—"

Illyris heard no more. The world grew quiet, and she closed her eyes. She opened them to see an old one above her, smiling. He had blond hair cut in a strange style, and wore clothes unlike any she'd ever seen. She was outside, and the air was cool.

"Oh Amber, now our love can be eternal."

Illyris stood. "The last one who told me that lay empty on a dirt floor twenty seconds later. Where am I?"

"You're in Seattle, at my estate. Do you not recall our—?"

"Where is Seattle?" Even as she asked, a flicker of a memory called out to her. She put her hand to her head. "I am…what?" She felt the world spinning around her for a moment, and then darkness.

CHAPTER TWENTY-FIVE
Concentering

Marcus, India, 1926

Marshall ate at the table, but Marcus let his plate lie and sipped the wine. A bottle was on the table, and eleven more were in the crate Michael had sent with him as a gift for Marcus's host. Marshall took a napkin and wiped his mouth. "Does our Indian food not agree with you, Mr. Auditore?"

The man had bright eyes. Marcus was surprised that he did. The job he'd undertaken in India was dramatic in scope and nearly impossible. Still, he imagined Marshall was one of the lucky men who had chanced upon a profession so utterly suited to him that years of backbreaking work didn't diminish its joy at all. Marcus smiled at the man. "You pronounce the *e*, Auditor-*ee*. Still, please call me Marcus."

Marshall chuckled. "Well, then. You must call me by my Christian name as well, and you must thank Mr. Reyns for the wine. That's the wine you're enjoying without any of the food."

"Thank you, Sir John, I will be sure to express your appreciation. Forgive me for my lack of appetite. I'm afraid the journey did not agree with me."

"Well, it is pleasant to have a visit from a benefactor, even by proxy. Mr. Reyns funded a dig in Crete some time ago. It would have been good to see him again."

"I'm afraid Mr. Reyns has been quite busy of late." *And not particularly interested in letting you see that he hasn't aged in the thirty years since you last saw him.*

"It's no matter. I received his letter and have gathered three items I believe he will find interesting. One of my men will bring them in a moment." He studied Marcus for a moment. "I must tell you, Mr. Auditore, I—"

"Please, Sir John, Marcus."

"I must tell you, Marcus, that this dig is not the result of private money, but of money from the Crown. I'm afraid I cannot let you take the pieces with you. I thought perhaps one of my men could photograph them for you from a number of angles."

"Perhaps there is an arrangement that could be made?"

"I'm sorry, Marcus. I have spent twenty-five years trying to keep such arrangements from being made. I remember Mr. Reyns interest in me when I was young, and the gratitude I feel is immeasurable, but I'm afraid I cannot compromise in this."

Marcus sipped his wine. "We, of course, understand, and I think I see why Michael showed an interest in the first place." A servant entered with a small box and Marshall gestured for him to put it on the table. Marcus reached for it but stopped himself.

"Go ahead, young man."

Marcus pushed his plate away and pulled the box, a small wooden crate, to him. He lifted the top and saw the top of a terra cotta bust. He pulled it from the box and put it on the table. "I don't understand why...oh." Above the carved lower lip was a stone fang. Its mate had broken off the bust, and the centuries had worn the survivor so that it was far less visible, but it was apparent.

"It was found with a number of others of no particular note, but…. You know, I thought in Crete that this was the passing fancy of a young man who'd read too many of the new books, but here we are."

An Indian entered and cleared the dishes. Marshall refilled his wine glass and Marcus's as well. "Mr. Reyns should read Burton's book. It will do much to explain the Indian superstitions about—"

"*Vikram and the Vampire.* Yes, Michael has a copy autographed by Sir Richard." He moved the bust to the side and returned to the box, pulling out a small, soapstone square about the width of two fingers. On it was a raised drawing of a woman holding a dead man by the hair while wolves danced beside her.

"At first," Marshall said, "We thought that might be a representation of Kali, but it's very rare to find her with only one set of arms. Also, you would expect to see the head severed, and many heads adorning her person." He reached forward and pointed at the man's neck. "There appears to be a wound here, like Stoker's count might have left as well." He chuckled. "Have you seen the German film yet?"

"*Nosferatu?*"

"*A Symphony of Terror.* I imagine Mr. Reyns wouldn't miss a film like that."

"He was at the premier in 1922." Marcus put the square down. "What is this?"

"It's a seal, for documents and goods."

"Like a signet ring?"

"More like what a merchant might use to make a clay impression on his goods. Take the other now, it's the most interesting of the bunch."

Marcus reached into the box and pulled out a small

figurine. It was stone, probably soapstone again, and it depicted a satyr of some kind. "Michael has no interest in satyrs or any of the Greek mythology, except perhaps for the Lamia."

"Oh, those aren't goat legs, Marcus. Those are wolf legs, and the creature has fangs."

Marcus raised his eyebrows. "Thank you for setting it aside. When may I have the photographs?"

"My man will take them in the morning. He'll develop them straight away and you'll have them at noon."

"I'm afraid I have pressing business tomorrow. Perhaps I could return in the evening at about nine o'clock?"

"Certainly." Marshall stood and extended his hand. Marcus took it and nodded to him.

"Although this project is funded, Sir John, perhaps there is another use for our money?"

He shook his head. "No. Tell Mr. Reyns that it was my pleasure to help a fellow archeology enthusiast, and he must visit me at his earliest convenience."

Marcus asked after Marshall's family and relations in England, exchanged pleasantries, and left. He moved quickly to the car he'd brought, nodded to the driver, and climbed in the back. Michael sat staring ahead. The driver pulled away and Marcus described the items.

Michael was silent for a long while. Finally he said, "You know they will try to kill her, Marcus."

"The queen?"

"Oh yes. The king removed her once, and even if he's gone or dead or wherever the hell he is, they don't want her uniting us with the wolves." He sighed. "The witches either, I suppose."

"But there are no wolves left."

"Don't be so certain of that, Marcus. I have seen one."

"But what will we do if they come for her?" Marcus leaned forward and told the driver to pull over.

"We will kill every one of them, Marcus. Every damned one." He glanced at the house they'd pulled up to. "Is this ours?"

"I bought it last year."

"You thought ahead, Marcus. We'll need that when the time comes."

Michael, Seattle, Present Day

Her eyes were different when she spoke to him, yellow like a cat's, but they flashed back to green before she collapsed. Michael looked down at her and finally lifted her up gingerly and walked her back to the estate. She mumbled along the way, sometimes talking about life in the orphanage, sometimes talking about wolves and fire.

What if I've been wrong all this time? He shook his head. He couldn't be wrong. It was unthinkable, impossible. When he reached the door, a servant rushed forward to take Amber from him, and Michael allowed her to be lifted from his arms. "Undress her, bathe her, and place her in my room."

Another servant arrived with a phone. Covering the mouthpiece with his hand he said, "A Mr. Gerard for you, sir." Michael took the phone. *This is it.*

"Hello?" He tried to sound pleasantly surprised by a phone call.

"Is she made?" There was an excitement to Gerard's voice that Michael hadn't heard before.

"I haven't even found her yet, Gerard. How would she be made?"

"The seers believe a dramatic event has just occurred, a prophecy fulfillment, Michael. What happened?"

"Nothing has happened here, Gerard."

"Michael, do I need to fly there and investigate my — ?"

"Gerard, you are always welcome in my house — as a colleague and a friend," *Asshole*, "but there is nothing here for you."

"But the seers said th —"

"I will search for any information I can find. In the meantime, see if they can give you any better information about the speed with which the queen will gain her power. I heard an interesting story that she drained her maker a few seconds after she was made."

"We've all heard that story, Michael. I think it's just a fantasy. Let me tell you what is not fantasy, Michael. If I don't get answers soon, I will find them myself." Michael looked up. Marcus was entering the room, a worried expression covering his face.

"Well, Gerard," Michael made his voice light. "If it is not a fantasy, you'll know the queen is made when you find me empty of blood in an alleyway. I'm afraid I have some matters to which I must attend. Goodbye, Gerard."

"Call me with answers as soon as you can. Goodbye, Michael."

Michael returned the phone to its cradle, and the servant returned it to a table in the corner. *I will have to kill Gerard sooner than planned. Too soon.* He shook his head and then noticed Marcus. "You look like hell, Marcus."

"Father, I...Michael, there's a sit —" He was breathing hard, almost hyperventilating. "A situation."

"Did you kill the witch? It will make the queen angry, but I —"

"I didn't kill her, Michael. I...I slept with her."

"You slept with a witch? Jesus, Marcus, what were you thinking?" Michael glared at Marcus for a moment, but then softened. "Ah well, you and I both know the queen will bring

all of us together anyway. Still, the risks are...wait a minute."
He turned suddenly and rushed up the stairs.

Marcus followed. "Father, there's more." Michael ignored
him. He entered the library and pulled books off the shelf,
letting them fall on the ground. "Father, she's asleep, or
something like that. When we...are you listening?" Michael
continued to pull books from the shelves. "If you tell me what
you're looking for, I—"

"The diary I sent to you from Hong Kong. Where is it?"

"The one from the herbalist?"

"No, the soldier, from the 1870s."

"It's in New Orleans, I believe. Wait, no, it's in a box with
books I had shipped from New Orleans."

Michael whirled on him, his eyes wide. "Where is it?"

"In the storeroom." Michael was off again. "Father,
I...damn." Marcus shook his head and followed. By the time
he reached the downstairs room the estate used as a catch-all,
Michael had torn the cardboard and scattered books on the
floor.

Finally, he held up a thin leather bound volume. He
flipped through the pages, stopped on one, and cried
"There!" He read for a moment and then handed it to Marcus.
Marcus took the book and read.

*October 9, 1874. Was retained to complete organizational books
for new firm Sharp and Danby. Architectural. Will take a day,
maybe two, and will pay for this holiday completely. I think
Margaret will appreciate a few days without me as well. Met a
strange woman buying bean curd in square. She had a cart with live
snakes and sold their organs to locals, who ate them with relish,
some health or vitality issue. That was strange, but I had heard of
the strange teas and potions eaten here. In fact, my host, who has
lived here for a decade, swears by a remedy for cough derived from
bark, mushrooms, and fish bones. A tall man, British by the look of*

him, walked by and the woman stopped him. She started shouting at him about a marriage. She screamed about a "sanpo" and "gonshe" and the man started asking her about a queen. My host says "sanpo" is the word for witch, but he doesn't know the other word. When the tall man left, I bought a snakeskin from the woman and will make a gift of it to Harold. It will make for an amusing anecdote over dinner when I return home.

A small piece of loose paper had been wedged into the spine next to the papers, and Marcus recognized Michael's handwriting. He'd written *goeng si* in black ink. "What is this, Michael?"

"*San po* is witch, Marcus. *Goeng si* is vampire. Evidently, your ugly Russian girl was right. You are part of the prophecy as well."

"She wasn't ugly, Michael."

"No, but your new witch looks like a hell of a good toss. How was she?"

Marcus's eyes grew wide. "Jesus! I forgot, she's asleep in the car and I can't wake her. I need your help...I don't know what to do."

"Bring her in, Marcus." Michael sighed. "Have one of the servants prepare a room. We'll take care of your witch."

Marcus left and Michael walked slowly upstairs into the office. Marcus's damned cat sat on the seat and hissed when he tried to move it. He shook his head, considered draining the thing, but instead sat on the desk itself. He took the phone and put the receiver to his ear. He hesitated but dialed.

He closed his eyes when the voice came on the other line. *Forgive me, Marcus.*

"Gerard, I believe I know what prophecy your seers saw fulfilled, and I'm afraid it involves my son."

CHAPTER TWENTY-SIX
Accumulating

Michael, Lisbon, 1918

Kabos entered the room with a burlap bag, something squirming within it. Michael looked at the bag and raised his eyebrows. "Live eels, Machiel; I bought them at the docks. Perhaps we can enjoy a meal without disposing of the body."

Michael smiled and took the bag. "You do know I'll have to feed on something—someone—else later." He brought the bag to the restroom and emptied it into the tub. "Should I put some water in here?"

"They won't want any freshwater. Just leave them, they'll be plenty fresh in a moment." When Michael returned, Kabos was searching through their luggage. "So, which did you kill?"

"The wine is in the canvas trunk, Kabos. It was Isabella, of course."

"What was the pretense?" Kabos found the bottle and brought it to the table.

"Oh, I complained about the wine and she made a comment about how I couldn't taste it anyway. I drained her and said that I could taste that." Michael looked wistful for a moment. "I don't like killing like that, Kabos."

Kabos stared at Michael for a moment before replying. "There are many sacrifices this prophecy will require of us. Be thankful when those harmed are not those we love. Believe me, my son, the time will surely come when your destiny and their comfort are in conflict."

Marcus, Seattle, Present Day

The night air had dropped five or ten degrees since he'd stepped into the house. The wind stung his face a little as he walked toward the car. *Oh, fuck. Not now.* Scarlet and Aleisha were leaning against the passenger door, Scarlet's hand under Aleisha's blouse, their mouths locked together. When she saw Marcus, Scarlet pushed the other away, then both looked at Marcus. They were painted for a night out, deep purple eyeshade on Scarlet, with Aleisha in powdery blue. "Who's the girl in the car?" Scarlet licked her lips and extended her fangs. "Can we have her?"

Marcus ignored her and walked to the door. Chloe was undisturbed, asleep, and still naked on the seat. "Go get me a blanket."

"Oh, come on, Marcus." Aleisha lifted her leg and put the stiletto heel of one of her thigh high boots against the door handle. "Let us play with her. You can play too." Marcus grabbed her ankle and flipped her to the ground. Her black skirt tore on the sidewalk.

"Go get me a blanket before I forget you belong to Michael."

Aliesha leapt to her feet and bared her fangs, but a simple dull stare from Marcus cowed her and she turned back to the house.

"You're such a buzz kill, Marcus. How come you never want to have us?" Scarlet had put on her pouty expression, the one she was certain made her irresistible.

"Does it bother you, Scarlet, that Michael never has you either? He should have let your pimp kill the both of you." He opened the door and gathered Chloe in his arms. Scarlet reached for her thigh but stopped when Marcus bared his fangs. Then, deliberately, she reached forward and stroked Chloe's leg.

A backhand sent her flying twelve feet to crash against the steps of the estate. Marcus held Chloe in one arm and advanced on the fallen girl, his other arm raised. "I think you have been a guest in my home for as long as you will be."

"Enough!" It was Michael's voice, and he stood in the doorway. Aliesha held onto his right arm, simpering and nuzzling his shoulder. He held a blanket in his left hand, and he tossed it to Marcus. "I still have use for these two." Scarlet rose and walked to Michael, glancing back with a petulant smile at Marcus.

"Come on, Michael. Did you even sleep with them when they were alive?" The two glared at him, but he ignored them.

"That's not the use I have for them, Marcus." To the girls, he said, "There is a houseguest in my room. Go to her and wait. When she wakes, one of you come to me immediately while the other attends to any need she may have." The girls' smiles disappeared.

"But Michael, don't you —?"

"But before you do, go to your own room and put on some clothes appropriate for this estate. I won't have Amber thinking I run a whorehouse." He turned back to Marcus. "I've made some inq—"

"But Michael, why do we have to—?" It was Scarlet's voice, and Michael didn't turn around but lifted his forearm.

"Well, Marcus, perhaps you could eliminate one of them for me. I think Scarlet is the more irritat...." He ended with a chuckle as the sound of the two disappearing through the door reached him, and then he returned his attention to Marcus, who had wrapped Chloe in the blanket and stepped to the porch.

"Don't bring her in. I've made some inquiries. Her—what's the word they use? Not congregation, no…coven, that's it. Her coven is located in Yakima; I spoke with a man named Tom a moment ago. Do you know where that is?"

"About two and a half hours southeast."

"Take the car and leave her with them." He reached into his breast pocket and removed a tiny leather journal. "Give this book to the leader there. A peace offering of sorts. The address is on a piece of paper in the journal."

"I may not see you for a few days. I'll have to get a room there and…." He shook his head. "I don't know why, Michael, but she must be safe."

"You won't be gone for a few days, Marcus. You will leave her in their care and return to me immediately. I have need of you."

Marcus looked at him. "I will not leave her!"

"My son, for two centuries you have quested with me. I cannot finish what we have started without you. She will be safe with them, far safer than she is here. You must return. Do this because I ask you. Don't make me compel you."

"But Father…very well. I'll be back an hour or two before dawn." He turned, walked back to the car, and placed her gingerly in the back seat. He started for the front, but Michael indicated for him to sit with Chloe and he did. A moment later, the driver walked up, his hair unkempt, still tucking in his shirt. He heard Michael telling the man to drive quickly both ways and moments later, they left the estate.

Marcus felt the rumbling of the car beneath him, and willed it go faster. Chloe's breathing was normal, not labored or shallow. He slapped her cheek, pinched her. No response. He heard the car accelerate as the driver pulled onto the I-90, and sighed. "Why do you matter so much to me, witch?" He hadn't expected a response, but he was still oddly disappointed that he received none. Reaching to the drink cabinet, he fixed himself a scotch. He gulped it down, feeling it burn for a moment, and marveled at how, even after all these years, he still expected the warm alcohol glow, and still found himself disappointed that it never came.

Time passed slowly, and he read the little journal, willing the miles and the minutes to move a little faster. It was interesting, a history of the migration of witches into North America in the 1600s, and then later into the nineteenth century. The first section dealt with the Salem witches. More specifically, he read that there were only two witches in Salem, Samuel Parris and Sarah Good. If the author was right, the whole hysteria was engineered by Parris, acting as an agent for European witches who were unhappy about the covens in North America and their attitudes toward unity. The children overcome by trances, fits, and immorality were charmed into it by Parris. Sarah Good had fallen into the trap more easily than any had expected, almost constantly muttering chants of protection as she walked the town, making her appear not unlike a homeless crazy woman. It took a few moments before he realized the journal wasn't condemning Parris but commending him. Clearly, the author's loyalties lay with the European witches.

Marcus drew in a deep breath when in the middle of the journal, he saw "Avalani" in the same flowing script.

The Avalani concur that the threats from the New World heretics are pressing, though not as pressing as the sympathizers. The utmost goal of the Covenant must be to disrupt the abilities of the rebels to press toward unification. The Avalani will continue to drive the extermination of the wolves while we will prevent any real power from developing among the rebel covens.

Marcus shook his head. He put the book down and looked at Chloe, who still hadn't stirred. He stroked her cheek, considered slapping her again to see if she'd wake, but ended up cupping her chin. Then, he slowly pulled the blanket from her breast. The mark itself was black, seared as though a branding iron had been pressed to her flesh. It looked like a symbol from the old tongue, and Marcus briefly wished he knew how to read it. Michael said Kabos hadn't taught him, and his father—Marcus chuckled, *my grandfather*—had spent nearly a century piecing it together himself. The skin around it was bright red, and Marcus was overcome with an urge to kiss it, to comfort. Instead, he put the blanket back over her and sighed.

He reached to the cabinet again and withdrew a small aluminum cocktail shaker, polished it with his sleeve, and used it as a mirror to see the mark Chloe had left on his neck. It was as black as the one on her breast, but his flesh wouldn't stay wounded, and the red inflammation around the brand had probably been there for only a moment or two. The mark was essentially a circle with lines through it, somewhere between a pentagram and a peace symbol. Still, he knew it. It was the mark of the witch. He pulled his collar over the mark instinctively, realizing as he did that the car had reached Yakima.

When it stopped, he didn't hesitate but lifted Chloe and rushed for the door. It opened before he was halfway there, and a flurry of figures came out, taking her from his arms and whisking her into the house. A lone man remained and nodded at him.

"As much as we speak about uniting, it's uneasy when we come face to face, isn't it?"

230

"Are you Tom?"

"I am."

"Michael wishes to make this book a gift for you." He handed the little journal over and looked to the door and then back at Tom.

"You may not go in there. Your presence does something to our senses, requires constant adjustment. We will all need our focus to help Chloe, and that means you must leave. As it is, we'll probably be able to do very little until you've driven for ten minutes." Tom stared at Marcus, who looked longingly at the door and finally reluctantly returned to the car.

As he got in, he noticed a fresh drink on the armrest. The driver smiled at him. "It's a shame, sir, that the only one of us who can drink in this car can't get drunk. You look like you could use it."

Marcus nodded, mumbled a thanks, and pulled the door closed. He lifted the glass and drained it. Again the burn; again no glow. He sighed and stared at the house disappearing behind them. They were a mile or so away when his vision blurred, and only a few feet farther when he saw only darkness.

Chapter Twenty-Seven

Barcarole

Amber, Seattle, Present Day

Illyris awoke. She sat up, letting the sheet fall from her shoulders, exposing her nakedness. In front of her was a concubine dressed in outlandish clothes. She thought briefly about how she might have been embarrassed, a long time ago, but she wasn't. The woman had painted the skin around her eyes the color of the sky.

Illyris swung her legs around the bed and stood. A looking glass stood in the far corner of the room and she walked to it.

"Oh look, Michael's little toy finally woke up." The concubine had an exaggerated voice, some artificial combination of sweetness and malice. She turned to her.

"What happened to me?" Illyris thought her voice sounded a little strange, not as deep as it should be, not as full.

The concubine leered at her, moving her eyes from her feet to the curve of her waist and up to her face. "Michael wanted a little whore that could keep up with him, and he made you." The girl licked her lips, pursed them, and blew a kiss at her over the palm of her hand.

Illyris covered the eleven or twelve feet between them before the girl had moved her hand from her face. She felt something brittle and sticky in her hand as she grasped the concubine's hair and pulled her head back. Her neck was warm, and her blood was sweet. She drank deeply and forced her words into the girl's mind. *I am no man's whore. I am no man's toy. I am your queen, and you will speak to me with respect.* The girl beat against her body as she drank, growing more and more feeble. Illyris ignored the blows and drank still. *Respect at all times.*

The concubine was panicking now. She still tried to fight, but her blood was nearly gone. She grew limp, and Illyris saw a tear fall from the corner of her eye. *Remember what I have told you.* She released the girl, who fell to the floor and sobbed softly.

Illyris returned to the looking glass and considered her reflection. It was the most effective looking glass she had ever seen. Even the polished silver from the East had never cast a reflection this perfect. The image in the glass was her...or rather, it was almost her. She was a little taller than she should have been. Her hair was more red, her lips a little more full. Her breasts were the same, but better proportioned with the taller body. She looked as an artist might draw her if she'd commissioned a painting.

"What is your name, child?"

"Aliesha." The voice was a whisper, and Illyris turned to her. She walked to the concubine, who still lay collapsed on the floor. She bit into her wrist and placed the wound to the girl's mouth. As she drank, the girl's sobs ended. Illyris let her drink for a moment and pulled away, walking back to the mirror.

"Whose body is this?"

"I don't understand. Uh...Michael brought you here

yesterday. He...I think he made you yesterday." Illyris turned to Aliesha. She was on her knees now, eyes on the floor.

"I was already four-hundred years old before yesterday, Aliesha. He turned another, and I have become her. It was foretold a long time ago, though perhaps not as clearly as I see it now. Who is she?"

"I...I think I remember he called you Amber."

Amber stared at the vampire kneeling before her. It was one of the dreams, because she was naked again. She stood in silence until she realized nothing was happening. *Oh, God! This isn't a dream.*

Don't be afraid. We share your body —

She held her hands over her ears. The voice in her head was her own, or something like it. Amber screamed. The vampire on the floor recoiled as though she were struck. The mirror cracked behind her; the windows shattered as well. From the side she saw movement, and Michael was there. She caught a brief glance of his red ruffled shirt and black pants, and then her mind was flooded with images of her mother — not Mother Stone, another. She felt herself being held, being placed to her breast to nurse, felt herself wrapped in softness and warmed in her arms.

"Amber. It's me, Michael. We left together from the restaurant. Do you remember that?" Amber nodded. She realized she wasn't screaming anymore. "I changed you. The life you once knew is over. The life yet to come is what I gave you."

Michael's hand reached under his chin to scratch it, and Amber realized his steel-blue eyes had never left her face despite her nakedness. *I'm naked!* She covered her breasts with one arm and dove toward the bed, clutching a blanket to herself and sitting on the edge of the bed. "What did you do to me?"

Michael smiled kindly down at her. "Amber, I am a vampire, and now so are you. You and I were chosen many centuries ago. Don't be afraid of me. I will not harm you. There are others, though. These others have dedicated millennia to prepare only for the day to come that they might destroy you. We won't let them, my beloved."

Amber looked at him and smiled. For a moment, he made perfect sense. Her lips parted but no sound came out. Something within her felt warm and comforted, and above all compliant. There was a strength there, too, and the strength was battling against the comfort. "Who gave you the right to do this to me?" Her voice was soft and calm, but the strength was gaining ground. "I have no choice?" Stronger still. "I was chosen?" She said that louder, the strength had won completely. *You filthy animal! You want me to love you? Get out of my sight!*

Michael didn't move, but he seemed confused. "You not only resisted my calming but also projected your own thoughts." He smiled. "Truly you are the queen. I will not leave you, but I will guide you in this life and love you for eternity." His eyes dropped to the floor for a moment, and then returned to her face. "If you will have me."

We will. Amber heard her own voice again, the deeper one, and sighed. The voice was right, of course; she knew it. "I will have you, Michael." She dropped the blanket. "Come to me."

Michael looked surprised and hesitated. Then, he knelt in front of her and lifted his lips to hers. He was gentle, almost timid at first, but she gripped his head and kissed him passionately. Michael ran his hands over her shoulders and down her back, and he felt her nails extending, felt her pulling at his shirt. Having pulled away, he stood and undressed. She backed onto the bed as he did. Her eyes had

236

shifted from green to a cat's-eye yellow, and her nails were out, as were her fangs. Michael smiled when he was finally naked and climbed above her.

They moved very quickly, urgently. She found his wrist while he moved above her and bit into it, savoring the rich, hot flow of his blood. It was intoxicating, but it was even more incredible when she felt him bite into her own wrist and felt him drinking. As they made love, she felt almost drunk with the blood. It was hours before they finished, Michael rolling to the side, Amber draping a leg over him. She glanced at her wrist, noticed her wound was closing. It was like watching one of those documentary films with time-lapsed photography. In a few seconds, she had no wound on her wrist at all.

Amber still felt the afterglow as she stood. *Aftershock's more like it.* She looked down at Michael and smiled at him. He smiled back. "I shall have to take you...how is it said in America? I shall have to take you out on the town tonight."

"That would be nice." Amber walked to the side of the bed, smiling as she did. She looked down and realized the vampire girl was still kneeling on the floor.

"Rise, Aliesha," Illyris said. "You may help me dress."

Marcus, Present Day

Chloe and Marcus swam beneath the waves above the reef. She was naked before him, her hair so damn long that he was certain as she moved that it would be caught by the long strands of orange coral rising like some kind of winter tree with pointy, prickly branches in all directions. She smiled at him, and he understood that he loved her. She was perfect, her eyes wide open, the water flowing around her. Her breasts seemed to be a part of the water, and the mark he had left was less harsh than he remembered. Small fish, bright orange with white stripes, schooled about her. A flat blue fish the size of his palm hovered in front of her crotch like some kind of a censor's bar. It was beautiful, almost hypnotic, with dark blue in the background and wavy white and light blue stripes rippling through its body like an optical illusion.

"Chloe," he whispered, and the man who watched him hit him across his face with his club. Bones broke, and deep red and purple bruising rose on the depression left where his face had been. In moments, the face had returned to its normal state, the features once again sharp, angular.

"This filth is waking up." The man checked to see that the silver chains binding the vampire were secure and stepped a pace back. Marcus's eyes opened and focused on a fat man with a thick wooden club. The man was bare to the waist and extraordinarily ugly.

"I will kill you for that blow." His voice was raspy, rough.

"Oh, sure you will," the fat man sneered. "But what will you have left to kill for this one?"

Marcus saw the blow before he felt the impact, and the world grew dark again.

***

"Filth," the fat man said again.

Beneath his collar, the mark Chloe had burned into Marcus's neck began to glow.

Chloe, Yakima, Present Day

Emily looked at the young witch and motioned for her to follow inside. Gwen nodded and entered the house. There were men and women everywhere, filling the room. Emily heard their chatter. All of them knew of Chloe's unimaginably quick rise to power, though Chloe didn't quite understand the gulf between her and the others. "Is she the one?" The excitement, and fear, were overwhelming. "Is she that strong?"

Emily spoke softly, but all other voices became silent. "We must remain calm. We must not speculate. For now, we are here to help Chloe. We...we...we...we...we....." She listed to the left and Gwen caught her, but struggled to hold her weight. A man came to help just as Emily's eyes rolled back until only her whites were visible. It was a louder, stronger voice that came as she said, "This is the witch that will damn you all if you allow her to fail. One witch, one wolf, three lives intertwined, a fourth to emerge. Do not forsake the chosen."

Emily swooned, and the man carried her to the couch and called for a glass of water. She sipped it and refused further attention. "Take me to Chloe."

Chloe lay in the back bedroom, still wrapped in the blanket. Emily reached forward and pulled an eyelid back, seeing that the girl still responded to light. She moved the blanket and saw the symbol burned on her breast. She reached forward and touched it. Chloe's body jerked. Her arms and legs pushed away the blanket, and Emily retreated in the face of her spasmodic dance.

Suddenly she stilled, and Emily watched as her face began to glow, and a white streak grew from her forehead and through the considerable length of her hair. Emily stared for a moment, then rushed from the room to an adjoining room. Shelves covered the walls, and books filled them. Her hands ran up and down the spines until she found an old cloth-bound volume. She sat on the floor and turned page after page, until finally she read.

When the fullness is reached will come the empowered one, dark hair revealing the mark of strength. She will be tried and marked and must endure. Abandon her to your peril, for her strength is yours.

The rest of the passage spoke of the vampire queen, or that was what tradition taught. Emily shuddered. The prophecy was always something that would happen someday, to her descendants maybe, not something to face herself.

Twenty-five feet away, the mark on Chloe's breast began to glow. She opened her mouth and breathed a word: "Marcus."

Chapter Twenty-Eight
Germination

Amber, Seattle, Present Day

"*Mon amour*, it is time to feed." His voice was sultry and intoxicating.

Amber took his hand, embracing the cool air, and allowed him to escort her into the night. The night sounds were enhanced in her ears, more clear and robust than ever before. *You will notice things now.* It was her deep voice again. "Who are you?"

"I am Michael, my dear. What do you mean?"

She started to say something but stopped. "I just wonder why I feel comfortable with you, that's all." The deep voice answered. *I am Illyris, and the prophecy is us. We are the queen, child.* Amber considered the response. She could tell now that she was certainly a child of the night; no, a lady of the night...a very hungry lady of the night. Amber breathed in the air and let her fangs come. "I could get used to this." *In fact, you already like this.*

Michael and Amber walked through the city, watching the people coming and going. Seattle was definitely a busy place this time of night. Pike Place Market had been closed for hours but the nightclubs, strip joints, and all night diners were packed with people. Walking a few blocks up on Pike Street eventually brought the duo to Westlake Park. In the background, they could hear the monorail moving across the town, as well as the concert at the Paramount Theatre. The sounds of Seattle were overwhelming to Amber's new senses.

Amber took a deep breath and tried to understand her new instincts. There was confusion inside and a rage so powerful that she couldn't understand it. *It is the hunger of the new, child — that, and thousands of years of prophecy calling us to act.* As they walked, they saw a man in dark clothes speaking on his cell phone. She could hear him though he was at least sixty feet away. "The gun is in the bottom of the Columbia River, and the fucking coyotes have probably already eaten the body, baby. You and I don't have to worry about him anymore." Michael glanced at Amber and then crossed the street. He spoke softly to the man, and soon, both he and the man stepped into an alley. Amber followed.

The man was calm when Amber arrived, and she was alarmed at how clearly she heard his blood flowing through him. She pushed Michael aside and tore at his throat. The man was calm no longer. His arms flailed and his legs kicked, but Amber held him tight. Blood seeped out from the corners of her mouth and soaked the man's shirt. She could feel his heartbeat slowing, then stopping. She dropped him to the ground and considered that the body was no more than an empty, hollow shell.

Amber looked at Michael. "More."

Michael reached into his pocket, pulled out a handkerchief, and dabbed at Amber's mouth.

"My love, this is not the way. We will feed when we must, and only on men like him, but now you are full. It is no more than the desire of a drunk man for more whiskey."

Amber felt drunk indeed. She stepped forward and

stumbled, but Michael caught her. *It will pass. You will learn to control it as you grow.* She thought back at Illyris, tried to communicate her confusion. *Relax child, neither you nor I can change what has happened.*

"I don't think I want to."

Good.

"Want to what, *amour*?" Michael stared at her.

"Want to wait until we get home." Before he realized what she was doing, she untucked his shirt and undid his buttons to his pants. She knelt before him and took him in her mouth. Michael looked to the alleyway opening worriedly, but soon was lost in the feelings. He realized he longed to be wanted and loved by this woman. It wasn't right. She should be unsure, unaware, and completely pliable—new.

Okay, Illyris, Amber thought as her hands reached around his waist and up his back, *I won't accidentally speak out loud to you now, but I want to know what's going on.* Her nails found the small of his back and she began to scratch.

We must gather the chosen ones, Amber. Michael moaned as she moved her head. *We will need to find them and....* Michael gasped and reached down, gathering Amber's hair in his hands. *I don't know how to find them, Amber.*

Michael cried out, and Amber grasped his thighs as he finished. She stayed in place and held him tightly until his breathing returned to normal. Finally, she pulled off and looked up at him. Michael stared down at her green eyes, her lips red from the feeding, her fangs bared and white. She kissed him a final time, stood up, and smiled.

"Where can we find the chosen ones, Michael?" *Yes, where?*

Marcus, Present Day

Marcus woke to the smell of burning flesh and a terrible

pain in his abdomen. He opened his eyes and saw another vampire standing above him. The vampire was sallow and deformed. He looked around and saw no one else in the room. Marcus bared fangs and hissed at his torturer.

"Ah, so you're awake." Then he assumed a singsong voice. "Wake, you vile vampire. Wake and wake and wake." The thing sneered, his strangely angled mouth forming an incomprehensible shape. "Sleeping with a witch, you prick. I will make you sing for your eternal death."

Marcus screamed as a hot iron pierced his flesh. The burning was too much for him, and he knew he was on the verge of passing out again. "Dannare. Succhiasangue sporco," said the deformed thing. Then, he stood back. Marcus saw the heated iron stake, white at the tip, then red, then coal black. The vampire leaned forward, and Marcus leapt at him, but realized as he did that he was chained to the floor. His leap was stopped a few inches from where it started, and the creature pushed the stake into his neck. The pain was overwhelming.

"We will break the bond to break the vampire, huh?" The man opened his misshapen mouth and ran a thick tongue along his lips. "First, we remove the mark. Then we give you to the Avalani, yes?"

The pain was overwhelming, and Marcus saw black on the edges of his vision. Then, he saw black everywhere.

When he became aware again, he was alone. His wounds had healed, and he felt no pain. Still, he was troubled. Why was he here? Who had — *Jesus, Michael gave me to them*. Would he? It was too much. As he thought, his eyes closed and he saw no more.

Before darkness took him, though, Marcus whispered, "Chloe."

Amber, Seattle, Present Day

Amber sat on the chair in the sitting room. Aleisha and another vampire had brought wine for her and she sipped it. *I'm not sure I understand all of this.*

Her other voice, the deep one, answered. *It will take time, child, but we are bound in the same body. We will fulfill our destiny together.*

But what is our destiny?

The room was gone. Amber lay naked in a field. She was twelve, her breasts just forming, hairless between her legs. The Roman soldier stood above her, laughing as he unbelted his tunic. She looked around for a weapon, but none was there, not even a rock. She screamed.

"There is no one to hear you, bitch." The soldier stood naked now, and Amber saw him stroke himself, her eyes wide as he moved forward. "But please feel free to scream. I will like it if you scream." Amber turned her face to the right and saw where her linen shift lay, torn now. She felt the man grab her leg and part it from its mate. She closed her eyes.

Suddenly the air was filled with a growl. She opened her eyes just as a large black shape threw the soldier off her. She crab walked backwards, saw that the black shape was a wolf, saw its jaws on the Roman's throat. The soldier thrashed about for a moment and finally lay still, and the wolf howled.

Amber stood and looked about for a safe place to run. The wolf turned, blood on its muzzle, and looked at her. Then, it began to change until a squat, hairy man stood before her. He walked to the shift, picked it up, and handed it to her. "What is your name, little girl?"

"Bircenna," Amber said.

Our destiny is to save the wolves, Amber. To end the fighting.

CHAPTER TWENTY-NINE

Gestation

Marcus, Present Day

Voices pushed at the edges of his consciousness, and Marcus lay still. He concentrated on them until they came into focus, a man and a woman.

"But why is it so important to remove the damn mark? Let's kill him and be done with it." That was the woman.

"The mark binds him to the witch. If we kill him before we remove it...well, we don't know all that could happen." He heard a rustling of papers before the man continued. "It may just alert the witch."

"Who cares? I'm not afraid of any one witch." *You'd be afraid of Chloe, bitch. Hell, I'm afraid of Chloe.*

"Of course not, but that's just one of the speculations. It could be some kind of a warding device, protecting him from damage."

"Haven't you heard him scream?"

"But it could also be a failsafe kind of warding, protecting and retaliating in the event of death. This whole place could go up like Hiroshima." *Too bad I couldn't see it.*

"What has he told us?"

"Nothing. We know the witch's name is Chloe, at least

that's the name he cries for."

"What of the queen?"

"We've learned nothing of her. Still, I know Michael's hiding something." *Michael. Why did you do this?*

"Why would he give us this one if he were hiding something?" *Oh, Michael.*

"You're right, of course. Still, I don't know how Marcus and this Chloe fit into the prophecy. Michael read me the passage and sent an old journal along. They're a part of it, and they're the reason our seers got so excited about fulfillment." *Michael, you could have told me. I would have come here willingly.* "We'll keep looking for the queen."

"You know, Gerard." The woman's voice dripped malice. "We could chain him to the ground somewhere remote. When the sun rises, there will be none around if the mark is indeed some kind of bomb or trap."

"You may be on to something. In the meantime, let's keep trying, and let's focus the questions on the queen."

Chloe.

Michael, Seattle, Present Day

None of this made sense. She should have been pliable, easy to handle, easy to influence. She was confused a bit, and that was normal. Still, she should be completely reliant on him. *It's the bitch queen; first she takes Amber and then the wolves.* Michael shuddered. When this was over he had to find a way to get rid of the king's thoughts and memories. They were too vivid, too real for him.

He crossed the office and looked through the books, but even as he did he knew he'd find nothing. The door opened and he turned to see Amber. She wore tight blue jeans and a white cotton blouse. "Where did you get those clothes?"

"Why, at my apartment. I picked up a great many of my

248

things and had Aliesha and...oh, I forget the other girl's name...."

"Scarlet."

"Yes, Scarlet. I had them unpack it all for me in a free room." Amber stepped up to him and brushed a kiss against his cheek.

"Amber, you are too new to be outside on your own! Anything could have happened." Michael shook his head. "You must stay at the estate until you've been trained."

Amber looked distant for a moment and then smiled up at him. "Okay Michael, I'll behave." She reached forward and pulled his mouth to hers. "Will you show me the garden?"

He sighed. "Of course I will, love. Come with me." He extended his hand and she took it. As they stepped out of the office he stopped her and looked at her. "You asked me where the chosen ones are...I think I may know something. But first, what do you know of them?"

Her eyes flashed to yellow again. "There are five, Michael. My consort, that's you. A wolf, a witch, her consort, and me." She let her eyes run up and down his frame. "Well, we've located two of them, but the rest are required."

Jesus. Marcus....

"I believe we may have a problem. Amber, there are forces against you, and I have gambled to protect you. I would not have done so had I known." Amber looked up at him, reached forward, and stroked his cheek.

"Tell me." She took his hand and began again to walk.

He did. He told her of Chloe and Marcus and the diversion he'd made to Gerard. By the time he was finished they had reached the garden. Amber looked around and smiled. "It's beautiful, Michael."

"Have you heard nothing I've said?"

"Oh, we will have to rescue him, and find a way to wake

her. What you did you did for me, however foolishly. Still, there are only a few hours before dawn, and we can do nothing now." She reached forward and plucked a rose from its stem. She inhaled its fragrance and turned to him. "Can you smell this, Michael?"

"Not as I once could. We can smell flesh and blood with an intensity far greater than before, but flowers, trees, not as it was."

"And yet to me the fragrance is stronger and more beautiful than it ever was before. Why is that?"

Michael took the rose and placed it to his face, breathing deeply. He shook his head. "I don't know. There is so much about you that isn't as it normally would be. I...." He sighed, and she kissed him.

Gently, Amber pushed him to the ground, climbing over him and holding his face in her hands as she kissed him. Suddenly, the soil and grass were gone, and he lay on stone. Amber stood naked over him, but she was different somehow. Perhaps she was shorter. Her eyes were solid black. She kissed him, and he realized he, too, was naked; but it was not his body but another's. He reached out to hold her, but she breathed a kiss into his mouth and he felt his consciousness fade.

By the position of the moon he could tell he'd only been out for a moment or two, but he heard voices from the wolf pens. *Wolf pens? Will I never be free of the king?*

"Who are you, woman?"

"Have you come to see your pets?"

"Plan to make us perform tricks, bitch...?"

Soon, the words degenerated into howls until they were suddenly silent. Michael leapt to his feet and ran to the stone door on the side of the castle. *Castle?* He flung it open and stepped into the room. There were cages lined up on the floor, side by side, each about five feet wide and deep and built from floor to ceiling. The cages were filled with men, woman, and children. *Wolves.*

Amber stood in front of the cages and turned to look at him. "What is this room, and why are these people in cages?"

He reached forward and gripped her arm. He heard himself say, "These people, as you call them, are filth. They're contagious filth and you are to think no more about them." Amber took his hand from her arm and casually swung him outward with it. He flew through the air and landed against the tree by the roses. He shook his head. It was his estate again. Amber stood in front of him, still in her jeans and white shirt.

"Michael, I feel so strange. I didn't mean to hurt you. I had one of the queen's memories. They come and go." She leaned down and helped him to his feet. "Are you all right?"

"I was pulled into the memory with you, Amber. I was the man, the king."

Amber looked at him a long while before finally kissing his cheek and whispering, "We must find the chosen, Michael."

CHAPTER THIRTY

Expectation

Chloe, Yakima, Present Day

Gwen sat in the chair and alternately watched Chloe sleep and read *A History of Far Asian Art*, her textbook for Art 104. Watching Chloe was exciting for the first three minutes, and boring every second thereafter. Art 104 was mostly boring, with an occasional painting worth seeing and one or two biographies of note.

She wouldn't have noticed right away had the blanket not fell at her feet. Her mouth opened as she noticed Chloe's body rising from the bed horizontally. She tried to yell, but her voice didn't work so she rushed out to Emily. When she saw her sipping tea at the kitchen table, she screamed out, "She's sleeping on the air! It's like Sigourney Weaver in *Ghostbusters*. She's up in the air!"

Emily rushed into the room and saw Chloe levitating. "Put that blanket over her, Gwen," she said, and reached out with her power. Almost instantly, she felt her power pushed back and disappearing. The mark on Chloe's breast began to glow, soon becoming a bright light, filling the room. The witches in the back yard saw light spilling out of the windows, and Gwen and Emily saw nothing but light.

As quickly as it happened, it stopped. The only light left in the room came from the lamp softly shining from the end table next to the bed. Chloe, from six feet above the bed, opened her eyes. The light that had filled the room just moments before now shone from her eyes like search lamps. She spoke.

"The life within this girl is the future of the world. Protect her. Keep her. Feed her."

Emily felt her power gathering although she hadn't gathered it herself. She noticed Gwen, eyes wide and jaw dropped. She sensed her power flowing outward and watched as Chloe jerked in the air like a heart patient under the paddles. Emily stood paralyzed as she felt her power pushed to its limit, channeled away and pushing, pushing.

Chloe screamed and fell to the bed, where she slept quietly. In the house in Yakima, in the kitchen and bathroom, in the living room and the garage, and in the front yard and the back yard, ninety-seven witches slept as well.

Amber, Seattle, Present Day

*In the hour of the wolf will come the queen of reconciliation. In the birth of her death, the joining will commence and great will be the hatred of her words...*was on the first page. Amber read the lines two more times to be sure she read the word "joining" correctly. She sat down in the chair and continued to read on.

"You don't read the old tongue, do you, Michael?" Michael looked up from the book he read as she spoke.

"No. Kabos knew a little, and he taught me a few symbols, but there is none left who read it, I think." He stood and walked to look over her shoulder at the scroll.

"You are wrong. I can read it. Or rather, Illyris can." She pointed at a word on the document. "This word is mistranslated. It's not the *joining* that will commence, it's the *mixing* or the *intermixing*, this word."

"What does that mean?"

Amber looked up at him and he saw her eyes had become yellow again. "It means that we need to get to Marcus. He and Chloe will have a child."

"Are you sure?" Michael shook his head. "It's unthinkable."

"Unless I'm going to have a wolf child, Michael. Where is Marcus?"

"I don't know. The Covenant has him, or maybe the Avalani. I know that he and Chloe are bound somehow. Perhaps she can help us find him." He walked to the tray on the table and poured himself a tall scotch. He downed it in a single swallow and cursed the lack of effect.

"Well, then, it's time to go to Chloe."

Marcus, Present Day

The pain was unending now, as was the constant heat and the smell of his own flesh burning. *I know why you did this Michael, but I swear to God I'll never let you forget what I'm suffering.* The pain eased for a moment, and Marcus closed his eyes. *If I make it through.* He heard a door close and waited for his body to heal again and end the pain.

The door opened again, and Marcus heard footsteps and the familiar voices. "Is he unconscious again?" It was the man, Gerard.

"Yes," the deformed vampire replied.

"What have you learned?" The woman asked.

"The queen's name is Amber Stone. She works at the museum with the witch. She is at Michael's estate in Seattle." *Oh God. I told them. Chloe.*

"The bastard. He intends the queen's power to be his own. I'll kill him myself." It was Gerard again, his voice rising to nearly a scream. "Gather everyone. We attack tonight."

"Everyone?" The woman queried.

"Everyone here. That will be enough." Marcus heard footsteps, and then from the doorway Gerard said, "Chain this one to the deck; when the sun rises, he dies." *Deck?* Marcus realized the listing and rolling he'd felt since the ordeal began wasn't from the torture. *We're on a goddamn boat.*

"What of the warding?"

"All of the Convenant members on board will be killing the traitors. Who the hell cares about the humans we leave behind?"

He heard the door close and moments later reopen. Arms gripped his and the deformed vampire slurred, "Let's get this cunt to his new home."

CHAPTER THIRTY-ONE
Impending

Michael, Seattle, Present Day

Amber sat in front of the computer and Michael watched the map printing. When it was done, she took it in hand and stood. "We should be in Yakima in a few hours."

Michael nodded. "That's what Marcus said when he left." He took the paper from Amber and stared at it for a moment. It gave turn-by-turn directions from the estate to the address he'd given Marcus with the journal just a day or so before. "How did you know how to print that map?"

"You have really not paid any attention to the changes in the world, have you?" She smiled at him. Then, she reached to his face and took his cheek in her hand. "Have you truly spent all of the last century doing nothing other than searching for me? So caught up in your books and your intrigue that you never used a computer?"

"Marcus handles all of that for me. I have not…needed to learn." He inclined his head to the door, and Amber nodded. The two left the office and went down the stairs. They crossed paths with Aliesha and Amber indicated their destination.

"We may be gone for some time, Aliesha. If we are—"

A piercing scream echoed from behind the house and

through the open windows. "That was Scarlet," Aliesha said. "She was at the pool house." She took off at a run, and Amber followed. Michael folded the map, placed it in his breast pocket, and hurried after them. *I have a pool house?*

Michael saw the fire as he exited french doors from the parlor. Orange and yellow flames licked along the walls of the structure. Servants were already racing to the scene with water buckets and hoses. Michael leapt to the front as he heard Amber shout, "Someone is still in there!"

Through the flames, he saw the figure of a man in a duster or a trench coat. He wore a dark brown hat with some kind of muted feathered plume. It may have been a hawk feather, maybe an eagle feather. Whatever the bird, it seemed out of place, like something he would have seen in Bruges or Paris before he knew of vampires or witches or of the prophecy. The man wasn't moving. He stood within and the flames raged on. There was something about him; the image brought a recollection, something he'd heard. *Something about Marcus…oh Jesus. What else will this damn prophecy bring?*

"It's Valentine, Amber." He watched her cross over to stand next to him, looked at the figure in the flames, and then back at her. "Damn it."

"Who is Valentine, Michael?"

Who indeed? He hadn't heard much more than occasional rumors, and the few comments Kabos had made offhand. A few years ago, though, Marcus had called in a panic about an attack and Kabos had been more forthcoming. "Vampire hunter, Amber. Kabos thinks — thought — he's older than me."

The figure within the pool house lifted his hand, and in it he held a bundle of some kind, obscured by the smoke. He wound his arm back and the bundle hurtled through the air toward Michael, Amber, and Aliesha. He realized what it was before it left the man's hand, and he muttered "Scarlet" before either Aliesha or Amber recognized her head bouncing on the grass in front of them.

Michael was through the door of the pool house and in the air before Aliesha screamed. He pushed through the flames and landed hard against the man. They flew together into the pool, and Michael lost hold of him. *Come on Valentine, I don't have time for this.*

The water coursed around them. Both struggled, but the attempts were feeble, the weight of the water turning savage blows into taps. Michael kicked to the side of the pool and pushed himself out. He turned, ready to kick at the man in the pool, but instead felt an explosion in his ribs. He flew up and backwards against the far wall. An impossibly large sword was lodged in his chest, slicing rather than piercing, but at least five inches deep.

He saw the man swimming for the side. With a scream, Michael grabbed at the blade and pulled it from his body. The effort sent the sword clattering on the floor until it slipped back into the pool. Valentine, still dripping, stood above him, and Michael willed the gash in his side to heal faster. Lifting a heavy boot, the man kicked the wound. Michael screamed.

"I don't need my sword for you." Valentine kicked again and Michael felt his world grow dim.

Marcus, Present Day

The sea air was a shock. The room in which he'd spent the last eighteen hours screaming had been sweltering. The blast of cold as he was lifted by his arms and carried on deck was unexpected and harsh. He opened his eyes, and saw they were on some kind of a yacht, seventy or eighty feet long. It was older, and the white hull had given way to yellowing and faded stripes.

There were at least twenty vampires there, as well as a number of others he assumed to be witches. They stood waiting while servants, human apparently, loaded items into a number of smaller boats with outboard motors. Marcus looked up and saw the Seattle skyline a mile or two across the water. The activity was constant and punctuated by regular commands from a large vampire Marcus assumed was Gerard.

Marcus's guards stopped and lifted him to his feet, then waited as a line of men walked by carrying life jackets and other sundries. One of them was the fat man Marcus had first seen in this place. Instead of a club, he held a tarp of some kind. He glanced at Marcus as he walked by and stopped. A sneer covered his face, and he said, "Well, pretty boy, now's your chance." Marcus ignored him, and the man spit on his face. Then, he bellowed a laugh, cruel and harsh, that filled the deck with the noise. A few others joined in, their laughs mixing with jibes and threats.

About two seconds into the laughter the guard on Marcus's left laughed as well. When he did, his hand relaxed its grip and Marcus moved. The left guard crashed into the right guard and both crashed to the deck. Marcus shrugged and stretched his arms.

"Don't let him escape!" Gerard's shouted.

No plans for that. Marcus looked at the fat man, who stood momentarily paralyzed, but then realized what was happening and dove for cover behind a railing. *None at all.* He was on the man before his feet left the ground, tearing into his neck. The man screamed and Marcus hooked his fingers into the man's mouth, extended nails gouging into the inside of his cheek. He pulled, and the man's cheek tore from his face and landed on the floor. Hands pulled at Marcus, but the blood gave him strength and he drank.

Finally, a blow to the back of his head stopped his feeding and he crumpled to the deck. He heard Gerard say, "Chain him to the top of the wheelhouse." Marcus heard steps approaching him and heard someone ask Gerard what to do with the body. "Throw that fat fuck overboard."

Marcus lay on the deck, his head exploding with pain, streaks of lightning dancing against the darkness overtaking him. He lay there and smiled.

Amber, Seattle, Present Day

Where are you, Illyris?

Amber waited for the deeper voice to speak, but nothing came. She stood on the tile floor of the pool deck. The walls on the left and right were burning, but the flames so visible from the outside of the pool house, the ones that had licked at the silhouette of the man Michael called Valentine, were already dying down. The man had ignited something and burned the pool furniture. He wasn't interested in the pool house. He was here for Michael, for her, maybe for all of them.

The man lifted his foot to kick again and Michael lashed out. He caught the bracing leg and pulled it off the floor, sending the hunter crashing to the tile. Amber watched Michael stand, but something was wrong; he staggered and fell to his knees. His wound had stopped seeping blood, but Michael's shirt was soaked in red. She watched him feebly try to rise, but the hunter had already gained his feet and walked to where the kneeling figure gasped in pain.

She saw him lift his hands above his shoulders, clasping them together above his head. She screamed, "No!" and the sound of her exclamation seemed to steal from the air all of the other sounds—the crackling of the flames, Michael's gasps, the soft lapping of the water at the pool filters, even the noises of the servants carting water.

Valentine stopped. He turned slowly to Amber, looking at her with a shocked expression. Amber looked at him. He stood on the tile, the width of the pool separating them. His arms descended, and Amber saw water still dripping from them. She found it strange that she noticed he'd lost his hat in his struggles with Michael in the pool. It bobbed next to the far corner, the feather making it look like some kind of misshapen duck. A few feet closer to Amber, she could make out the broadsword, a brute of a weapon at least five feet long and six or seven inches thick, but the refraction of the water made it seem twice as large. Droplets of water mingled with blood covered the tile where it had splashed into the pool.

"Illyris?" Valentine's eyes narrowed. "I thought you were gone. Dead." He brushed water from his brow and his eyes and then shook his head. Amber was amazed to see a tear fall on his cheek, but it could have been the pool water. "I spent nearly a century searching for you, trying to see if you were really gone." The voice was surprisingly tender. He reached into his coat and pulled out a silver cigarette case. He opened it, threw several wet cigarettes at his feet, and placed a relatively dry one in his mouth. He lit it against the burning wall and inhaled deeply. "A century...." He exhaled a long plume of white smoke, strangely visible although smoke and flame covered the place. "Until I was convinced that you were no longer on this earth."

"I am here." *At least Amber is here. Where the hell are you, Illyris?*

"Yes." He gestured to Michael, who still knelt woozily. "Then this one must be your consort."

"He is."

He put the cigarette to his lips again, took a long drag, exhaled, and flicked the butt to the tile. His face went from tender to vicious. "Well, then, it appears I can cause you a measure of pain before I kill you, you vampire bitch!"

He walked to Michael and clamped his hand over his neck. With the other, he grabbed his thigh just an inch or so above the groin and lifted Michael over his head. Michael lifted an arm weakly but couldn't protest. Valentine extended his arms their full length, and Amber thought of how he looked like some kind of bodybuilder finishing a clean and jerk lift. He lifted slightly, and Amber realized with horror that he intended to bring Michael down on his knee.

"Noooo!" It wasn't Amber this time. She saw a blur and Michael's body was thrown forward even as Valentine's was thrown backwards. Aliesha clawed at the hunter's face and bit at his arms. Michael landed in the pool and Amber dove to him. Grasping his neck, she pulled him back and onto the tile opposite Valentine once more, helping him crawl out. Even so, one leg still lay over the top of the water when he collapsed, the toes of his shoe submerged.

Aliesha fought furiously, but Valentine finally found her throat and wrapped one of his hands around it. His other hand gripped her hair and he wrenched both hands in opposite directions. A sickening crunch sounded and Aliesha grew limp.

"You see," Valentine was panting hard. "There's almost nothing you can do with a vampire they won't survive." He tossed Aliesha's body to the tile and stood staring at Amber and Michael.

"Come on, Michael—you must wake up!"

Michael moaned softly but didn't move.

"The only real way to kill one is cut off the head, or to break the neck." Valentine reached into the water, took his hat, shook it, and put it on his head. "I tried stakes for a while, but they just don't offer any guarantees. For you,

Illyris, I think I'll cut off an arm."

Where are you, Illyris?

"And then another."

Amber saw him reach down toward the sword. He lay over the side reaching in. *I need your help!*

"Then your legs, and finally your neck."

Amber reached down and pulled Michael's shoe out of the water, pushing him fully onto the tile. She felt the water in her hand, cool but not cold, temperature controlled by thermostats that probably…she stopped and put her hand on the lip of the pool, her fingers lightly touching the edge. She closed her eyes and began to speak strange, guttural syllables.

Across the pool, Valentine's hand closed onto the sword's hilt. He lifted it out and stood. "Now, Queen Illyris, let us play."

Amber looked at him. Her eyes were dark, as black as the charred pine of the walls. Her eyes too, were streaked with flame. She chanted the syllables a second time as Valentine stepped into the pool. His scream was inhuman, and she watched him leap back. His arms and face were red, his hand clutched the sword, and Amber saw blisters rising on his neck and cheeks. Steam rose from every part of him.

In fact, steam filled the pool house. Amber looked down and saw the pool rage. Water rose and fell in great boiling bursts of spray. She felt splashes stinging her cheeks and arms, and watched blisters rise up on her hands, only to see them fade back to clear, white skin. She reached down, lifted Michael in her arms, and dragged him from the pool house.

As she passed the servants still battling the flames, she told them to let the place burn. She entered the door she'd exited just minutes before and crossed to the front. The car was waiting still, and she pulled Michael into the passenger side and took the wheel.

Chapter Thirty-Two

Joining

Chloe, Oak Harbor, 2004

The kids played in the surf and Chloe laughed at the boy who did his best to appear nonchalant and above the play of the rest. She could hear his flip flops. They spoke of the Guatemalan mother who fastened thong to rubber to make shoes for fourteen hours per day, making just enough to pay for the food her family of five would eat. She was alone now, her husband killed eight years prior by a man who knew as little about the reasons for the conflict as his victim. He died just months before the violence finally ended in the Central American country, and the bitter irony wasn't lost on the woman who toiled endlessly to make ends meet.

The boy, on the other hand, came from privileged parents. His sunglasses cost more than the woman had earned in a week, and yet just that morning he'd complained that his parents hadn't bought the new video game console he wanted. He stood on the beach in bright clothes and sulked about his deprivation.

In the distance Chloe saw an eleven foot boat bobbing. She couldn't see them, but she knew a forty-two year old man had his twenty-three year old mistress with him for a pleasure cruise. She lay next to the Jacuzzi on deck and sipped a cocktail while the paramour steered the boat. *I wonder if I could swim out that far? Just swim out and climb on board.* Before she'd finished the thought she was running to the shore, the pebbles and rocks and sand breaking away beneath her bare feet. Ankles, knees, waist, and the finally all of her was beneath the water and moving furiously.

She felt the cold water against her face and opened her eyes. Small tufts of seaweed floated in front of her and then away with each sweep of her arms. She saw a crab crawling beneath her, greyish brown with a bluish tint, nearly matching the sand beneath it. It was twice again the size of her head, a Dungeness, and it lifted its claws defensively as she swam above it.

She dove beneath the surface and kicked again and again. The water flowed around her and she smiled. Ahead, she saw the silhouettes of large fish, salmon, and she kicked toward them. The school parted but regrouped around her, and she reached out to stroke the side of a four-foot chinook. Its body was lean and strong, and she felt the muscles of its tail as it slipped through the water.

Farther, the water grew deeper and she lost sight of the bottom. Vaguely, she realized she'd been beneath the surface for some time, but she didn't feel any strain on her lungs, felt no lack of breath at all. A stray salmon swam near, and she smiled and reached for it. She knew it was travelling to the Columbia to spawn, that it would leap the rapids and return to its place of birth. The fish nuzzled her neck and disappeared behind her.

Still she swam. How far from shore was she now? A few hundred yards? A mile? She contemplated returning to the surface, but a glinting up ahead caught her eye and she kicked toward it. It was a fish she didn't recognize, squat and large, scales silvery against the last powdery vestiges of sunlight in the water. She touched its dorsal fin and smiled.

Then arms were pulling her from the water and the soft ethereal glow of the sea was replaced by the harsh rays of the sun.

Marcus, Coast of Seattle, Present Day

The boat bobbed in the water. The last of the small boats had left the yacht hours before. Marcus strained against his chains again. Nothing. Not a damned inch of play. He stared at the sky and wondered if he'd see the sun before it consumed him. He thought of Michael and found that he couldn't hate him. *I know why you did this, Father. I would have sacrificed you, too.* He realized even as he thought it that he wouldn't have. *Myself, yes, but not you.*

Of course, he'd never had the single-minded focus on the prophecy that was as much a part of Michael's being as his hair or his eyes or his steadfast refusal to be limited by any external factors in the procession of events that drove him to Seattle and to Amber. *You're stronger than me, Father.*

The wind rose, and Marcus felt it against his face and neck. He smelled the salt mist from the ocean and wondered why the change of two centuries ago had distorted the smell of everything living, but enhanced everything inorganic. He felt his eyes watering and realized it wasn't the mist or the wind.

Goodbye, Chloe.

Probably three hours left until sunrise.

Chloe, Yakima, Present Day

Chloe screamed. She opened her eyes and saw Amber and Michael standing over her. Amber was different, her hair a deeper red, almost the coppery red of blood. Her eyes were a deeper green than before and her lips were darker, more pronounced. She touched the mark on Chloe's breast and whispered, "Chosen."

Chloe sat up on the bed and looked around the room. Emily, Tom, her mother, and thirteen or fourteen other witches were crowded into the room. A younger girl — she thought her name was Gwen — handed her a dress and Chloe realized she was naked. She rolled off the bed and pulled it over her head. "Where is Marcus?"

"The Covenant has him." It was Michael who spoke. "Them, or the Avalani. We don't know where he is. We're...we're hoping you can help us find him."

"Water...." She breathed the word softly, and in a moment her mother was handing her a glass, and Chloe drained it, a measure of color returning to her face. She dropped the glass, and it shattered on the floor. She ignored it and stepped forward, leaving a trail of bloody footsteps behind her. The crowd, led by Amber and Michael, followed her from the room, down the hallway, and into the living room, where it grew with more witches and continued through the kitchen, out the sliding glass door, and into the back yard.

Chloe looked out into the night, the cool breeze sending wisps of hair up against her face. She saw the dogs against the far fence nearly a half mile away, saw the rows of corn and potatoes, the apple trees. The mark on her breast shimmered and began to glow, and she lifted her face to the sky and screamed again.

When her face dropped down again, her eyes were open and again were illuminated with the search lamp rays of light. She lifted her arms and began chanting a charm, inclined her head, and the light from her eyes flowed out up to the sky, the clouds seeming to gather around the beams.

She was shaking now, her arms moving in concentric circles, her hair bouncing against her back and thighs. Her feet were sinking into the grass and dirt beneath, nearly two inches already. Chloe's voice rose, and the sounds of the chant grew more intense, the syllables seeming to flow in a great stuttering flurry from her mouth until she stopped altogether. The mark on her chest shone so fiercely that the dress caught flame and the fabric over her breast blew away. It glowed there, a fierce and angry orange red, and she lifted her head again and screamed.

All but Amber brought their hands to their heads and clamped them over their ears. A teenage boy screamed, and blood trickled from beneath his palms and over his neck. Amber walked to Chloe and touched her face.

And the sky opened.

Marcus, Yakima, Present Day

He saw the light in the sky and wondered at how quickly the sun had come. He closed his eyes and prepared for the rush of pain that would precede the oblivion, but instead he was falling. No, the whole boat was falling. He opened his eyes and saw the ground hurtling up at him, and suddenly he was thrown in a mass of twisted metal and fiberglass. The chains that held him broke from the wheelhouse as it crumpled and flailed about him, striking his chest and winding him as he fell to the grass. He staggered to his knees and pushed the chains, now loose, from his shoulders.

He was on the ground and surrounded by a crowd. His vision was clouded, but he blinked hard and saw two figures rushing toward him. He bared his fangs and prepared to leap, but another blink revealed Amber and Michael and he stopped, breathing heavily and disoriented as hell. They reached him and Michael threw his arms around him.

"Marcus, I...."

"The plan worked, Father." Marcus's voice was husky and strained. "There is much we must discuss. There is much to...." He trailed off when he saw her, standing like a statue a few yards away. He pushed Michael away. "Chloe!"

By the time he reached her, she had already collapsed on the grass.

CHAPTER THIRTY-THREE
Reconciling

Four Chosen, Seattle, Present Day

The car slowed as they exited the freeway and Chloe awoke. Marcus sat beside her and smiled, and she smiled back. She felt strange, and tired. He leaned forward and kissed her, and she stroked his cheek and returned the kiss urgently.

"My dress?" She looked down at herself and realized her clothes had been changed. She wore a green silk shirt over black pants. "I don't look good in green."

Marcus laughed. "You'd look good in anything."

From the front seat, Amber said, "You had to borrow some of my clothes. Lucky I still had some at the apartment. We couldn't return to Michael's estate."

The car came to a stop at a service station and Michael turned to face the other three. "I don't know what our next steps are. I know that Gerard will not rest until we're dead."

"Maybe Valentine killed him when he came to the house." Amber sounded hopeful, but then shook her head. "No, Valentine would have retreated to nurse his wounds."

Marcus took his lips from Chloe's and turned to Michael. "They know about the museum."

"What?"

"I must have told them under the iron, but they said that Amber Stone works at the museum with the witch. That must be their next stop." Marcus looked pained, and Chloe stroked his arm.

Michael looked at Amber questioningly and she nodded. "Even if they're not there, we can gather some of the Macedonian artifacts. They mean something to Illyris, to me. Maybe they can help us know what to do next."

"Can we take them, Michael?" Marcus looked at his father. "Or is this a fool's errand?"

Michael laughed bitterly. "I'm sure it's a fool's errand, Marcus. Still, after two centuries with me, could you really expect anything else?" He turned the ignition and the car roared to life. "Gerard is mine. The rest, well, it's open season. Gerard, though…that son of a bitch is mine." He turned on the headlights and pulled onto the street.

Amber closed her eyes. She felt an uncomfortable pain in her leg and realized something in her pocket, her crystal, was poking her thigh. She vaguely remembered removing it as she changed before printing the map to Yakima.

"How much longer before dawn, Michael?" Marcus sounded tired.

Michael glanced at the radio clock. "About an hour and a half. Maybe a little less."

"We'll have to find somewhere to spend the daylight. We'll…."

Amber realized Marcus didn't want to state what the four all thought. In an hour, daylight might be irrelevant to any of them. She took the crystal from her pocket, adjusted the chain, and clasped it around her neck.

Illyris spoke.

Amber, Blackbird State Forest, Delaware, 1990

The woman held her to her breast and Amber felt calm and secure as the warm milk flowed into her. The tall man was back, and she heard him talking to the woman. Amber's infant eyes flashed yellow and she understood his words.

"She cannot stay here, Miriam. The blood drinkers come ever closer and will discover our camp soon." He noticed the crystal Amber grasped in her hands and pointed at it. "Place that on a string for her and put her in a basket. I will drive her to New York tonight."

Miriam stroked Amber's hair. "Such a dear little girl. I had hoped to keep her a while longer."

"It's not safe for her here. We can leave. We can live as wolves for years if we must. She would be helpless against them, and they want her even more than they want us."

Miriam pulled Amber from her breast and looked down at her. "Do you think she could really be the girl? How do you know, Nikoli?"

The man sighed. "Our memories are long, Miriam. They're long and not bound by generation. I will hunt for you before we leave." He turned and Amber watched him change, a large grey wolf pushing open the flap that served as the tent door and disappearing into the night.

Miriam looked down on her and Amber heard her say, "Well then, my little Amber, we must prepare you for your journey."

Four Chosen, Seattle, Present Day

They stepped into the foyer of the museum, Chloe and Amber leading. Chloe walked to the side of the door and used her key card to deactivate the security alarm and to turn on the soft overhead lobby lights. They cast a light glow over the center of the lobby, just enough to keep from stumbling about. "We should head to my office." Her voice sounded loud, echoing across the empty lobby.

"Illyris and I are together again," Amber said. "It's getting easier to distinguish my memories from hers. They're starting to align chronologically, and our thoughts are beginning to meld. We are becoming one." She heard Illyris's deeper voice in her head speaking in unison with hers. *We are becoming one.*

The air conditioning was on. The museum kept it running to keep the lobby exhibits, the stuffed elephant by the information desk, and the stuffed sperm whale hanging from the center of the ceiling, from growing musty and rotting at night. It left the air cold and dry. The four walked across the lobby, tentatively at first and then gaining confidence as they headed to the elevators.

Amber heard the click first, and the lights above the patio style café flooded to life. A large, almost fat vampire stood between the tables. *Gerard.* She and Illyris thought the name in unison. He stared at the four and then said in a theatrical tone, "The king charged me with killing you millennia ago, Illyris. At the time, I regretted the necessity. Such beauty and grace. To kill it seemed a waste, but it was a right and wise decision." He turned his focus to Michael and glared at him. "Killing you, Machial of Bruges, will be a joy I will relive time and time again."

Michael started forward, but stopped as more lights came on and illuminated the entire lobby. Vampires, at least a score of them, stepped from the shadows. Their fangs were bared, and while a few seemed uncertain, most of them smiled maliciously. From behind Gerard came more figures, a dozen or so witches, already chanting and gathering their power. "Tell me Michael, what would make you end your quest here as a failure instead of in endless glory at the right hand of the king? Are you so foolish?"

"Our quest is not at an end, Gerard." Michael's voice was soft but cold. Gerard ignored him.

"And you, Illyris, the would-be queen." Gerard spat on the floor in front of him. "How does it feel to finally walk the Earth again, an Earth all but rid of your precious wolves? You know, I think I must have killed nearly a hundred myself."

Illyris hissed and sprang at him. Chloe watched her clear nearly seventy feet and descend toward Gerard. The vampire recoiled, but a yard or so before reaching him, Amber flew backwards as though hit by a mid-air car, and Chloe felt the power of the witches lashing out. She began chanting herself even as the vampires closed the gap toward the three and toward Amber.

Her first charm sent streams of fire into the faces of the six or seven dark figures that rushed Amber. They screamed as the flesh melted from their faces, but the rest were upon Marcus, Michael, and her in moments. She flung one backwards against the hanging exhibit, and it crumpled to the ground. It staggered up as another took its place and that one, too was cast against the whale. The first helped the second to his feet and they stood for a moment. Chloe saw the whole animal shaking above them and cast out at the chains that held it. They broke with a crack that echoed from the walls, and the giant creature crashed down. Chloe watched the head of one of them being crushed beneath the giant frame, thick red blood flowing over the floor beneath it. She turned to survey the rest of the battle, but a woman with short, spiked black hair and crooked fangs was upon her, and she felt the fangs sinking into her neck.

Michael leapt from one vampire to the next, and three fell beneath him, their throats torn by his nails and teeth. He was a crazed vision of blood. It dripped from his hands and covered his face. He roared and leapt to where two of them had cornered Marcus.

Amber ran toward Gerard and leapt at him again.

As Michael dispatched the two in front of him, Marcus jumped over him and pulled the woman from Chloe. He sank his fangs into her neck and ignored her nails, which slashed into his face over and over.

Chloe staggered to her feet, muttering a charm of healing as she did and feeling it dull the pain at her throat and bring strength back to her. She saw Amber leap and felt again the power of the witches behind Gerard. This time, though, she was not cast backward but instead stopped in the air as though held by a thousand invisible hands.

Marcus stood up from the drained woman and looked at Chloe as two vampires leapt upon him. They lifted him like a rag doll and threw him to the wall, where he collapsed in a heap. They turned on Chloe and two more joined them. She pointed at the first and barked a single syllable, and the vampire exploded, just vaporized into a red mist that splashed against the others and covered Chloe in sick goo. There were too many, and one jumped at her and she felt an exploding pain in her chest as he sent her flying to join Marcus at the wall.

She looked up weakly and saw that four vampires held Michael against the floor. From the café, she heard Gerard yell, "He's mine!" Michael struggled, but they held him firm. Gerard walked calmly to Amber, who was suspended just inches above the floor, straining against the invisible vise that held her. Chloe's three attackers, still covered in red, turned and watched as Gerard bared his fangs and sank them into Amber's neck.

Michael screamed, "Noooo!" but even in his scream, Chloe could tell he had lost all strength. She tried to gather

her power, but the pain in her chest, the exhaustion of the last two days, and the hopelessness that descended upon her kept her from it.

Suddenly, growls filled the air and black shapes poured from the balcony, the hallways, and the doorways. Chloe watched as one, and then two, than all of the witches fell beneath them. *Wolves*, she thought, *wolves!* The vampires on Michael started, but the massive jaws clamped onto their throats, making sickening crunching sounds and turning their bright eyes into dull, empty orbs like the glass painted marbles that filled the sockets of the stuffed beasts tourists paid $11.95 for adults and $7.95 for children 6-11 years old to see.

Illyris opened her eyes and Chloe saw them change from green to bright yellow. She opened her mouth, and Chloe thought she was smiling as she sank her fangs into Gerard's neck. The fat vampire took his mouth from Amber's neck and cried out. He beat his hands against her back, but she showed no sign that she noticed.

Marcus was above her now, and he helped Chloe struggle to her feet. She never took her eyes off Amber as Gerard's movements slowed and then finally stopped. Still, Amber's mouth stayed on his neck.

Michael was there now, breathing heavily and watching as the wolves tore at the carcasses around them, biting off legs, arms, great chunks of torso and even heads, until only the four remained whole—the four, and Gerard's lifeless body. Finally, Amber lifted her head. Her eyes were bright and she licked blood from her lips. With a laugh that sent chills up and down Chloe's spine, Amber lifted Gerard's body and threw it amongst the wolves, who dove on it and continued their orgy of gore.

Michael rushed to Amber and embraced her. Chloe and

Marcus limped along after him. Amber smiled at them as she disengaged from Michael and ran to Chloe. Michael called after her, "I should be angry with you. I thought I was pretty clear that Gerard was mine."

The friends stood together and watched as the frenzy gradually died down and wolves began whimpering rather than snarling. Soon they gathered and walked to the four, transforming as they did and kneeling in front of Amber. Chloe recognized a number of them as museum employees. *Even the bitch from accounting. I will never complain about how you want purchase orders completed again.* Finally, a giant of a wolf, fur dark black and glistening with gore, padded in front of the others and gradually assumed a familiar shape.

"Malakai Ridgewater?" Marcus stared in disbelief. The man stood before Amber, smoothed his sideburns, and knelt.

"All these years," Amber whispered. "All these years and you waited for me."

Ridgewater pushed the hair from the side of his neck and revealed a dark black symbol. Marcus glanced at his own, and then at Michael, who shrugged and inclined his head to reveal one of his own. "I would have waited another thousand years for you, my queen; and I'm not sure the mark gave me much of a choice anyway."

Amber smiled at him. "Then rise, friend Giorgos. I told you lifetimes before the tile was laid in this lobby that no wolves need ever kneel to a vampire again." She looked at the others kneeling. There were at least seventy, maybe as many as a hundred of them. "That goes for all of you." Slowly they stood. Ridgewater stood last.

"I'm afraid I've been Malakai for so long that I no longer recognize my name, Illyris."

"And my name is no longer Illyris. I grieved for Domator as Bircenna and for Illyria as Illyris. The time for grief is done.

I am Amber…or rather, *we* are Amber now."

Ridgewater nodded. "Well then, Amber. By the way, you'll be happy to know I made sure a clause was hidden in your contract that allows you to work nights."

Michael was the first to laugh, then Marcus. Amber smiled as Chloe and the wolves joined in until she, too, giggled like a schoolgirl. The laughter was cleansing, and even covered with blood and flesh and gore, Chloe felt innocent and new.

Finally, the laughter abated and Amber turned to them. "Well, the five are united. It's time then to make the prophecy more than ink gracing the parchment of Eshmun'azar's scroll."

Far to the east, the first rays of the sun were trickling over the horizon.

ABOUT THE AUTHOR

Having been born and raised in Hawaii, I loved telling stories ever since I was a child about vampires, werewolves, angels, demons, and witches. I was a little girl who loved scary stories, much to my mother's dismay. The scarier — the better. Hawaii was a perfect place for stories until I moved to Seattle. I decided to turn a love for the supernatural into writing stories to see if others would love them as much as I do. Currently, I live in Florida but since I'm a Seattle girl at heart, my stories take place in the Northwest. I continue to write supernatural stories of vampires, werewolves, witches, and more while enjoying the beaches and sunshine.